Gil Hogg

BILL BATLEY'S NOTEBOOK

Limited Special Edition. No. 6 of 25 Paperbacks

Gil Hogg graduated in law and later became a Crown Counsel in Hong Kong and a senior lawyer and executive in British industry. He has written a number of contemporary novels and he writes about what he knows, like the lives and loves of the Bill Batleys of this world.

To Maureen

By the Same Author

Fiction

A Smell of Fraud
The Predators
Caring for Cathy
Blue Lantern
Present Tense
The Cruel Peak
Codename Wolf
Don't Cry for the Brave
The Unforgiving Shore
Rendezvous with Death
Night Shelter

Non-Fiction

Teaching Yourself Tranquillity
The Happy Humanist

Gil Hogg

BILL BATLEY'S NOTEBOOK

AUSTIN MACAULEY PUBLISHERS™

LONDON • CAMBRIDGE • NEW YORK • SHARJAH

A CIP catalogue record for this title is available from the British Library.

ISBN 9781528926539 (Paperback)
ISBN 9781528926546 (Hardback)
ISBN 9781528964722 (ePub e-book)

www.austinmacauley.com

First Published (2019)
Austin Macauley Publishers Ltd
25 Canada Square
Canary Wharf
London
E14 5LQ

1

Do I Need a Vacation?

On the advice of my retirement counsellor, Ms Biggs – actually, she's my redundancy counsellor engaged for me by my caring ex-employer, but she always declines that title – I should keep a notebook to record, reflect and plan ahead.

"What shall I record?" I asked her. "My life is very ordinary."

She looked at me tolerantly. "Mr Batley, you will be surprised at how extraordinary your life is when you come to record it."

I didn't believe Ms Biggs, but I humoured her by buying an A4 sized notebook which I placed prominently on my lap at our next meeting.

"Oh, very good, Mr Batley. A conventional diary with a day on a page would be too limiting for your project."

Ms Biggs' advice was given a year ago. I've made a slow start – the story of my life – but I now feel that I am taking the first steps toward capturing that state of enjoyable, but orderly and constructive leisure which Ms Biggs has promised.

My mention, at breakfast this morning, of going away for a week's walking in Wales was not well received. Ann is usually eating her cereal and reading *The Times* in the half hour or so she allows herself before dashing off in the car to the Castleton School at Shepherd's Bush. I have often found this a propitious moment to open difficult issues. Ann, a housewife, now trained as a teacher of teenagers, is considerate and reflective at this time. Not this morning.

I am a kitchen-hand in the morning routine. Having dutifully brought the newspaper in from Mr Bhatta's shop, prepared the fruit and cereal and made the coffee, I leave the newspaper to Ann. I will clear the table and the kitchen when she has gone – after all, I have all day. What a contrast to breakfast when I was working: I rose at 6 am, had a bite of toast and was on my way out of the front door when Ann was entering the kitchen.

On this occasion, she frowned slightly when she heard my Wales bid and looked up. "Do you think you need a vacation, Bill?"

There was something chilly in her response, as though the only persons qualified for vacations had to be dropping from exhaustion. "It's not that. It's not a matter of need. The weather's good now, and I know you've got your commitments."

"I couldn't get the time off work. But you never asked, anyway," Ann spoke coolly enough. She was noting the facts, not really annoyed but perhaps startled.

"Well, it's like your summer schools and conferences," I said. "You don't ask permission to go or invite me to go with you. You tell me when you're going."

"Conferences and summer schools are different," she said, emphatically.

I searched for what the difference might be. "Union policy weekends and seminars on disruptive pupils? Why are they different?"

"They're part of work. Learning something serious, Bill."

"Come on, Ann, I've been to a few summer schools and conferences too. Dinner with drinks. Plonking in the bar every night and a party in somebody's room." I didn't add that there could be some discreet or indiscreet sex on the side, because I didn't want Ann to think I'm jealous. I'm not really.

"I don't go away for dinners and drinks, Bill. Is that why you're going to Wales? To have a bit of a knees-up?"

Suddenly, I was on the defensive. I'm no match for Ann when it comes to argument. "I'm going for the walking and besides, from what I know, most of the people on these trips are nearer 70 than 50."

Ann smiled stiffly. "Not too old to climb the Brecon Beacons and put away a few pints in the bar. You might be surprised at how much energy they have left over."

"Left over for what?" I asked but she apparently didn't hear me as she gathered her bag and left the room.

No peck on the cheek this morning.

I was pensioned off at 53 by the company I was employed by for 30 years. Let me describe myself as I see myself. I'm white and not very posh middle class, born in Putney. I went to a comprehensive school. I don't have any material achievements that would stand out in print. I'm better defined by my attitudes and preferences which are pretty much the same as those of the many people like me. I have a wife, an adult son (the question whether he behaves like an adult is one I will deal with later) and daughter, a grandchild, a South London semi and a dog. And the pension from my ex-employer.

After the experience of almost a lifetime, I confess I'm still unsure of myself. I'm an optimist, willing to go along with other people's ideas until I work out how barmy they are. I enjoy life and Ann, my wife of 30 years, says that I am not a serious person. I'm not quite sure what she means, but I will be examining it in this notebook. In part, she contends that I don't have coherent social and political views. That is certainly true. How can one? I support the left, the centre and the right or none of them depending on the issue, but only in the kitchen dialogue with her. I don't go to rallies with a placard, as Ann sometimes does, write letters to *The Times* or make points on social media.

Ann is just 50, a schoolteacher, a member of the Women's Institute and chair of a local play reading group. We met at

Reading University, where we each gained undistinguished bachelor-of-arts degrees. We were married when I was 23 and Ann 20. At times, we are a little out of touch as a couple, but we get along. I vow to get back in touch, and I hope to record progress here. Our marriage, up to now, has been quiet, uneventful and I would say in one word – happy – including our sex life. We are in good health.

What can there be to write about in this uneventful life?

My perspective on my life is the ordinariness, the lack distinction that I share with hundreds of thousands of others. I know that if you put individuals singly under the magnifying glass and begin to construct their intimate story, as novelists and poets do, you will be confronted by many unique twists, but it is the ordinary pattern of my life that I like and want to sustain. I want to record it here. I have an uneasy feeling that it is fragile – hence this notebook.

Before I begin in earnest, I will note one small matter nagging me from last night. Ann and I had dinner with our neighbours Jim and Sally Clitheroe (my turn to treat). I chose the Brasserie in Fulham Road. I found that a raffish crowd eat there now, and I couldn't help noticing that we were not a fashionable foursome. Jim and I wore dark jackets. Sally and Ann were in cocktail dresses with necklaces and fresh hairdos. To be *in* at the Brasserie, now, you have to wear a t-shirt with *I climbed the Great Wall of China* on it, or a black body stocking with green lipstick. My yellow tie, figured with camels, could not redeem us.

I made the mistake of choosing the wine as host and then inviting Jim to taste it – a Cotes du Rhone 2013. It was apparently a bad year for the particular vineyard but I didn't know. Jim's a wine buff. He goes cycling in France. And I suppose I'm secretly embarrassed by hardly being able to tell the difference between claret and burgundy. Jim wrinkled his nose, swallowed as though the wine had lumps, and eyed me as a fool. You'd think I'd offered him sulphuric acid.

"It's not very good," he said, making sure I understood that this was the understatement of the year.

"Oh, well," I said, "I'll get a different wine for the second bottle and you can choose it." I was determined we weren't going to go through the palaver of sending the bottle back – the charade of putting on an astonished face and sniffing the cork under the eye of a touchy waiter.

I said to Jim that the Cotes du Rhone tasted all right to me. Not good, but all right. That's the kind of measure I use.

Jim looked sour. He ordered lobster, the most expensive dish on the menu. And when it came to ordering a second bottle of wine, he chose a chateau vintage costing nearly as much again as my humble Cotes du Rhone. I smiled my way through the evening, vowing that I would make this note and refresh my mind with it when he invites us in return. One thing should have been clear to me. When you're a host offering wine, taste it yourself and proclaim that it's good.

Am I being mean-spirited? As Jim's host, shouldn't I ignore, even bless, his exercise of his appetite?

I need to think carefully about this. I'm helped by the fact that at the end of our street is a string of shops including a small convenience store run by a Nepalese man named Prakash Bhatta. I don't have much occasion to go into the convenience store as a customer, except to buy a copy of *The Times* (weekdays and Sunday) or *The Guardian* (Saturday). Ann takes the car and does the shopping at Waitrose and is not attracted by Mr Bhatta's store. But I am a regular visitor at the laundry next door, because Ann has gradually retired from looking after my clothes and doing my washing. She is too busy now to wash anything but socks and underpants, which go into the washer-drier with her clothes. I have never been able to submit to the discipline of ironing my own shirts, despite encouragement. Thus, I deliver my washing to the laundry-man and take the time to chat to Mr Bhatta next door.

In his scantily provisioned shop, Mr Bhatta is fighting what I fear is a losing battle with the giant supermarkets; he has few customers. The business is imploding: the less items he can afford to offer, the less customers are inclined to come in. I see the shelves are becoming emptier. When I have been given the task of buying a few additional groceries, I try the shop, but he either doesn't stock what I want, or it is inferior in quality and Ann complains.

Mr Bhatta's round face and limpid eyes radiate calm. He's not worried about supermarket competition or whether I'm a big spender or not. We are drifting in a cloud. Relax. Accept. When I get into difficulty, which is frequently, I try to summon Mr Bhatta's cloud. For example, I don't let my irritation with my son show and I earnestly, but unsuccessfully, attempt to eliminate the feeling. Should I accept and forget Jim Clitheroe's behaviour? I'll have to think about it later. A small meanness by a friend often remains in the mind like a grain of sand whether you've got big worries or not.

2

With Ms Biggs

It is now over a year since I retired, although it seems like a week. I say retired, but I was given a *package*. Everything that obviously can't be packaged now comes in a package: like a job, a vacation, a new car, a government policy or in my case arrangements for my redundancy. Yes, I was redundant. That means superfluous. I don't feel superfluous, so I prefer to think of myself as a retired man.

I'm not going to moan about becoming superfluous early in life. I think it's early in my life. I'm fit in mind and body – I could go on working for years. I was a senior executive in an insurance company, but I've had to realise that there are hundreds of people with skills like mine. I thought I was unique, or rather too accomplished to be vulnerable. I would go on into the sunset. I've variously been a clerk, supervisor, manager, senior manager, regional coordinator, human resources director and divisional director (not a board director, alas) as I made my own limited climb up the greasy pole of corporate advancement.

In the predatory world of commerce, my employer was taken over. Suddenly, in the newly merged company there was an oversupply of senior executives. I lost out. My fancy job titles didn't mean anything beyond my desk at the office.

It's frightening, at first, to learn that you're not wanted any more. I had overlooked, in my own case, how people are conditioned by the skills they exercise, like Jim Clitheroe. I recognise him as a blustery public relations man. Ann has taken on some of the fussy, directive persona of a schoolteacher. Without realising it, I had developed the senior executive mentality. In my last post in my career, I had an assigned driver and a company car. I'm not fond of driving or of being driven. It sounds grand to talk about 'my chauffeur', but it became a nuisance because I'm not used to handling servants. I was too friendly. John recounted his whole life and all his troubles to me. This made it easier for him to obtain privileges from me.

It's like that in Amherst Street too. We get somebody to do a few hours' housework, become friendly, and in no time they come in, read *The Mirror* before they start and don't mind taking lengthy calls on their smartphones. But whatever you think about having servants, I will admit that there is a lift in having this obvious sign that you are a big dick, entitled to have somebody driving you around.

I was used to moving in a business crowd where people expected me to speak judgementally and were respectful of what I said. Take away that status and what was I? *That's what I'm trying to find out.* Suddenly, I appeared to be nobody in particular. What a contrast with retired members of the House of Lords, wining and dining at the House into their dotage and pretending to govern the country. Some of my colleagues who were also losers used the word 'gutted' to describe their feelings. They felt that they were limping along with some vital parts removed. When I had a chance to think about it, I was disappointed but not gutted. I have had to rebalance myself – with Ms Biggs' help.

At the time, I was told by Ms Biggs that far from being the end of the road, I should see this as an *opportunity*. Ms Biggs was a vivacious young woman who had not yet reached 30 and was quite confident of her understanding of an older generation. She said, "You can now do all the things you've always wanted to do – you're free, Mr Batley, with the company's generous package ..."

"I'd like to go on working," I said. "I enjoyed my work. It was very interesting."

Ms Biggs didn't scoff at this but dismissed it as valueless. "You've already had a long and successful career, Mr Batley, and with the company's generous package…"

I wouldn't have described my career as particularly successful, but it depends on your personal point of view – I allowed her poetic licence. And I didn't think 30 years was a long career. Ms Biggs fixed me with her earnest eyes as though she was privy to my thoughts and knew I had a secret list of exciting ambitions. She even researched and placed before me three job opportunities. "You could probably get any one of these posts, Mr Batley, if you want to go on doing the same thing."

She seemed slightly contemptuous of doing the same thing. I wasn't. I seriously considered these posts. They appeared to be in line with my experience, but I realised that 'the same thing' could never be the same thing. Being released in a different company hierarchy would be like being a chimp parachuted into a different jungle – confusing and demanding. Did I really want that after 30 years?

I protested, "But I don't know what I want to do. I've thought about it and I can't make up my mind." This was true. Perhaps, I'm not very convincing.

Ms Biggs smiled in a superior way. Apparently, I was behaving immaturely or concealing my real thoughts. Whatever textbook Ms Biggs used must have specified my kind of evasion because she took it in her stride. "You can take a villa in the Algarve for a while. You and your wife can go ballroom dancing," she urged, as though any sane middle-aged person must be busting to do these things.

I wanted to say I disliked the Algarve, but I don't. The coloured pictures of villas in the holiday brochures may be true, but as a retirement *opportunity* the Algarve didn't seem to be right.

"Do *you* go ballroom dancing, Ms Biggs?" I pressed, knowing the answer. I could visualise her in a leather mini-skirt under the strobe lights in a club. She had probably never heard of the military two-step, let alone the Tower Ballroom. I didn't want to admit that I can't dance – well, not real ballroom dancing, the kind they advertise sniffily on activity holidays as 'not for beginners'. Ann and I manage to stumble around, but it's not dancing. Ann tolerates me. She's actually quite accomplished.

If ever I'm in Blackpool, I like to go into the Tower and watch the old couples with their chalky bones and white hair circling so lovingly under that grotesque ceiling. But doing a fox-trot with a double reverse pivot, a fleckle and a cross-chasse and lock-step is and always will be, quite beyond me.

"I have no time for dancing, Mr Batley," Ms Biggs said patiently, expecting me to believe she was in bed with a cup of cocoa at 9 pm, memorising her notes for the next day.

I completed the quality assurance questionnaire which she sent me following our meetings giving her excellent marks. I particularly ticked the box which said, *Did you get a sense that this is a time of opportunity for you?* I did my bit to keep Ms Biggs in work, but I remained confused about precisely what the opportunities of my position were. And I have to confess that a year on, the fog hasn't entirely cleared. I may have made *some* progress and I want to document it here.

I have to acknowledge that I have wondered about Ann's conferences and summer camps. I've averted my gaze from them, so to speak. I never watch her preparations or try to divine her feelings when she returns. My thought has been that I can't keep her on a leash and if I try she'll slip the leash and go anyway. She's a voluptuous, kind-natured woman, and it isn't hard to imagine men pursuing her.

I ought to admit too, that my booking for the Wales walk, which needled Ann, followed a conversation with my daughter, Jane. It happened on one of my weekly visits to her flat to see my 12-month-old grandson, Benedict.

Jane lives with Barry Macklin, father of Benedict. He's a go-ahead builder with his own business. He's bright and a generous provider. I like him, but Ann has reservations which arose when the pair met.

When Jane told us she was going to move in with Barry, whom she met at a pop concert a few months before, Ann was upset. But apart from raising her eyebrows and asking Jane if she was sure she knew what she was doing, Ann kept quiet. Barry only got conditional approval from her, although she never showed it. She was comforted by the fact that he apparently had a good income and seemed mature. She was very impressed with the apartment the couple were to share – in a purpose built block in Thames Reach, near here, state of the art and with a river view.

"But he's a builder," she said to me disconsolately.

"He's modest. Yes, he's a builder who doesn't call himself a property developer. Nick would." Nick is our son and not slow to gloss his achievements with a word or phrase.

"Barry's formal education finished when he was 16," she said in a critical tone.

"Darling, they are only going to live together."

"I'd prefer it if Jane found somebody of her own intellectual level."

Jane is a graduate in social studies and a trained community worker. "I wouldn't call Jane an intellectual, Ann. And Barry is clever, an achiever. They're together. It's happenstance. We have to accept, my dear."

With this exchange between Ann and me, we saw Barry and Jane begin to cohabit and it went on for a year. We should have been prepared for the next event. Jane called in at the house one evening and flushing, but quite level-eyed, said to us that she was pregnant.

"What are you going to *do*?" Ann said in consternation.

"Nothing but have the baby, Mum. Barry is delighted."

17

"It was an accident?" Ann pressed.

"No, Mum, we decided on it."

"Is he going to marry you?" Ann asked.

"I don't want to get married at the moment," Jane said this with a pained expression which implied, 'You two wouldn't understand, and I'm not going to try to explain.'

I could see that Ann was baffled and wanted to ask why, but perhaps realised it was too intrusive. So Benedict was destined to come into the world without further reference to us.

After this meeting, Ann complained to me, "We will have an unmarried daughter with a baby living with a man who isn't entirely suitable as a husband."

"Are you sure you're not more concerned with the way Barry uses his knife and fork?" I asked.

"Barry is a bit rough, and I'd prefer he wasn't," she said defensively.

"But you must admit he's a nice guy. And good-looking."

"Oh, sex," she said, as though it could be disregarded.

I didn't want to get into a debate about the importance of sex with my wife, because it would have to be illuminated with examples from our personal life – that could be awkward. "And he's generous," I said. "Making a pile of money. He'll probably go further than Nick."

"Nick's in a different league!" she retorted swiftly. Nick was inviolable in her eyes.

Recently, Jane made a further assault on our flimsy conventions by announcing that she was pregnant again and happily going to have the baby. She had given up her job at Hammersmith Council to look after Benedict.

"We'll have an unmarried daughter with two babies!" Ann said to me. "And Barry." Barry grates on Ann uncomfortably. For her, he's between being a decent bloke and a bit of rough.

"They will be lovely kids and she and Barry seem very happy," I said.

"Bill, you just don't care!"

Jane and I don't have a soppy relationship, but we can talk and I enjoy seeing her and Benedict. On this visit, I was sitting in a chair at the kitchen table, playing with the kid in a high-chair next to me. Jane was at the bench mashing baby-food with her back to me. Our trivial talk died away.

"Dad?" she said, without turning round, in a voice which alerted me; it had a higher note than necessary and a forlorn ring. I've heard it occasionally over many years and it usually heralds either trouble, or a request for an excessive favour.

I looked up and released the child. "Yes, dear?"

"Why don't you stop Mum going away to these school activities and go off together on a decent holiday, like Peru or something?"

"You know we've been on quite a few overseas holidays."

"Maybe, but I'm talking about these conferences."

"I can't stop her doing anything, Jane."

She sighed and struck the fork she was using on the bench top. "Oh, Dad, that's you! Don't you understand about women?"

"I guess not, dear."

Jane had touched an important point. Although I have studied the subject earnestly and continue to do so, Ann and Jane, my only private and personal experience of women, are like a patch of quicksand on a boggy moor to me – recognisable in their dimensions but difficult to negotiate and dangerous to cross. For example, I went into our bedroom this morning and noticed a rather elaborate, gold-coloured perfume bottle amongst others on Ann's dressing table. I said innocently, "That's nice. Where did you get it?"

"You gave me that for my birthday last year, Bill," she replied, with a hopeless look, as though her past birthday was a forgotten matter of no importance to me. The thing is, I'm not a very thingy person. I know Ann is very attached to the rings and other modest jewellery I have given her, but they don't mean anything to me except as far as they please her.

Now, Jane was determined to put me right: "Women like a man, Dad, a macho guy who puts the bite on them sometimes. They want you to be gentle, honest, all that stuff, but they want to know there's a steel edge in there – you have to show it occasionally. Women don't respect you if you're a doormat."

"If I ever had any steel in me, it's probably corroded. What's so bad about Mum's summer schools?"

Jane still had her back to me. She raised her head and looked out the window. She didn't answer for a moment and I knew something I didn't want to hear was coming. "Bernard Chandler," she said, in a croaky voice.

I concede I had a stab of pain in my chest at the name. "Is Ann having an affair with him?"

"I don't know. I think you and she ought to be careful."

The vision of Bernard Chandler loomed before me, heavy, with square hands, in an Arran sweater, corduroys and soft moccasins, his beard greying. He is a history teacher, heavily into psychology, counselling and recovered memory. Whenever he stops by the house to pick Ann up and we speak, I have the uncomfortable feeling that he is trying to get inside my head and that he knows there is something wrong in there.

"I've never thought seriously of Chandler as competition," I said. I hadn't. He made me shiver.

"He may be a prat," Jane said, turning round with a bowl of mush for Benedict, "but don't be complacent."

It's curious how children slip naturally into the role of counsellors to their parents. If I dared to advise Jane about how to handle Barry Macklin, she'd explode. But Jane's very forthright when it comes to my marriage. No beg pardons. She moves right in.

"I have to whisk Mum away to foreign parts to stop her falling into the hands of Big Bummed Bernard, the seducer?"

Jane laughed. "No, Dad, you have to rekindle her affection and this would be an opportunity."

"Hell, the fire's gone out! I hadn't noticed."

"This is serious, Dad."

"Did she tell you that the fire had gone out?"

"I'm not going to tell you anything she said. I'm worried and you should be."

Is it that children, having watched as their parents' marriage was unfolding over the years are inevitably experts on it? Whatever the answer, my verdict is that Jane is worth listening to. Now, I'm worried – no, I'm concerned.

3

The Potting Shed

On one point, at least, I have followed my counsellor's instructions precisely. Ms Biggs was emphatic that *every retired person must have a potting shed.* "You need this personal space, Mr Batley, where you can keep your notebook, be alone and think."

"How do you think my wife will react?" I asked.

"She will appreciate that you can't be together all the time. She will want her space and allow you yours," Ms Biggs spoke with the confidence of somebody who knew Ann thoroughly.

I had misgivings but nerved myself up a few months later to establish my potting shed in the first-floor spare bedroom of our four bedroomed Fulham semi. Desk, office chair, easy chair, lamp, filing cabinet, PC, printer, bookcase and one of the portable phones.

We do have a neglected and deserted garden shed, and Ann said I should use it. "Nobody has a potting shed on the first floor of their home, Bill."

"I'm not in the least interested in gardening, dear."

"I know. So what is the purpose of the potting shed?"

Ann was going to get me to commit and bind myself on the exact purpose of my invasion of the spare bedroom. "It will be my office, my study. I will run my – our – affairs from there."

"Our affairs? Are you going to turn paying the household accounts into a business?"

I ignored this. Ann evidently thought that there was nothing useful I could do at a desk – despite having kept her and the children by my desk-bound efforts. "I'm going to develop my – our – opportunities," I insisted, groping for words that had flowed so easily from the tongue of Ms Biggs.

Ann's face crumpled like a used brown paper bag at my remark, and she then looked very unattractive. Except in times of tension like this, she has a relatively unlined complexion, silky mahogany hair and a generally cheerful expression. "Our opportunities?" she asked, her eyes wide.

I had a sinking sense that an interrogation was about to begin. It was as though I'd suggested that we go into pornographic film-making. "I now have the time to do all the things I've always wanted to do," I said, trying to sound blasé and stealing another line from my counsellor.

Ann eyed me suspiciously. She sniffed and looked as though she could smell alcohol. "What do you want to do, Bill?"

I couldn't help hesitating. "I'm not quite sure."

"But you said there were things you've always wanted to do."

"I only meant that I have complete freedom to decide – anything…" I tailed off feebly.

Ann gave me her super-rational 'you haven't thought it through' look. "Let me know before you get me involved in any of your opportunities, Bill."

Ann is as formidable in verbal fisticuffs as the driver of a black cab. There was no point in exposing myself further. Nevertheless, the potting shed is established. I have a place of retreat, where I can surround myself with books and papers relevant to my opportunities (as I develop them) and contemplate my destiny.

One decision I have made is that I will see my solicitor, George Cutler and discuss my will. I've known him for years and I trust him. He's not in practice now, but he'll cobble up a new will for me. And that brings me to my son, Nick's part in this. He's 29, an investment banker as he describes himself and a workaholic, but absolutely brimming with hubris. I think his conceit outdistances his ability. He has what seems to have become a habit, of dismissing as fools people who disagree with him. I haven't quite been dismissed yet, because I suppose I have been too timid to tell him what I really think.

My thoughts about Nick came into sharp focus with the death of Ann's mother, a widow, three years ago. She left a will which was fair and conventional – she willed her home and all her assets to her four children equally. However, she appointed one of them – her beloved, only son, Raymond, a civil servant – as executor. Raymond is a sensible guy. All he had to do was to arrange to sell everything and divide up the money.

In Ann's peaceful and affectionate family, arguments flared like bush fires about who had been promised what from the family home. During her life, Ann's mother had made a variety of nebulous and probably contradictory comments to the children individually, about them having some of the quite valuable articles in the home 'when I'm gone'. Each of the children, including Ann, thought they were entitled to this or that. A certain amount of wishful thinking had led to them having a sense of title to some of these family possessions. Instead of reaching agreement with his sisters, or in the last resort selling everything and dividing it up, Raymond became as much involved in the disputes as his sisters were and the fires continued to smoulder and sometimes raged.

When the final distribution was made, there were winners and losers. Ann was a loser. She never got the original tiger painting by David Shepherd which she so much wanted to hang in the hall – thank goodness (I prefer the Leger print which we have always had). But much worse, there were scars within the family which will take a long time to heal completely.

This made me think about my own will made several years ago. I left everything to Ann if she survives me and otherwise to Nick and Jane equally. As a proud father, I ignored my solicitor's advice and appointed my son as executor instead of my solicitor. I felt very satisfied with this arrangement at the time.

Now, having witnessed what a flashpoint a will can be in a happy family, I asked myself: can I trust Nick to deal equally and equably with my daughter? Equally, eventually, yes. Equably, no. He doesn't do equable with anybody. He would probably want to put the money into one of his funds operating out of the Cayman Islands promising his sister great rewards. She might even be taken in. He's a bit of a bully. I concluded that I should appoint somebody as my executor who will get on with the business, namely, George.

The first time I saw Carol was in the coach at Victoria Bus Station. She was blocking the aisle of the bus. She had a haversack too big to go under the seat and too awkward to go in the overhead rack, until I helped her. She took a seat across the aisle from me. At first, I thought she was just another passenger, but she produced a wallet to replace her bus ticket, and I saw a folder in the light green colour of the Trail Walkers' Company. I was too diffident to point out our mutual holiday destination and buried my face in a book.

As a matter of fact, I wasn't too impressed with her. She was small (I'm nearly six feet). It was difficult to see much of her under the lumpy layers of clothing she was wearing. Her face was partly hidden by spectacles with bluish glass. Her straight hair was brown with some grey threads. She had to be 50 or more because these trips are exclusively for 50-year-olds plus. Anyway, I didn't arrange this holiday to meet a woman. I'm here because I enjoy hill-walking – and yes, all right, because I was cheesed off with Jane's mention of Bernard Chandler about which I feel powerless to do anything. Big bummed Bernard. I knew I should not be responding in this way, but I had to do something.

One of the other points about Chandler is his hair. He has a lot of it, grey-black, curly and thick, like an astrakhan hat. You can see it's the sort of hair that never falls out on the comb. If he lives to be old, it will be like a silver halo.

My hair, mousey grey-brown in contrast, is fighting a battle with time. It hasn't yet been routed. I've been tonsured. Ann tells me not to complain. She says, "It looks OK from where I stand," which means that the shine on my crown isn't so visible if you're a few inches shorter than I am. I have plenty of hair at the sides and a little in front. I try not to comb it over my baldness too obviously because that's a giveaway about your sensitivity. I make the most of it, a little longer at the sides and back to compensate. To do this trick, I've found I can use one or other of the barbers in Fulham Broadway. No fancy salons for me. I'd feel embarrassed. I'd say I'm marginally better off than men (like Jim Clitheroe) who go bald from the front. A big, shining forehead is what you fear in your forties or fifties.

I believe men's head hair is a sexual turn-on with women. I had little experience of women before I married, but I've observed how they openly admire big hair. It's hard to become a successful politician without a decent mop. Ann used to grab my hair when she was getting close to orgasm. Now there isn't much to grab. I try to keep her hands off my head at this time because I don't want her damaging what's left. I sometimes wonder if this change, my receding hair, has made a difference to her feelings about our sexual relations.

Then there is facial hair. That is somewhere else where Chandler is also heavy. Facial hair may be sexually attractive to women too. Clean-shaven men like me call it a pussy-tickler. Certainly, it is common now. Chandler has plenty. He must spend as much time trimming it as I do shaving. The other possibility is fashionable stubble. A young man, 20 years younger than Chandler, can give a manly emphasis to his jaw line with a stylish dark stubble, but an older man, who also wants a shadow, only gets a grey fuzz and looks as though he's had a drunken night out. But fashion is all. Many my age are tempted.

The argument that shaving is a nuisance to be avoided won't work, because, if you elect to have stubble, or something more elaborate, you have to mow and trim it regularly to get the effect.

And when you get egg in your beard or tash, you need a wash rather than a table napkin. I estimate that facial hair is most common with bald men, but it's not good to invite the thought that you're only compensating for lack of head-hair.

At Cardiff, we left the coach and boarded the Walkers' bus for a run through the cold twilight to the hotel at Merthyr Tydfil. Carol and I found seats at the back, quite close but still not speaking.

The Walkers' rep, a pear shaped woman with straight blond hair, tied tightly back in a ponytail, had a pair of spectacles like a car windscreen across her face. She began an introduction to the area around Brecon Beacons as the bus jolted on. She spoke in carefully measured sentences like a schoolmistress with an infant class: population, weather, local customs, timings for briefings, breakfast and dinner. I learned that of the 20 of us, seven of the ladies were singles and three of the gentlemen. That didn't mean the singles were single. Women frequently travel in pairs on these trips, like nuns. With one or two exceptions, most of my companions looked decidedly old-world, with silver hair and parchment faces.

As a male, I reflect on the mortality statistics sadly. I've sometimes been engulfed by streams of female grey panthers with cropped hair, pouring out of a tourist bus, in t-shirts and track-suit bottoms, fancy free as they spend their dead husbands' pensions. I guess from their nunty dress and shouty behaviour, that the greater number of them have closed the sex shop. What they seem to want is a few sherries, roast beef and Yorkshire pudding for dinner, a hearty walk and a chummy chat in the bus. Nothing wrong with these objectives, of course.

At the hotel, which was more like a boarding house and in need of a coat of paint inside and out, our keys were distributed. A moment arises when nobody in the group wants to get the last room because it might be the worst. Some jostling for position occurs. Fate had already played its part when, last in the queue, I clasped my key in my hand. If I was going to be beside the lift shaft or the machine room, or have the air-conditioning fans whirring outside my window, it was too late. Be calm, inspect the room and complain if necessary with a kind of unanswerable, logical sincerity. And be prepared to be rebuffed. Monstrous behaviour passes with the phrase, "I'm sorry."

4

The Virtue of Planning

Plan your time was another adage of Ms Biggs with which I've had some difficulty. Of course, I already knew the virtue of planning. As an ex-commercial man, I'm used to schedules and plans. Ms Biggs reminded me gently that the most valuable commodity I had was time and I should plan to use it skilfully. When she said it, I didn't like the implication that this was a commodity in short supply in my case. Like a 30-year-old I'd been reckoning on working and living forever.

Now, as I lay on my bed in Merthyr Tydfil, I made a preliminary action plan:

Clean up the PS: The name potting shed has stuck to my room and Ann utters it with particular bite at times as though I do disgusting things in there.

And organise household and private files. All those old bundles of paper, photographs, holiday brochures and maps.

Hold talks with Ann re re-allocation of household chores: I should offer generous help in our partnership. I mean *more* generous.

Seek voluntary work to help the less fortunate: I have guilt feelings when dodging *Big Issue* sellers.

Review financial affairs: I have paranoia about being ripped off by the cherubic ex-public schoolboys who manage my ISAs.

Make a radical lifestyle change: Consider whether to sell the house and move elsewhere.

Consider whether to become a consultant: Congenial and occasional work for select clients might be attractive.

I have completed this schedule after weeks of thought, and I have decided it needs yet further work. There is no immediate hurry. The odd thing is that without a plan I am busy all the time. I'm doing the things that I used to do in my lunch hour at work – posting letters, or writing emails, shopping, arguing with the gas company or getting angry with automated telephone answering services. This trivia seems to take a lot longer now.

I have the leisure to read too and I regard this as a pleasant introduction to a more rigorous (planned) regime of reading. I like crime fiction, but I am thinking of more classic works. Although Ann makes no overt comment, I think she feels it verges on the indecent for a fit, mature man in the prime of life to sit in an armchair reading a book in the middle of a working day. Yesterday, when I described a few much worn shirts and trousers in my closet as "my workaday clothes", she laughed heartily. "Bill! You don't do any work!" Is this the Protestant work ethic in her? We are both nominal Anglicans which I think means that neither of us are religious. Ann finds me all sorts of little jobs to do, writes me lists that fill my days. Although she has never said so, idleness will not be tolerated, but I have found idleness is a pleasant, healthy state. I have time to notice the wallpaper and take in what is happening around me.

The difficulty here, which is not a real difficulty, is that I don't have a real job. What I do have is a company pension (I should be so lucky!). Yes, it's generous. I am one of the fortunate ones in this age when black holes in funds and tax raids on them are forcing schemes to close or be less generous.

The problem with a pension, which shouldn't be a problem, is how much you *think* you need to live on. My observation is that no matter how generous the pension, people tend to believe they need more. I'm thinking of people who are already well off, often retired public servants, politicians or business executives (like me). Ann and I could live comfortably on less than I get. I'm not acquisitive. I don't want any particular *things.* If Ann asks me what I want for my birthday, I usually say that I think I have everything. But I'm not saying, I would decline a ten million pound win in the Euro Lottery. I buy the occasional ticket. You can't win more than £25 on Premium Bonds, I know that from years of experience!

Suppose, I did want more income. I could add to it with some consultancy. I have a lot of experience about how to conduct insurance business. Then I start to wonder whether I want the hassle that would entail. It's nice to feel valuable and wanted for your abilities, but companies and governments don't pay you fees to sit around and dream. They expect advice, opinions and written reports. You have to be on the ball. You have to visit the site, be it Milton Keynes or Malawi. You have to get up early in the morning.

I certainly don't need this money. Why work if you don't have to? It might be better if I devoted my time to good causes and enjoying myself. After all, I worked for that pension and there shouldn't be any shame about taking time to relish the fruits of my labour. But there is, slightly, in the eyes of others; it seems like indulgence to them. And I question whether there is anything wrong with indulging myself, provided it's not too decadent.

Now that I have the notebook with me in Wales, I have settled down to make a list of things that are bothering me. I was going to head it 'Principal Worries,' and then decided that 'Principal Concerns' is better. Even my worry about Bernard Chandler is really a concern.

I have a theory about personal worries, anxieties and concerns. Since they are always with us and they are innumerable, we have a mental A list. At the top is *the* worry or anxiety of the moment. You think, 'If only I didn't have this worry, life would be fine'. But when that worry ceases and you overcome the euphoria, it is immediately and automatically replaced by the next worry in order of imagined gravity. The disconcerting thing is that the number two worry becomes as important, as big in the mind, as the former number one. This effect means that when your worry about say, angina is eliminated, thanks to modern medicine, you are just as much possessed by a worry about a misunderstanding with your neighbour over the position of his fence. The pressure of worries, anxieties and concerns is unrelenting. Therefore, according to Mr Bhatta, I must disconnect. Accept. Drift in the cloud. Very, very difficult.

I have no actual concerns about my health, but I have had a slight sensitivity (or is it a pain?) in my chest recently. I can't help wondering whether this is anything to do with a heart condition. You can't tell what deterioration has occurred in your arteries at 50 plus. When I explain some difficulty of mine to my doctor, she smiles, dismisses it and says, "When a man gets older…"

I remember all the years I smoked 20 Players Plain a day and ate fish and chips and mushy peas at least twice a week. My entire bachelor of arts degree was fuelled by hamburgers. Riddled with guilt, I don't smoke or eat McDonalds now. Ann provides a reasonably fat and sugar free diet. I don't have a bulge. Once, I hiked with a doctor from Taiwan who said the human body couldn't metabolise red meat in a healthful way. Perhaps the damage is done. I could be a ruin waiting for the last tick of my genetic clock. *My resolution*: carry on with the bathroom exercises.

And then, to be more specific, there's that waterworks question. I was told that if you have to get up in the middle of the night to pee, and it takes a long time, it could be the pressure of a growth narrowing the tube inside you.

I have a friend who survived a urinary operation. He announced a benign growth. He wanted to find out if I had the symptoms he had. Oh, yes, he positively wanted to check out all his friends. His eyes gleamed in an accusatory way when he asked me if it took me a long time to pee in the night. It's a natural question when you're standing side by side in the loo of a pub or motorway café. He knows it always takes a long time when you're half asleep. But he was going to scare me. If I had admitted slowness, he's would have clapped me on the shoulder, told me with a brassy laugh not to worry and recommended a surgeon. Admit nothing is my policy.

But I *have* been getting up from bed more than once in the middle of the night and it does take a time. Does it take longer than it used to? *My resolution*: I will count how many times I get up to pee every night over six months and then consider the matter further.

The worry list is not complete without the suppressed worries. You could call this the B list, but the letter B doesn't do justice to the severity of the worry. Suppressed worries are thrust to the back of the mind, but they lurk there. Into this category comes my trouble with the police and my problem with my son, Nick, but I can't bear to make a note of them now. This category of worry leaps out at me, with unimaginable distortions, at 3 am. As I return from the bathroom, I say to myself, "Well, that's absurd!" But I can't get to sleep afterwards without picking the whole affair over in my mind.

I had what is truly a single room in the hotel; a narrow bed on a carpet tile floor. A small mirror on the wall and a chair. A rack of coat hangers served as a closet. There was no room for anything else. The bathroom contained a shower, a tiny hand-basin in a corner and a lavatory. It's not possible to walk into the bathroom and shut the door. I had to enter, step on the shower tray and close the door behind me. Only then could I access the hand-basin and lavatory. I couldn't sit on the lavatory without resting one leg on the shower tray.

Having tried out these inconveniences as I swigged sherry from the bottle I had brought with me, I decided not to complain. I am a little shaken by the sheer cheek of this accommodation, but you can't expect the Ritz in Merthyr Tydfil.

The rough plastered walls which appear to be stout and stony are actually flimsy. I could hear everything that the couple next door, newly arrived, were saying. I have no neighbours on the other side, only an air shaft which is lucky. But listening to one couple for a few nights might be disturbing. One or both may snore. And what of my behaviour? The mere release of wind could give offence.

As I listened to the voices next door, I was on the brink of ringing the desk and demanding another room. While my eyes searched the few spaces where a telephone could be, I became aware that there was no telephone – and no television either! We had already been told that there is no mobile coverage or Wi-Fi. Isolated, I had yet another sherry while I considered whether I could be bothered to go down to the desk on what would probably be a fruitless errand. I would be likely to be fobbed off with sing-song Welsh blandishments. And if I stayed here, I might learn something from my neighbours. I am naturally curious about what other couples do when they're alone together and out of their household regime. With these thoughts, I fell asleep on the hard bed until 15 minutes after 7:30, the hour that dinner was to be served.

5

Walking with Carol

Saturated on the walk today. Our leader, the glib Stan Jenkins, insisted that we press on and my attempt to foment a rebellion which would have swept us into the nearest pub, failed. Even the most expensive walking gear eventually lets in the water.

On the two previous days, Carol had chosen a group taking a different route and I had to check with the walks list this morning to find out which one she had chosen for today. It was easy for me to make her acquaintance now that we were on the same path. At some point, you fall into step with one of the party and get into conversation. I cruised alongside Carol at the start and reminded her – if that was necessary – that we had travelled a long way 'together'. And we stuck together during the seven hours we were out, which made my wet feet and cold legs more bearable. She's a divorcee, no children. She's lived overseas, daughter of an RAF officer who had foreign postings. She was formerly married to an oil company engineer working in the Middle East. I liked her. All this easily elicited without being intrusive.

We exchanged life stories, although mine doesn't take long to tell. I asked her very diplomatically about men-friends. She said she drew the line at married men. One question she asked me stood out above all others. She wanted to know if I had false teeth. I told her I had all my own gnashers in good order. I thought about this. Why would it be of any interest to her if I removed my teeth every night and soaked them in a glass of water in the bathroom? Only if she envisaged going to bed with me, I decided. I was heartened.

One subject we touched on was the ramshackle hotel. I explained that the trickle of hot water in my room wasn't going to be enough to have a decent shower when we got back.

"Have you complained, Bill?"

"No. I think it's the plumbing system. It doesn't work well on the top floor I've heard from the couple next door, through the wall."

We plodded on in pouring rain, a little society of two. Our pace was dictated by the oldest woman in the party who must have been near 70. At a point, we had to straddle the trunks of several pines which had fallen across the path. I helped the woman and after a particularly awkward step for her, she said to me regretfully, "I can't seem to get my leg over like I used to."

Carol and I exchanged a look. "You can use my shower, Bill," she said, with a grin.

I was surprised, and momentarily troubled, by how this squared with drawing the line at married men, or whether it was merely a generous offer of help, but while the bitter Welsh rain chilled my chest, a red coal burned in my loins. "Thanks for the offer, Carol," I said boldly. "I'll bring the bottle of sherry I've got in my room, and we can have a drink before dinner."

"That would be nice," she said.

I made this note when I returned to my room before dinner with something on my mind.

Sex: There's no point in keeping this notebook and then being too timid to record the facts. I have concerns about my sexual performance. I don't get as many erections as I used to. I thought this might get worse if I don't have sex very often. My penis might shrivel up permanently. This isn't mentioned in any of the books that I've read. I discount those confident articles in the broadsheets quoting medical studies which say that ageing in men affects the testosterone level.

The assumption in these reports is that although you've been married for 30 years *with a bit of therapy* you and your partner will be raring to get at each other and can carry on bonking until – until when? I don't want therapy. I hope I don't need it. That's why I'm anxious to see what my abilities are with Carol. She's a test case. This could be good for my marriage.

It may be that many men my age have the same uncertainties and are working their way through a list of blind dates in the contact mags. There are columns of them in our local papers and I understand that business online is roaring. There's a certain sameness about the ads. "Mature, urbane, fit, good-looking unattached man, GSOH, WLTM…" There are so many of these mature, good-looking unattached 50 going on 65-year-olds just in one borough in one city. What would they LTM for? Not companionship. Rivers of semen are flowing out there.

Ann and I have sex which, now sometimes, seems to me to be perfunctory and not as often as I would like. Somehow, she doesn't want it when I do, and I don't want it when she does. I have read that you have to make sex a priority because it's important. It shouldn't just happen because you always do it when you get into bed on Monday night. You've got to think about the most auspicious moment.

I've found that a regular time doesn't help, say Sunday mornings (like we do) after we've had breakfast in bed and read the morning papers. By the time I get to the book supplement, I'm thinking whether I should stop reading and make a start. I can see Ann eyeing me as she hesitates over the travel pages. When we got married, I suppose we did it at any time one of us wanted. Now, we know what each other is thinking. It's marital osmosis. If I read the signal that she's not all that keen, I cool off.

So it's either this mental sparring match, or there's a Premier League game on Match of the Day, and I have to watch it. Often there simply isn't time to make breakfast, eat it in bed, read the papers, bonk and see the match. I believe our priorities must be wrong because I can't remember ever sacrificing breakfast, or the papers, or the match.

I don't want to give the impression that there aren't spontaneous sex moments in our lives. They are treasures but, like treasures, relatively scarce. "What shall we do next?" is my code for "Let's make love". I don't know precisely how it came about. I think it was on a holiday cruise or hotel stay. In one of those moments, when you are both feeling satisfied with eating and drinking and you go back to your cabin (called a 'stateroom' of course) or bedroom (called a 'suite'). You have nothing specific to do and are feeling well rested. The mind turns to sensual things. You embrace. Ann never uses my phrase or indeed any words at all. She signals her feeling in similar circumstances by a big bright-eyed grin and an embrace. I don't miss these moments, so I can be sure that when I say, "What shall we do next?" her face lights up.

I hope that what's in store for me isn't having wild sex thoughts running round in my head, while I'm dead below the waist. Impotent is the word. It's fearful. A dead willy. I decide to stop thinking about this. Make the mind a limpid pool. *Resolution:* I will re-read one of the sex-instruction books in the suitcase in the garage and consider buying a later edition for new ideas.

That was it, an arrangement between sensible adults sharing scarce resources. I wasn't kidding about the lack of hot water in my room. I did in fact shower as best I could and put on fresh underclothes and a clean shirt and with what was left of my bottle of sherry I went to Carol's room. I found she had bathed and was sitting on her bed wearing a transparent cream silk shortie nightie over scanty underwear. I was astonished. She had moved the game on very quickly – but we had so few nights left.

It occurred to me that she had brought these delicate clothes on a walking trip. Not what I would have expected her to wear in an indifferently heated room on a cold night in a ramshackle hotel. She'd removed her glasses and looked quite girlish. I showered hastily and sat on the bed in my underpants. It would have been rude or falsely modest to do anything else. Events were racing ahead, quite out of my control.

I poured two sherries which were quickly forgotten as we lay down together. I found myself beside a small but shapely and firm body which could have been 15 years younger. It had been well hidden in those shapeless outdoor clothes. After a few minutes of kissing and cuddling, Carol said, "Bill, do you have a condom?"

It was quite right of her to ask, for both our sakes, although she certainly wasn't going to catch anything from me. Was I going to catch anything from her? She'd told me she saw a man occasionally. She had really downgraded her liaison with this man in her manner of commenting on it earlier in the day. I read her words as, "Yes, he's decent enough, but I wouldn't mind an upgrade." At that particular moment, the other man wasn't a subject which troubled me, but I did remember my son, Nick's, graphic remark to me: "When you sleep with a girl, Dad, you sleep with all her previous partners," he probably said, fuck.

"No, Carol, I don't have a condom. I'm sorry," I said thankfully, "and you wouldn't expect me to, would you? I told you I didn't come on the walk with the thought of getting laid." Actually, I had thought getting laid might be possible, but I didn't think of a condom.

She smiled enigmatically.

Suddenly, the brakes were on! What a relief. Carol's question allowed my mind to move from a position in my groin, to its rightful place behind my eyes. We had an exciting time, cuddling and drinking sherry and being late for dinner.

After dinner, Carol went up to her room without saying anything to me, and I thought perhaps I should follow. I couldn't phone her. Our mobiles wouldn't work in this primitive countryside. If I knocked at her door without a call, it might not be convenient for her, and it would be embarrassing to be sent away. And there was the condom problem. Instead, I bought a pint at the bar to think it over, and talked to a computer consultant who kept complaining about his sore feet. I couldn't get away. We had two brandies each after the pint, and I went up to my room with my head fuddled but clear enough to make more notes.

Drinking: Ann says I drink too much and it's a waste of money. She drinks but more modestly than I do. She might have a point about me.

If I'm out with friends, I'll go into a pub and have a few pints but that isn't regular. I'm not a pub man. My habit at home is to have a hefty gin-and-tonic while I listen to Channel 4 news. I'm sceptical about the news. It's like a graphic form of fiction and incredibly biased (whichever station you watch), not I hope in misrepresenting facts, but in arranging them for effect. Skilful work in the cutting room and script writing.

The TV disappointingly dries up at Christmas, New Year and other public holidays when I want it most. The news cameramen and presenters are on vacation (national disasters and the deluge of stories about the poor and needy excepted). Two hundred years ago, I wouldn't know much about a war in Syria or a famine in Africa. But today I'm there, at the TV, for nearly an hour most nights, poking my nose into the farthest corners of the earth – with my gin-and-tonic, occasionally more than one. Ann often joins me. We have plenty to talk about afterwards. The presenters become characters in our lives and not always much loved characters.

Then I go into the kitchen, ostensibly to help Ann with the dinner. I light a candle for the dining table. An odd habit domestically but it does focus the small world around the table as it does in a restaurant. We lower the lights. I put on a CD and pour a glass of wine but otherwise I'm at leisure. I hold forth on subjects in the news, reshaping the world and pointing out mistakes. I think Ann quite enjoys this while she's finishing off the cooking and dishing up. She can certainly talk while manipulating the various pots and pans and maintaining their devilish timing. Later, I drink about half the bottle of wine or perhaps two-thirds while Ann stays with one glass of white. If it's a bottom-half night, I may have to open a new bottle. Too much? Possibly, yes.

Very good news. I read a recent article in *The Guardian* backed by medical research which said that red wine is healthful to the arteries. I know that Thomas Jefferson wrote that a bottle of red wine a day, which he made himself on his estate at Monticello, was positively necessary for his health. I am going to stay with Jefferson, Homer and Omar Khyam on this.

A friend of mine wrote to me that he stopped drinking for two months to prove he could do it. And he started on the eve of a trip to Hong Kong. Imagine the self-punishment involved. Whenever I used to get on a long haul aircraft (business class in my executive days!), the first thing I asked for was a strong G&T. Water is wonderful, my friend said. Superior so-and-so! What he was really saying to me was, "You know I'm stronger than you, don't you?" Well, he is.

But I wonder whether I should do the same. And then I think, why should I have two miserable months to prove a point? If anybody was so indifferent to alcohol that stopping made no difference, whether he stopped for two or ten months wouldn't matter. But if it's part of your enjoyment, stopping does matter even if it's only for a day. Unless you're a masochist. And another angle not to dwell on is whether I *could* stop at all if I wanted to.

Resolution: carry out research into how much our friends drink and review at year's end with a view to varying consumption.

Serious thoughts: I know I can't have Carol without a condom, but the problem lurking in my mind is whether, if I had one, I could use it effectively. All that messing about with slimy rubber might make me go soft. I haven't used a condom since I was a kid. I was never any good with them then. How will I perform now? Perhaps, I'll look like an old fart who can't get it up. It's hard to think of anything more pathetic than an old man who wants to mount, but can't. The lion turned into a pussy cat. All natural juices dried up. That really is old.

I could look pretty silly, and I would cringe inwardly forever if I failed to have sex with Carol. It's become a contest, a peak I have to climb. More seriously, suppose I had a condom and supposing I could master it, should I proceed? The precept from Mr Bhatta is that harmful sex isn't permissible. Well, this wouldn't harm Carol because she's a free and single woman. Would it harm me or Ann? It might hurt Ann if I fell for Carol, which is different from having sex. Is it really? Perhaps love (which would include sex) and sex both come with such a web of entanglements that there's no material difference. Or an affair with Carol might give Ann a greater sense of freedom with Bernard – if she knew. I asked myself whether I would ever tell Ann. Answer: never.

These questions swirled in my mind as I fell into a lurid sleep in which Carol's firm and fragrant body engulfed me.

In the morning, I woke up with the clear intention of forgetting Carol. I had a hasty, early breakfast, took a cab to the railway station and the train to London. I never even saw her.

6
My Day

I thought I should sketch out my day (Ms Biggs' recommendation) so that I can examine it in say a year's time and see how it has changed.

On weekdays, I am out of bed by 7 am. I splash my face, clean my teeth, feed Rex and go down the street to Mr Bhatta's for *The Times*. Often the pages of the newspaper are soiled or creased because Mr Bhatta seems to get the remnants of the delivery. I could get a pristine paper along the street at Tesco, but I don't. I walk back home briskly. By the time Ann is dressed, I have the coffee, grapefruit and cereal on the kitchen table. We eat together, glimpse the news on our I-pads and, perhaps, talk about a household item. Ann glances at the newspaper. Then she is gone.

Now the day is mine. I tidy the kitchen, stack and start the dishwasher and walk Rex to the dog area by the Palace Road. I watch his antics with other dogs. He has a macho arrogance and impertinence, despite his small size. I nod to faces I know. Dog-walkers are more than friendly if you compliment them on their animal. They're like mothers with babies.

When we return home, I cease to be a kitchen-hand or a dog-walker. I am not denigrating these roles. I find the opening sequence of the day pleasant in its certainty and repetitiveness. I try to think of the everyday as extraordinary.

Now, I do my bathroom exercises. Most of our friends go to a gym, but I have a dislike of the machines. I see people pounding on treadmills, looking mindlessly into the wall, or watching stock exchange screens. Others are bending their bodies on a variety of racks. Sweat is running. It's torture.

My exercises started when I was about 30. I realised that I was withering away as a result of the sedentary life I led. The demands of work had pushed my walking pursuits aside. I moved the furniture to help a maiden aunt and hurt my back. I needed to get these bones and muscles moving. I found a copy of a little book amongst some old papers in the shed, titled *24BX*. It dated from the 1939–45 war and was a keep-fit guide for aircrew. I based my 20 minutes of exercises upon it, throwing my arms and legs around and doing sit-ups and push-ups. Yes, I do use some modest weights but I keep that quiet from friends.

Jim Clitheroe has a big belly and is envious of my shape. One day, he questioned me about how I managed to keep it. He's always struggling with his weight and wondering why a game of golf twice a week with a golf cart doesn't seem to help. When I told him about the *24BX*, he said disparagingly, "Hoping to live to 105, are you?"

A long time ago, I made a decision that exercise had to be enjoyable. 'No pain, no gain' as a principle didn't appeal to me. The very sight of a gymnasium with its torture devices repelled me. The *24BX*, in contrast, gives me a feeling that I am setting myself up for the day. My body always feels springy and active afterwards. If I miss it for a day or two I hardly notice, but after a week I start to feel flaccid and weary.

Exercises done, I shave and shower and dress. Ann maintains that the whole process takes an hour and a half. And she says this with a hint that I am idling my time away. I assert that it takes 45 minutes.

My first stop now is the potting shed where I review the business on my to-do list – all the minutiae of daily living. There are usually half a dozen items, bills to be paid, emails to be sent and phone calls to be made. And a number of household things, bulbs to be replaced, locks to be oiled, laundry visits, forgotten grocery shopping.

It is an unwritten rule of mine to defer everything I can, for as long as I can, without making things too difficult for myself. Ann has some caustic remarks about the time a task has to spend on the to-do list before it is done. I contend that tasks have to mature on the to-do list before they are ripe to be tackled. The real test is how long I can sensibly delay them.

Now, for my emails. I'm slightly computer-phobic, although I have used one for at least 20 years. The introduction of the web is change enough in that time, but that is matched by changes to software which seem to happen every month. The screen changes almost before you can get used to it. So many nerdy apps, so many alleged improvements and so much interference with your screen by the people selling the software and apps. There is something slightly sinister about committing your communications to a machine that is routinely interfered with by others. Who owns it anyway? So I have a phobia!

My first computer sat on a side table by my desk in my office and quietly, almost unnoticed over a period of many months, subverted dictation to my secretary. I began to send her draft letters from my computer to *her* computer which she typed and despatched. I started emailing colleagues with whom I worked. I expanded along with everybody else to emailing outside the company. No need for letters! My secretary was diminished. Lo, over very few years, without any trumpet sounds, the computer had arrived, settled in and changed much. But I did not reject entirely the luxury, particularly on urgent matters, of calling her into my room, letting my head ease back on the head-rest and *composing*. And then without bothering about titles, names, addresses and postcodes, say to her, "Please get that away now."

Before I retired, I could be called or texted as I sat down to lunch on Sunday afternoon and I was on occasions. Computers had sneakily extended my hours of work, as well as that of a big chunk of the population. Twenty-four hour shopping! But the real capabilities of these devices have always remained beyond me, an undiscovered territory.

My next action of the day is to devote some time to this notebook, entering new items, reflecting on what I've done and where I'm going. No clarity emerges, but I have a feeling that I have engaged usefully and that I am edging closer to certainties.

I get *The Times* from the kitchen, and if the weather is fine, put it under my arm and walk to the Café Nero in Fulham Broadway where I order a large Americano which I have black with a cake, preferably a chocolate cake, or if it is close enough to lunchtime, a chicken sandwich. I read the paper for half an hour and walk home.

I question whether I've learned anything from the newspaper. The important news can be absorbed in minutes, but I look for the particular opinion columns which I prefer. I disregard the journos whom I tend to disagree with. I shouldn't do this. It's a failing, avoiding ideas you don't like, but I want to be calmed and reassured. Somebody said that rather than read the newspapers, we bathe in them as in a warm bath. I do.

At home, I read more instructive work from my bedside selection if there is any time left before lunchtime. This is part of my self-improvement project. I am more than half way through Dickens' *David Copperfield*. I have just finished George Orwell's *The Road to Wigan Pier*. At 1 pm, I make a sandwich and have a banana unless I've had lunch at a café.

Afterwards, and weather permitting, I take a longer walk, perhaps an hour, with Rex. I can walk for miles from Amherst Street along the Thames without having to dodge cars. I am a walker. I think and dream and walk. One of my favourite ways is along the Thames Path from Bishop's Park to Fulham Reach near Hammersmith Bridge. As the year wears on and the sun gets lower in the south and west, I have the sun (if any) behind me and, more often than not, a light south-westerly too. On a winter's day with heavy grey clouds and no sun, this is a scene I imagine I might have painted with black ink and wash, the dark line of trees on the far bank, the oily water and the mere silhouette of the Hammersmith Bridge in the distance. On a fine day in summer, it is a spectacle of delicate colours.

The afternoons are varied. I play poker with a friend every three weeks. He lives in Hammersmith. We generally play at his house. I went to school with him. We play for pounds and I know the shape of his mind. He is cautious but usually succeeds in taking me for a fiver or a tenner. He has a better memory for the cards that have been played from the deck than I do, and consequently judges his chances more shrewdly than I do. My method is to be unpredictable, to alarm him into backing down.

I have a drawing class at Putney School of Art twice a week. That class, for me, is about really seeing the objects that are in front of me as models, a vase of flowers, a bowl of fruit. I'm not hooked on producing art myself. No, I don't go to a life class with nude female models, but I might in future.

Ann arrives back from school at 4:30 or so. We talk about the day and watch the 7 pm Channel 4 news. I take her out to dinner usually twice a week. Sometimes we go to a classical concert, a show, a play or a gallery. I'm not into this scene except as an interested and amateurish observer, but I do like to criticise plays in discussions with Ann and with friends.

I cook an evening meal for us at times and it's usually rather basic, like baked chicken in tomato sauce (bought pasta sauce, warmed up), boiled potatoes and frozen peas. Ann, on the other hand, is a skilful cook and produces a starter and a main course; it seems by magic. She's clever with sauces while I have to co-opt pasta sauce for every dish. I'd rather dine on her cooking at home than go to a restaurant, but I remain agreeable to dining out because five tasty home dinners out of seven in a week is a good score.

We usually have a martini before we eat, if we are at home on Saturday or Sunday and wine with the food every night. That is, apart from special nights. Any night can be declared to be a special night by either of us. We have a gin and tonic or whisky and dry – or two. A special night can be caused by any event we choose – usually when we have had an unexpected piece of luck, like Ann getting a rise, or me having completed a somewhat delayed DIY task.

The weekends don't have a pattern. Saturday is for the usual home chores but we sleep in. On Sunday, we watch Andrew

Marr on BBC1 and read the papers in bed (I have to throw on a few clothes and go out to Mr Bhatta's to get them). Sometimes, we don't get up on Sundays until noon.

Even though I am said not to 'work,' the weekdays have a different quality than the weekends. There is an impression of a calendar of activity. I like dining at home best on Saturday and Sunday nights because the day brings a sense of relaxation, a few glasses of wine and some old CDs. I have a tin ear when it comes to music. Rap and the incoherently mumbled lyrics of the present day pass me by. I'm back in the time of Elvis Presley, Frank Sinatra and Ella Fitzgerald. I can go as far as Rod Stewart or even Freddie Mercury and the protest songs of Bob Dylan, but that's about it. I listen to classics, popular ones like Beethoven's Fifth and admire them, and as I say, even go to concerts with Ann, but music is just not my thing. I know I have missed something, it's a kind of language and I'm shut out from it.

I walk the dog at 10:30 or 11. The streets are quiet and well lit. These are good days (subject to my anxieties).

7

I Reach out to Carol Again

Shortly after I fled from Carol and returned home from Merthyr Tydfil, I received a letter from the police. I can't express my angst as I opened the letter. My fingers were trembling. But there, on the page, was the definite statement that they would *not* be prosecuting me on a charge of failing to stop after an accident – a very serious charge. I was flooded with relief.

I had had an experience like the character in the Tom Wolfe novel, *Bonfire of the Vanities,* getting embroiled with the police. I unintentionally roused malevolent feelings.

I was driving back from the shops on a Saturday morning, with Ann, at about 20 mph, along Weston Street in Fulham. This is one of many streets which are parked on both sides with cars, leaving only a central passage. I had to stop suddenly because the driver of a parked car flung open the door of his car in my path. I stopped inches from the door. I backed up a few feet. The driver, standing in the road, paid no attention, but busied himself with a baby on the back seat. The nerve!

At this instant, I made a serious mistake. I was irritated and I hooted my horn. The man was infuriated. He stormed up to my car window. "You hit my car and endangered the baby!" he shouted. "You pull over. I'll settle the baby and get your details."

I began a trenchant denial of his demented claim, but he didn't stay near the window. He returned his attention to the child. In a few moments, he had to shut the door of his car because traffic was beginning to bank up behind me. Drivers were hooting and tooting.

I looked at Ann. "He's a lout!" she said.

"It's not going to be helpful to talk to such an unreasonable man," I said. I shrugged and drove home. Over four months later, I received a summons for failing to stop after an accident. I couldn't believe it.

I denied that there was any accident and a detective took my written statement at the Fulham police station. He cautioned me that it could be used in evidence against me. I didn't like him. He had a ratty face, a greasy tie and his tone carried the assumption that I was a liar. I was partly strengthened by the fact that I was telling the truth, but I was very worried. Indignation was not going to do me any good. It was going to be Ann and I versus that lying driver and the woman in his car. I knew you could toss a coin to determine the outcome of such a contest. I found it hard to understand that anybody could generate the malice that had led to this.

I went home from the interview with the detective feeling very low. I was filing the police papers away when I noticed that somebody had pencilled 'not W6' on the envelope enclosing the summons. I live at SW6. In a moment, I understood the delay. I worked out that the summons had been wrongly addressed to W6, eventually returned to the police, and then readdressed to SW6. I checked on the time limit for this. I saw that the date of issue of the summons had been changed by the police, to make it appear that it had been issued and served in due time. If I was right, the charge was dead.

Not only was I the victim of a liar, but of a cheating police department. I wrote in strong terms to the police saying that the first thing I would raise in court was their malpractice. And after toasting me on a griddle of silence for months, they had backed down.

I have to accept responsibility for having provoked an ill-tempered and probably unbalanced driver, who knew that a complaint to the police could cause me considerable pain, win or lose. The nastiness of the threat made me wake on many nights in the darkest hours in a sweat. The threat was like a septic sore, buried in my consciousness. I lived with it silently and painfully – until this morning's letter. Mr Bhatta reminded me that consequences may be entirely disproportionate to actions. "There is no natural justice to events, no necessary balance between people," he said, with a smile which itself said, 'You already know this.'

I have been scrupulously honest in the few facts I have told Carol about my married life. I'm mindful of a friend who had a fling with a girl at a summer school, having suggested to her that he was unattached, only to be pestered by her at his home. His wife found out and he nearly lost her. I've told Carol that I'm married and have no desire to disturb the relationship with my wife, so I'm not expecting her to pester me – unless she's a stalker. She's not a pushy kind of woman anyway. And of course, Carol and I are not really an item. I conjecture about whether we ever could be, while I try to counter the malign spell that Bernard Chandler has cast over my life.

I have tried to follow my daughter, Jane's advice, to interest Ann in a holiday abroad. I thought I had made adequate allowance for the fact that she likes to be at home around Christmas and New Year for family reasons and has her teaching commitments and meetings. But Ann has viewed my approach as slightly menopausal as well as inconvenient. We have both enjoyed travelling in the past, but it is as though our marriage had now progressed beyond holidays abroad and I ought to know that.

It has been on the tip of my tongue to say to Ann that I will not be patronised by Big Bummed Bernard any longer. He acts as if he and Ann share insights which I would not understand. He moves around our kitchen as though it's his, opens cupboards, helps himself to a glass of milk or a biscuit. It's him and Ann, with me on the outside. However, I remain silent – for the time being.

As a consequence, I have put my reservations about Carol as a stalker aside. All I can do in these circumstances is seek consolation with her. Yes, I think I'm justified. *I have called her* to re-establish contact after nail-biting concern whether I had the nerve to call her. She seemed delighted to hear from me. We have agreed a walk in Yorkshire. She has some leave owing to her from her employer. Our trip will be four days long and a group affair. All we have to do is to book into the same walk. Meals and accommodation are part of the deal. We will have separate rooms.

I have spent some time gently getting Ann into a frame of mind where she will accept my absence on another walk so soon. She becomes slightly suspicious when I voice my thoughts – they have not been translated at this moment into an actual booking, they exist only as a proposal to Carol. In one way, Ann's attitude is comforting. She is at least interested in what I do outside the house. My defence to her enquiries is robust. I say, "If you can't get away with me, isn't it fair that I do something, rather than sit at home?"

"I suppose so," she says, reluctantly. That is the gist of her attitude.

One evening recently, before dinner, I saw what I thought was my moment. "I'm thinking of walking next month. It's in Yorkshire. Looks good."

She was preparing vegetables on the kitchen bench and she turned her head toward me, staring. "Really?"

There was something ominous in that look which I should have anticipated. I wanted to interpret it as indifference, but it may have been suspicion.

At Merthyr Tydfil, I mentioned Nick in this notebook. I had a disturbing phone call from him before I left home for that trip which I tried not to think about. I know parents often subsidise their children even as far as buying flats for them, not to mention paying for school and university. But Nick, presents a different problem. After a lacklustre school career (minor public school and a lot of costly coaching), he acquired an indifferent law degree from Leeds University. He found work in a law office dull and after a row with the partners, declared that he was 'unemployable'. He is certainly a very difficult man (although he will always be an adolescent to me).

His first venture as an entrepreneur was a restaurant which went broke after a year. I was never called upon to contribute, but I imagine a number of his friends were. The point to me (which I never made to him and should have) was that he knew nothing about the restaurant business. Admittedly, he was only the promoter and financier, but he seemed to me to show a profound disrespect for the complexities of operating a restaurant; as though it was only necessary to find the money, rent premises, employ staff and the takings would roll in.

In this, I recognised something that had not changed since his school days. He and three friends once spent all their savings on musical instruments – guitars, drums and keyboards.

They were going to be a pop group. But none of them could read music or play any of the instruments they had bought. Their few gigs were a disaster. It sounds incredible. It was certainly incredibly stupid. They willed the end without thinking about the means. And again, with an implicit disrespect for the art and expertise behind the making of any kind of music. At that time, I calmly put the incident down to boyish eagerness.

I have said that Nick is hubristic and absurdly over-confident. He would have been a good second-hand car salesman. Instead, he solicited money from anybody he could and set himself up with friends as an investment banker. The money he elicited went into one of his funds and was spent on small start-up companies. As he conceded to me, four out of five of them would fail but the fifth, he maintained, would be a bonanza.

Nick holds forth to me when we meet about his investments. He likes to talk about himself. I suspect that these small start-ups are in fields of activity about which he knows little or nothing. He has a facility with computer and 'app' technology which is often the vehicle for such companies, but not the underlying businesses. If you are going to produce an app about farming chickens, you have to know about farming chickens. It's not much of a solution to say that the people you employ have the knowledge.

I thought I could see, in Nick's career so far, a man with his eyes dazzled by the golden pot at the end of the rainbow. A man who didn't understand that he didn't know how to get there. I should have advised him to get a proper job a long time ago.

Nick is basically honest. I say basically because he is given to exaggeration, but I think he sincerely believes in his schemes. When he called me on the phone, he sounded smooth and agreeable. "Just calling for a bit of a chat, Dad."

"Any time, son." Nick never calls for a chat. Something bad was going to come out.

"Got a couple of writs."

Not surprisingly, Nick, who is custodian of a lot of other people's money and seems to owe a lot, is always being sued. Once, when I remonstrated with him about this way of doing business, he brushed it off saying, "Where there's brass there's greed and where there's greed there are lawsuits."

"So what's new," I replied.

"These are biggies," he laughed.

"Tell me?"

"Around 350,000. Thought you might be able to give me some advice. It's a frame-up but they could bankrupt me."

"Give you advice? You mean give you more money?"

I had already lent him 30,000 pounds about three years ago and never heard another word about it. Ann told me to forget it. "He's just getting on his feet," she said. So I did 'forget' or rather, keep quiet. But the 'loan' is like a slice of old Gorgonzola cheese. It begins to smell more strongly to me, and I believe to him, as time goes by.

"Well, yes, Dad," he said in his assured way, as though 'advice' and 'giving' were synonymous.

"I'll have to talk to Ann," I said, very calmly in the circumstances.

"Don't leave it too long, will you?" he replied ungraciously.

I was cooled by Nick's approach. In view of his blind spot about himself and his schemes, I wasn't sympathetic, as I might be if he was suffering from a malady which affected his judgment. He is a healthy, intelligent, tolerably well-educated man. I certainly wasn't going to commit myself. Talking to Ann was my first line of defence.

"By the way, Nick, you said there 'a couple' of writs. Do you mean two at three fifty each or a total of three-fifty?"

"Yeah," he said, agreeably, avoiding the point.

"So we're talking about a liability of nearly three quarters of a million?"

"We are indeed, Dad." Again, that assured tone.

"And you mentioned writs. These are not writs, are they? They're judgments against you."

"They are. Forgive my loose phraseology." His clipped reply suggested I was niggling.

"I hope your maths are not loose too. I'll talk to your mother and get back to you."

The call ended in a taut atmosphere. Nick wasn't grovelling for a favour. He was taking it as read that he was entitled to 'help'. He is however aware that although I discuss everything with Ann, I am the money manager in the household.

Phew! I was staggered, but I stayed calm – outwardly. Nick knows very well that I don't have the kind of money he needs in cash. He knows that relatively big as my pension is, it's untouchable as capital. Yet he's coming at me.

Naturally, this exchange flared into a heated conversation if not a dispute between Ann and me. I recounted the conversation to her that night in the kitchen when she was preparing dinner and we were having a glass of wine.

She was upset. "Bankruptcy. It's a horrible stigma."

"He'll get over it," I said.

"He'll never be respected in financial dealings again if he's been a bankrupt."

"I think people are a bit more blasé about it now."

"That might go for the US, but not here, Bill. Besides, he's our son."

"I don't feel any deep tribal link with Nick."

I saw Ann's face fall. That is a slightly shocking truth. Nick is good in parts. I'm ambivalent about him. I grew up, an only child, without the so-called benefit of a father. I found I had more freedom to determine my own course. My mother was quite enough. Ann chastises me for having no concept of 'family' in contrast to her affectionate brother and sisters – although they are a little less affectionate now, after distributing the gifts in their mother's will.

"You don't feel anything very much, Bill. It would be shameful for the whole family."

"Hang on, Ann. There's only four of us including Nick. Unless you count Benedict aged one."

"It would be shameful anyway."

"Are you thinking how you will feel in front of the ladies at your play reading group when you've told them what a brilliant and prosperous son you have?"

"Yes, I damn well am and why not!"

"I think we're bigger than that, my dear," I made this pompous pronouncement without any confidence at all. I suppose I'm as protective as she is about the way we 'look' to Amherst Street and our friends and family. But I felt that there was implicit disrespect in what Nick wanted. It stuck in my throat.

"You've already made up your mind not to help your son. Your only son. I can't think why I married such a cold fish."

"It isn't *only* about money," I protested.

"Not much."

Nick could do no wrong according to Ann. His improvidence haunts me at 3 am, but at 12 noon, in the daylight, I'm cold and fishlike.

8

I Volunteer at a Food Bank

The idea of volunteering at a food bank was not mine. Ann and Susan Clitheroe have been compiling a list of voluntary jobs I might do. When Ann refers to these possible jobs, I hasten to defend myself quietly by listing my domestic chores. I am solely in control of all clearing up in the kitchen after eating. I am solely in charge of rubbish disposal from all bins in the house to the gate. I occasionally do the supermarket shopping if Ann can't. I manage the servicing of the car. I manage the cellar – our wines and spirits. I carry all heavy items which are destined for upstairs or down. And I am on call, with a fully equipped toolkit, to deal with any do-it-yourself technical problems 24/7. Admittedly, my rating as a DIY person is not high in Ann's eyes, nor is my contribution to domestic chores, considerable as it may be. Hence these 'suggestions' about what I might do.

I knew I would have to yield, and I liked the food bank idea. This is in part because the sort of people I know refer to food banks in a tone of disgust and embarrassment (with our society). I want to find out more, because I would have thought the more food banks the better. But no, 'food bank' seems to be shorthand for government incompetence.

I have enough trouble managing my own affairs, and I can quite understand that there have always been, and will always be, people who are temporarily broke, unable to pay the gas bill to heat up a tin of baked beans. What do they do? I expect that thousands of community friendly societies have been wiped out over the last 200 years by industrial change. Some ethnic groups and religions continue to look after their own. The food bank of today may be nothing embarrassing or disgusting, but a different solution to deal with a perennial problem. This was merely an idea in my untutored mind and I wanted to experience the reality.

I was directed (by Susan Clitheroe) to an appointment with Mr J D Pullen, manager of the food distribution centre at Shepherds Bush. I waited for 20 minutes in an old building on King's Road. I sat on a chair in a narrow, grey corridor, facing a notice board with peeling papers. The door of Pullen's office at last expelled two bonny young women with clip-boards who would have no need of a food bank. I waited. Fully five minutes later he who must be JD Pullen appeared in the frame. He was large and uneven, laced in by a tight waistcoat. His head was jug-like, a high forehead and a smear of dark hair with a wide jaw. He waved me to enter and settled before me, too big for his desk. He flapped a piece of paper – my application.

"Any experience of voluntary work, Mr Batley?"

"I'm married and there's a fair amount of voluntary work in that."

"Don't try to be funny, Mr Batley. You're not auditioning for a show at the Palladium. This is serious."

I shrivelled up inside. "I'm quite serious, I assure you," I said modestly.

Pullen's eyes were slits. "*Quite* serious?" he questioned.

"Very serious, absolutely serious and deadly serious."

"Mmm. Your CV says you were an insurance company executive, not a stand-up comedian."

"We're not getting on well, Mr Pullen. Do you want me to stay?"

"Let's see how you get on. You need seriousness, Mr Batley, and a conviction that the work is good and necessary."

"I have that."

He looked at me doubtfully. "I was a stationmaster in my previous life, Mr Batley, and you get to know people, meet all kinds. I *know* people."

He apparently had a gift of instantaneous appraisal. He knew me and I didn't measure up. "Certainly, as a stationmaster... was it one of our city stations?" I was seeking something agreeable and neutral.

"It was a very fine, clean, efficient station in Buckinghamshire, Feldenbois."

I had never heard of Feldenbois. I had a mental picture of Pullen, tyrant of the ticket clerks, peaked hat low, shading his eyes, commandant of a 50 yard stretch of concrete in a desert of suburbia. If I could show Pullen I was a railway buff and even claim to know Feldenbois, perhaps, I could make a friend for life, but I couldn't.

"Swept away by the road lobby!" he went on, "Redundant at 48, but with a portfolio of skills and experience, Mr Batley."

"A portfolio?" I said, wide-eyed.

Pullen paused, eyed me balefully, as though I had insulted him, and then unwillingly it seemed, began a long lecture on the processes of the food banks. When he talked about volunteers, he appeared critical. "What makes you want to work here, Mr Batley?"

"I have the conviction that the work is good and necessary," I parroted. Wrong remark.

Again the baleful stare. "You only remembered half of what I said. Seriousness, Mr Batley. No room for dilettantes."

"Does it hurt to approach a grim task with a sense of humour, Mr Pullen?"

"Your humour is misplaced. Remember that." He led me away like a dog to the kennel. "You have to start at the bottom, Batley.".

I pondered whether the change from Mr Batley to 'Batley' was a comradely sign, as it is with a certain class of person, or whether he had consigned me to the depths. I concluded it could only be the latter.

When we entered the store, he stopped and flung his arms and chest out. "You must get to know the stock. Know where everything is. Then you can fill baskets quickly," his voice boomed and the other volunteers who were present in the room – which was like the back-room of an old grocery store, crammed with racks – heard all and were silent.

"We don't want clients loitering on the premises, Batley, drifting down the aisles, choosing whatever they fancy. This is not the Garden of Eden. This is an efficient service. There is a prescribed entitlement and a small space for options. It's all written. Nothing more. Sad stories belong elsewhere." He handed me a bundle of rules and regulations.

"I get it," I said, but I didn't like it.

"Read, and study this well, Batley. It isn't a comedy script."

When Pullen had gone, one of the volunteers snapped his heels together and said, "Heil Mein Fuhrer!" I walked around the store introducing myself to my fellow workers and familiarising myself with shelves of canned spaghetti, baked beans and sardines. I felt very small.

We have a gravel garden instead of a lawn at Amherst Street – Ann's idea. It has select plants which require little maintenance and a large flagged patio. The main advantage I see is that I'm no longer enslaved by lawn-cutting as I have been in past years. The garden is completely secluded in trees and bushes, some of which are our neighbours'. This privacy is rare for London and we enjoy it, but it is dependent upon the neighbours being of the same mind as us.

I was sitting in the potting shed on Saturday morning writing up my notebook, aware of the whine of a chain-saw, but not seriously disturbed by it, when Ann came in.

"Take a look over the Foster's fence, Bill. They're cutting everything down."

The Fosters are our neighbours on the opposite side to the Clitheroes. I looked out of the back bedroom window. I could see the Foster's overgrown garden. Various brawny men were sawing, slashing and piling up green branches. The boundary line which had once been, with its vegetation, about eight feet high was now reduced in places to the four foot level of the brick fence. Our privacy was fast disappearing on that boundary.

"I'll go and see the Fosters now," I said.

"Can we do anything?" Ann said anxiously.

"Not if they're cutting their plants on their side."

"Oh, dear. I did so love it the way it was, Bill."

"I shall have to plead for mercy."

The Fosters were a remote old couple. Good neighbours, but we could only be distantly friendly with them. They settled in the street many years before us and represented a generation which was dying out in Amherst Street. Mr Foster was in the printing trade at a time when fonts had to be hand set. They had one son who was now my age. Tom Foster had never worked consistently. He still lived with his parents. He was an alcoholic, harmless enough, but always in trouble with the police. He used to knock on our door when he ran out of money, or ask for a can of beer. I used to make a donation in cash or kind, incurring displeasure from the Foster parents, our other neighbours and Ann. I stopped. Unfortunately, it was Tom who was directing the chain-saw massacre, as I found when he confronted me on the doorstep of his home, red faced and bloated.

"Is your Dad or Mum here, Tom?"

"Not if you've come about the cutting."

"Why is that?"

"Because I'm in charge."

It would have been much easier for me to speak to his father. "I must ask you to let me speak to your father, Tom."

"You can't. Dad's upstairs, resting. He's 90 years old, remember. And Mum's out, in case you want to try her."

"OK, Tom. Can I ask whether you're going to cut down all the trees and bushes on your side along our boundary?"

"I'm perfectly entitled to do so if I want."

"I'm not disputing that, Tom. We value the privacy, that's all, and I thought I'd let you know."

"What you really mean is you don't want to look over in our direction. It's too awful for you. And you don't want us staring at you, because you're so private."

"Never," I said. "Not at all," trying to be cheery.

That was a lie. Tom had hit the point. We didn't want to see over the fence. Mrs Foster was certainly the only person in Amherst Street who hung her washing on a line. Ann was particularly irritated by the sight of Mrs Foster's oversize knickers and other unmentionables dangling from a line which stretched across the yard, visible from our upper floor windows. While our rotting garden shed was shielded from all view by a laurel bush, the Fosters' was plonked in the centre of their yard (it was never a garden), caving in, and surrounded by bins also in full view from our upper floors.

"Ann and I like the seclusion, that's all," I added, retaining my smile.

"Well, you'll have to get used to us clocking you. Too bad," Tom replied.

I think Tom held it against me that I had stopped his supply of beer or petty cash. I retired as gracefully as I could. When I got home, Ann was agitated. "What did he say?"

"Tom Foster very deftly put his drunken forefinger on our middle-class sensibilities."

"What on earth do you mean?" Ann said.

"Mrs Foster's knickers, flapping in the breeze."

Ann sighed, adding, "Bill, this is not Tasmania."

In the Tasmanian countryside, as we knew from our visit, people do their washing on Mondays and hang it gloriously on lines in the wind. It makes an uplifting sight, like flags and streamers as you drive along the roads.

I didn't know where I stood with Ann on the holiday venture, but I went ahead in tandem with Carol and made the booking. I drove to Merrivale House, a country house near Swaledale in Yorkshire. I checked in, put my bag in my room and found Carol in the lounge. We exchanged rather polite and distant 'hellos' at first because other members of the group were sniffing around each other curiously – as they usually do. But we were all soon chatting.

It was rather comforting to sit through a briefing about the walks from our guides and know that Carol and I could retire after dinner from the dozen or so of our group, instead of getting involved in quizzes and party games.

When dinner was served, Carol and I were at the back of the crowd going into the dining room. There was the usual dive for chairs beside new friends. We had to separate to take the only available seats for our group. I talked absently to the people on either side of me during dinner but could hardly wait for the meal (which was tasty but had three courses) to end. I caught up with Carol afterwards as she went back to the lounge. "Do you want to stop for coffee and games or shall we slip upstairs now?" I asked.

"Oh," she replied, appearing surprised. "Yes, we can go upstairs if you'd like, Bill."

I had taken the precaution of bringing a bottle of whisky to get us in the right frame of mind for our encounter. I envisaged a quiet talk with a few shots, and then, when we were mellow… That part of the evening would take care of itself. My earlier reservations about what I was doing had not gone away, but were deeply submerged, perhaps suppressed. I stopped by my room to get the bottle and went to Carol's room.

We were looking at each other in her small, neat, twin bed space quite suddenly. She was standing between the beds uncertainly. She hadn't made a move to take off her clothes. I knew that I had made a mistake. She was going along with what she didn't want to do.

I fussed about getting two glasses from the bathroom, pouring and watering the whisky. I handed her a glass. She sat on the edge of one bed, while I sat on the edge of the other. Our glances had a chance to meet but didn't connect. We were distant.

"Here's to some good walking," I said.

"Bill, aren't we rushing it a bit?" she said, coolly.

Perhaps I hadn't made the hit with her that I thought I'd made. "If you feel that, Carol, we can go downstairs – and play games." I couldn't resist a derisive note, but I don't think she noticed.

"Well, let's finish our drinks first," she beamed in a forced way.

The conversation was halting and awkward. Carol did go downstairs when we finished the drinks, and I went to my room bidding her a terse goodnight.

9

The Delight of a Second Home

When I returned to my room, I picked up the notebook. I began to write to relieve my annoyance. I was more annoyed than understanding, but the feeling soon wore off. The fact was that I had pushed progress with Carol a little too hard.

When you're alone in a hotel room, especially one as mean as this, it's natural to think of other people enjoying their hotels and holiday cottages. Before the May bank holiday, I was whiling away the afternoon with George Cutler and a glass of cold sauvignon blanc, in his garden shed. I asked him what he and Penny were going to do in August. Most of the streets around Amherst Street tend to empty while the residents go off to their holiday homes or hotels.

"I'm going to have a lovely time carrying out maintenance and repairs on our place in Devon," he said. "Hours on the road – and then a lot of boring work with tools that won't obey my wishes."

"Can't you find a local tradesman?"

"Oh, sure. You have to submit to being soaked, and I can take that. But you know you can't call a tradesman for every bloody thing that goes wrong in a house. One minute it's the drains, the next the electrics. When you arrive from London, you have to be prepared for disaster. You open up the place and find the rain has soaked the sofa. Somebody has thrown a brick through the kitchen window, the gas cylinder is empty, the refrigerator has failed. You name it."

My experience of second homes wasn't wildly different. Some years ago we used to have a small holiday home in the village of Sedgwick, in Yorkshire. It was a terraced artisan's cottage on the village green. Very small. When we first saw it, it was a two-up and two-down basically, looking bright and cosy under a new coat of white paint. Ann fell in love with it from 25 yards away before we had even been inside. The surrounding Dales promised superb walking, but the house was a problem from day one. I bought it in a fit of enthusiasm, much of which was provided by Ann and colleagues at my office. They all had cottages somewhere. Why couldn't we?

In my hurry to purchase, at a time when such places were at a premium, and there were plenty of would-be buyers around, I omitted a survey. My own cursory examination revealed no defects. The reality was that the plumbing and drains were broken, the party walls on each side were damp and even soggy in places, the roof had seemingly undiscoverable leaks and there was a threat of subsidence at the rear. There was even a dispute with the neighbours on one side about the line of the boundary.

After my offer had been accepted (afterwards!), I got a local surveyor to make an examination and the defects were revealed. He bent down close to the front room wall and inserted the blade of his pocket knife into the brickwork. The blade sank in, as it would if the wall was made of cheese. He turned his tanned, bald head and looked up at me. "Not fust cluss," he said.

I should have cut my losses and taken issue with the vendor, but I was absurdly held on course by my pride. When I told Ann, rather diffidently, about the renovations we would need, she merely nodded. She added that we would also need another bedroom at the rear, a new kitchen and a conservatory and two new bathrooms. She was assuming I knew perfectly well what I was doing. She thought that the work I had mentioned had already been anticipated by me – we had already agreed that we would like to enlarge the purchase to make space for Nick and Jane. I hadn't the gumption to tell her I'd made a complete bollocks and been fooled by a splash of new paint.

Everything about *Rose Cottage,* yes, it really was named *Rose Cottage,* started in a bad place for me but not for Ann, Nick and Jane. They were excited and committed to the restoration of the cottage. I kept my secret, engaged the tradesmen and paid the bills. And ludicrously maintained my position as the businessman of the family. I also made many long, tedious and wearing journeys to the property. At the beginning, we were going to Yorkshire every weekend.

I had torrid meetings with surveyors and the owners on either side, who seemed to view me as a con-man from London. I thought the con-men of Sedgwick were well up on the London variety. But, eventually, the work was done. I could experience the Dales without worries, or sit in the conservatory and take pleasure in the flowers Ann had planted in the garden. I could also raise my eyes a little and delight in the sturdy lines of the reinforced concrete wall which stopped the hillside collapsing upon us.

We enjoyed what I could call the summer of *Rose Cottage* for three years or maybe four. But after this I had the feeling that we were going to the cottage because it was there, when both of us would have preferred to do something else, visit another town, take different walks, or go abroad. Our visits dwindled to twice a year. I decided to strive for freedom.

One evening, Ann and I were at the cottage and it had rained all day. "You know, I could do what I've been doing here, at Amherst Street – reading."

"It's just bad luck, Bill, the rain."

"The weather is worse here and more unpredictable than at home."

Ann considered this. "Yes, probably. We always knew that. The walking is great."

"Wouldn't you sooner do something different than come up here, like take a cottage in Devon or Wales or Majorca?"

68

"At times, Bill. But we've put a lot of work – and money – into the place."

"Is that a reason to keep coming here?"

"Yes. You can't invest and then neglect it."

It was a change for Ann to make a financial point. "Investment doesn't guarantee enjoyment," I countered. "We could sell and probably break even, and then the whole of the rest of the world would be our oyster." In reality, I wasn't confident about breaking even but I had got past caring.

"Nick and Jane love the place."

"Very convenient for their partying. But does that oblige us to keep it? They can always find a place for their wild weekends, my dear."

"Bill, apart from our own visits, we have spent a lot of quality time with Nick and his friends and Jane and her friends here, now that they've left home. We wouldn't see so much of them otherwise. I love that."

"Ah-hah! This is the home away from home, where the maternal fantasy can continue."

"What a cruel thing to say!"

"As far as I'm concerned, dear, what I get when they are here, is a lot of loud, cacophonous music and drunken revelry very late at night, while you labour over the cooker during the day, and I fix leaky taps, blocked drains or dispose of trash. We're body servants to these kids and prisoners in a demanding house which is always going wrong somewhere."

When Ann thought this out (it took three months) and agreed with me, and I announced to Nick and Jane that I was selling *Rose Cottage,* they heard me with scarcely a comment. I remember, Jane said, "It's such a long way, Dad."

I think our chicks had left the nest, in their own minds, years before without Ann wanting to admit it to herself. *Rose Cottage* had become a merely an incidental and increasingly occasional convenience to them. When has a chick left the nest? I remember the disappointment Ann and I felt the first time the children said they didn't want to come with us on our annual holiday abroad. On the sale of *Rose Cottage,* I felt sorry for Ann. Part of the rite of parenthood for middle class mothers had passed. And I judge from our friends, that there are a lot of holiday homes which provide an extension of the nest for mothers, until the children shatter the maternal illusion conclusively.

"Mr Batley?" the caller, a woman, asked on the phone with a timbre in her voice which I thought I should have remembered, but couldn't place.

"Yes."

"Oh, Bill! It's Cath Bell."

"Hey, I thought I recognised your voice, Cath," which was something of an overstatement. Cath had been my secretary when I left the company. She had never called me Bill to my recollection.

"I wanted to get in touch. I'm married now. I've got a new job and things are going well for me. I hope you and Ann are OK. I thought we might update a little."

"Oh, sure," I said. "Glad to hear from you. Well… you and your bloke could come over here. Let me have your email address and I'll get back to you."

We chatted briefly while I turned over in my mind how I would put this to Ann. It required a certain delicacy. Ann had met Cath only once before when I invited her to tea at the house on my departure from the company now over two years ago. At the time, it seemed to me to be the right gesture to make. To Ann's knowledge, I had, before that, taken Cath to the The Wolsey for lunch, again to mark my departure. Those two occasions were the only times I had ever socialised with her outside the building in which we both worked.

Ann's reaction on that first meeting was not an entirely placid one. She had to accept that a young woman was familiar with a large part of her husband's life which was completely outside her ken. There was a natural emotional mismatch between Ann and Cath, and it might have shown at that afternoon tea. I noticed it. I thought Cath might have noticed too and I was therefore surprised that she wanted to get in touch again.

When I explained the call from Cath, Ann received it silently and with a very small wrinkle in the centre of her forehead. "It seems a bit unusual. You said your goodbyes a long time ago."

"Maybe," I said, thinking I might be blundering. "I only want to do the right thing. The polite thing. I can't brush Cath off."

I hadn't expected to ever see Cath again. She was a good secretary but unattractive to me as a friend. I thought from what she told me of her love life in the past that she was slightly vulnerable. She was unhappy. Living with an unsatisfactory man – but I had been careful to listen and not to advise.

"All right," Ann said. "We'll look at some dates and you can email her."

Cath and her husband, Ben, agreed to come for afternoon tea at 3:30 pm one Saturday. They arrived with a photograph album. They had covered ground in the US where Ann and I had holidayed, but in their case on a motorcycle. This, and Cath's new job as a receptionist in another big company provided for plenty of conversation. The tiny cucumber sandwiches which Ann had made were soon consumed and the teapot emptied. The talk was faltering at half past five and both Ann and I were politely trying to close the meeting with phrases like, "It's been very nice seeing you."

Mr and Mrs Jones, Cath's new name, didn't seem to want to go. Cath enquired what we were doing that evening. Ann was quick to respond that we were clearing out the cellar (a lie).

"We wondered what you were doing for supper," Cath said with a laugh. "It's a long time since dinner!"

"Well, we don't usually have supper," Ann replied. "About eight o'clock I'll cook dinner (the truth)."

Cath thought about this and looked at Ben. "Never mind, love," he said. "We'll get something on the way home."

Ann stood up and began removing plates from the coffee table. When Cath and Ben went out the front door, there was a stiffness in the farewells.

I was in bed in the morning, looking at my iPad, and I read an email from Cath: *Thanks for your hospitality. Nice seeing you again. We called in at Pizza Hut on the way up the road.*

"What do you make of this?" I asked Ann.

"Don't you see there was a misunderstanding, Bill? Supper is what Cath and Ben have. They probably had their dinner before they came, at 1 or 2 pm. Not a sandwich like we have. Then they would expect supper in the early evening. We invited them for a late afternoon tea which they took as including an early evening meal. They were miffed that we didn't provide it."

"Are we too posh to have suppers?"

"Not at all. It's the different ways we live."

"It didn't go very well, did it. Yesterday?"

"Well, I got tired of watching her looking at you with adoration."

"I think that's permissible, dear. After all, you do – at times."

"And when she said her years with you were the best years of her working life!"

I couldn't help a smirk. "I was chuffed. It was only about five years."

"And that bloody photograph album, Bill. You just don't arrive with a photograph album on an occasion like this. A hundred grinning selfies."

"I thought it was a homely gesture," I protested.

"It was, and an indication of how Cath has misconceived your or our relationship with her."

"I see. No room for friendship."

"No basis for friendship. They are different people, Bill. Ben seems a nice guy. He rides a motor-cycle and works in a grocery warehouse. Cath is a pleasant woman who was your servant for a few years. Cath wants to translate a relationship from servant to friend at a snap of the fingers. We can talk casually with Ben and Cath about places we've visited in the US but we don't have common interests. Our backgrounds are different to theirs."

I never thought of Cath strictly as a servant. She was a rather nervous young woman, technically good at her job. But of course she was, in human resources terms, a servant.

Although, I felt that both the afternoon teas we shared were the right thing for me to have agreed, and I quite liked Cath and Ben, I didn't warm to them enough to imagine committing more time to being with them. I thought Ann was probably right; it was a mismatch. I was sure we wouldn't hear from Cath again.

I turned on the TV for Match of the Day.

10
I'm Heartless

The next day, at Merrivale House, was clear sunshine and we walked along a ridge high above Swaledale. Most of the time I talked to Carol, embarrassed by my pushy behaviour last night. Inevitably, I told her more about my work when I was employed and my family. She told me about a childless marriage and a mutually agreeable divorce. She works as a secretary for a consultant surgeon in private practice. He is an urologist. Maybe she knows more about a certain part of the male anatomy than I do.

We covered 12 miles of the path, up and down the hills. I'm fit but not used to walking that far in a day and when we returned to Merrivale House, the only thing I could think of was a long, hot shower and a double whisky. I was struggling to remove my boots in the boot room when Carol sat down beside me, very close. "Don't forget the condom, will you, Bill? she whispered with a wicked little laugh. Her coolness of last night had gone. It was hard to keep up with her changes of mood.

Even in my enervated state, I felt a surge of energy. We went to our rooms to get ready for drinks and dinner. I had the shower and perhaps more whisky than I ought to and then a beer in the bar with Carol. We seized chairs together in the dining room in spite of looks which said, "I sat there last night and it's my chair." Dinner was a mutually jovial affair.

Afterwards, it was hardly necessary to invite Carol to go upstairs. She led me to her room. I wasn't bothered about bringing the whisky. I had also had a big glass of red wine with dinner. I know when I've had plenty. We embraced. She had changed completely to the decidedly warm after-dinner person.

We undressed and slipped between the sheets. We cuddled. Events seemed to be moving fast. I had a resurgence of tiredness. I *was* tired. My legs ached. I had a thought – which I pushed away – that I would like to drift off to sleep. *Now,* at this crucial time!

Carol's cheerful face was in front of me and she said, "Bill, that thing…?"

Oh, yes, that thing. I hadn't forgotten it. I had placed it discreetly on the bedside table. I felt around for it. I knocked the clock off the table on to the floor. It fell with such a noise that Carol sat up in bed. She saw what had happened and slid back beside me. But I couldn't find the condom which I had also swept on to the floor! I had to get out of bed and start looking under the bed in half-darkness.

"Bill, are you all right?" Carol asked, as I hastily patted the carpet-tiles in the shadows without my glasses.

I found the damn thing and got back in bed, naked and cold. "I'm sorry, Carol, I feel pretty flat after that lot." That was the literal truth.

"Never mind," she said, casually, "we'll catch up."

I already knew I wouldn't be able to get the condom on. Here was a woman who was welcoming me. She was not in any way put off by my antics and yet I couldn't do it. My shame showed itself in open exasperation. "Bloody thing! Haven't tried to use one of these since I was in my twenties…"

"Take it easy, Bill."

"I feel a bit tired, Carol. I think I'll just go to bed."

I got up, dressed and left the room. Carol lay still, staring at the ceiling and didn't say another word. In my room, I gulped a few mouthfuls from the whisky bottle and threw myself into bed.

The next day, I was too ashamed to even glance at Carol waiting by the door of the breakfast room. She took my arm and sat beside me at breakfast. She talked as though last night never happened. She also made a point of sitting beside me on the bus and walking beside me when we reached our starting point and set out along a lake. For a while, she took my hand.

I had to thaw. We walked the day and turned for home. "We'll go up straight after dinner," she whispered. We had dinner and yet again, we were heading for her bedroom, and I was riven with doubt.

As soon as we were in bed, Carol said, "Don't worry about that thing, Bill. Just forget it."

I took this as a signal that we were limited to affectionate embraces. And of course I was, despite my weariness after covering 12 miles during the day, superbly strong. It was perverse, as though a different person was in command of part of my body.

And it happened, whether it should have happened or not.

We both drifted off to sleep afterwards. I woke up at 1:30 am, dressed hurriedly and scuttled off to my room. I felt I had crossed some kind of Rubicon. What was the new situation I had got myself into? I couldn't sleep. And I couldn't work out any satisfactory answers except that I had gone too far, and my marriage might be in danger. I'm not the feeble sort who has to confess his sins to whoever he's sinned against. I could keep what has happened from Ann, but could Carol? She might ring me at home supposing she knew my number or knock at the door supposing she knew my address. The thought gave me a headache. I was sure she wasn't a leech by nature, but a woman in a passion can do unorthodox things.

I climbed out of my sleepless bed in the morning with a resolution that I must be very clear: first, that I had gone too far, and second that we had to stop.

Carol was at breakfast before me, seated between two of our fellow walkers. She didn't look my way, and I tried not to look her way. We walked apart on a glorious day, sun, a light breeze riffling the lake below and a yellow path winding over the sunburnt hills. I kept others of our group close to me to prevent any intimate talk, including the lunch break when we all spread out on the grass with our packages of sandwiches and fruit. We covered in all 10 miles and 1500 feet of ascent. Toward the end I was, as usual, tired and anxious for a whisky and a shower.

Carol homed in on me in the boot room afterwards and whispered, "See you after dinner." This suited me. We had to have a sober talk. I did not count the whiskies I had while showering and changing, or the pint I had in the bar with the crowd, or the very large glass of cabernet sauvignon I had with my beef en croute. Carol sat at another table beside an 'unattached' man whom I noticed she had talked to for much of the day – I suppressed a possessory twinge. However, she rose promptly from the table after her jam tart and custard and I followed. We trooped silently up to her room.

Once inside, Carol gave me a wan smile and disappeared into the bathroom. I sat on the edge of one of the beds, considering whether I should undress. I held firm to my resolve and poured two whiskies instead. When Carol emerged, she was in her same semi-transparent shorty nightie but without knickers.

"Aren't you going to get undressed, Bill?"

I hesitated and handed her a whisky. "I thought we should... have a word, first." It was a mistake to say 'first', because that presupposed there was undressing to follow. But I couldn't unsay it.

"What on earth about?" she whispered, pleasantly.

"I mean, where is this going, Carol? I told you about my marriage..."

She put her head on one side. "Mmm, not very successful."

Had I given her the impression that my marriage wasn't successful? Yes, I suppose I had, in the heat of seduction.

Actually, it was a good partnership with Ann – so damn good that I didn't want to do anything to jeopardize it.

I said, feebly, "I don't want to wreck my marriage…and you're a lovely woman…and…" This pathetic wheedling should never have been spoken. I was presenting myself as a mouse as well as a louse.

"We're not going to wreck anything," she said, sadly. "Let's be close, Bill."

I sat still, quiet, my blood was rising. My head reeled. One last cuddle. I clawed my clothes off and leaped into bed with her. I made love hungrily, fiercely. And we fell asleep.

When I was back in my own bed, about 2 am, I felt mighty. It had been good lovemaking, but I had made myself very clear as the politicians say. Although, they also say it when they don't mean it! I slept soundly.

In the morning, I checked one or two points in my memory. Carol 'drew the line' at married men. She couldn't tolerate my teeth in a glass which was only relevant to the bedroom. She gave up on the condom. She wore a nightie which was designed to make her look good and facilitate sexual encounters. She could really be a subtle temptress.

I dismissed these unworthy thoughts. She was a nice woman making the most of herself – and I would hold her to her statement that I was beyond the line, a married man.

I dressed and prepared for the new day. In my confused mind, the events of this day were remarkably similar to yesterday. It was a splendid, long walk in cool sunlight, only shaded for me by my need to part from Carol amicably but finally. I chatted to her much of the time, trying to be brotherly rather than romantic. She stopped me as we were walking up the path to Merrivale House from the bus. She leaned close. "Bill, let's meet… You're a marvellous lover and… I want you tonight."

My tired blood throbbed again at these words. A man who refused would be a prig, a worm. "OK," I said, and when we had taken off our boots, I followed her up the stairs. The lighting was dull in these old premises with their narrow halls. Nobody was around. I succumbed to an urge. I pushed my fingers between her trousered thighs from behind.

She stopped and turned. "Let's do it now," she said.

We bundled into her room and tore our clothes off, although I didn't get to my socks and my underpants were round my ankles. But that didn't matter.

Our parting at 7 pm, in time for dinner, rising from Carol's bed, was a scene of misery almost too pitiful to record. Carol was crying and declaring her love for me. Having had sex, I was as cold as a toad, and guilty that I had evoked feelings in her which were painful. I was frightened that those feelings could shake the world at 67 Amherst Street, despite our understanding that this was the end. I was in territory I didn't understand. How could she love me? She scarcely knew me, and I certainly didn't know her.

We sat together, miserably silent at dinner. Her last, most abject question, was whether I could give her a ride in the car back to Wimbledon.

"I don't think that would work, Carol. I have to make a detour to Scunthorpe on the way back to see a relative," I concocted this outright lie in an instant.

11

Ann's Suspicions Are Aroused

Ann and I had to attend a compulsory funeral recently. I suppose everybody has these occasionally. It's usually somebody whom you know only very remotely but feel that as a mark of respect to them or your peers, you ought to attend; you ought to be seen amongst the mourners. Humans have always made a ballyhoo about funerals throughout history and today, at least, a conveniently sited crematorium can add brevity to the proceedings. But that does not take account of the wake to follow. Depending on the largesse of the providers, this can range from lemon cordial and biscuits to a veritable feast. Even the compulsory funeral can generate interest in the spread to be revealed, especially if the timing coincides with lunch.

In this case, my connection was with the long-serving treasurer of our retired employees association, Alan Burton, whom I knew very slightly. As a relatively new retiree, I had taken no part in the REA proceedings but I was interested to meet former colleagues, curious to see how they were getting along; some had been shocked by their redundancy.

I drove Ann to Mortlake Crematorium, parked the car and we joined the throng in the waiting rooms ten minutes before we were to go into the chapel. I read the notice on the wall scheduling four ceremonies at 30 minute intervals, which seemed very efficient. We waited in the crowd not recognising anybody we knew. We were sharing the standing room with mourners for other funerals.

We were five minutes late in being admitted to the chapel and slipped into a pew at the back. The chapel was full, and I had recognised one or two faces. The flower-decked coffin was on a stand before the curtains. The chairman of the REA and Alan's son said good things. His daughter read a poem. Part of a record of a Beethoven symphony was played. A Baptist minister gave a blessing. More Beethoven. The curtains parted slightly as the coffin moved of its own volition it seemed, through the aperture. The curtains closed. Beethoven continued as we were motioned to leave by a side door.

"That was brief," I said. I couldn't help thinking about what was happening to Alan behind the curtain.

"Yes, but very nice," Ann replied.

We came out into sunlight, and a solemn, darkly-dressed crowd viewing the wreaths and floral tributes of various funerals. I had a look but couldn't find the area devoted Alan's tributes. Actually, we were looking for our own contribution but neither of us said so. When you pay a large sum of money over the telephone for a confection of flowers you may never see, you may be curious.

I noticed that the known faces had disappeared. "I think we need to get back to the car and join the others, Ann."

When we were in the car which was parked in a row facing the chapel, I could see the two black limousines reserved for the family and chief mourners, standing in front of the building, about to move. "I'll follow the cortege," I said. "I know where St Hilda's is. I assume the church hall is nearby but this will be easier."

We wended our way at a stately pace in a line of six or so cars to Richmond. The limousines stopped outside a hall, and I drove on beyond them looking for a park. When we walked back to the hall, cars were pulling up outside with guests. We went up the steps and into the lobby. A line of three people was waiting to greet us. I didn't know any of them, but apparently neither did some others who were coming in with us. The hosts looked awkward and shook hands weakly with those who proffered a hand. I shook all three.

When we were inside, we were approached by a girl with a tray bearing orange juice, white wine and Champagne. I handed Ann a glass of Champagne and helped myself to one, saying to her, "This is in the best traditions of the company."

As we moved deeper into the hall, I looked around at the knots of people chatting, but I couldn't see a face I recognised. That wasn't surprising. There were many members who had put in years of retirement whom I would never have known. We shuffled about, trying to looking cheery and engaged.

A man came up to us, smiling. He looked authoritative. He had a black suit and a celluloid collar, perhaps a master of ceremonies. "Hello, how are you?" he said.

"Fine, thank you," I said. "A very fitting ceremony at the chapel."

"Very carefully crafted," he said. "Particularly the Vaughan Williams."

"Lovely," Ann said, her fingers nipping my forearm.

The man moved away.

"He needs a musical appreciation class."

"This isn't the time to contradict him," Ann said.

We moved further down the hall toward the tables laden with buffet food as yet untouched. "Quite lavish," Ann said.

I was helping myself to yet another drink from the tray when Ann said, "Bill, look over there. That large photograph on the lectern."

I looked. The photo wasn't hard to see; it was placed beyond and above the buffet, looking down the body of the hall. A commanding position. It was a studio portrait of a grey-haired lady.

"Oh, no!" I said.

"Oh, yes," Ann replied. "And she was fond of Vaughan Williams."

"How in hell did this happen. Seriously? I mean, one ceremony at a time, everybody in a line."

Ann shook her head, nonplussed. "The limousines weren't our party? They could only be the party in front of us and slow to get away after looking at the flowers."

I thought about it. She was right. I couldn't help grinning. "Yeah. That makes sense. We followed the wrong cortege. What shall we do?"

Ann too was in a good humour, "We'll have to withdraw as gracefully as we can. We'll go and have lunch in Richmond on the way home."

I could smell the food from the buffet and the servers were getting in position to help guests. "Do you fancy some cold baked salmon or maybe a chicken salad?"

"Bill, we mustn't."

"Ann, my darling, we must!"

Not many people in our street clean their cars, but the cars always shine. A sign of prosperity. Not many people here do anything menial except gardening. On any day, you can see the white vans arriving with men from Bulgaria or Hungary or Romania (university graduates, all of them) who will clean the oven or replace the fancy halogen light bulbs or clean the car. But one man down the street does clean his own car, Mr Daniels. I don't know his first name. I speak to him regularly when I'm walking to the shops, and he's polishing his vehicle, a weekly task. And this is what we talk about – his car. He extols the virtues of it, the smoothness, the power.

He performs the cleaning with the help of a young man who could certainly do the whole job himself. This must be what gives the car a double shine. Mr Daniels is usually dressed in an immaculately ironed shirt, sometimes double cuffed, with links.

His trousers, too, aren't baggy black corduroy like mine, they're more likely to be tailored cotton chinos with knife edge creases. His grey hair is cut short and neatly combed. His thin face is red, lined and pressured. He's a retired travel agent. Here he is messing about with a bucket of soap suds, a hose and a variety of dusters and tins of wax and abrasives. His car is not merely clean, but gleams and not merely like glass; it has a deep sparkle of a precious gem (this particular Mercedes). There is not a speck of dust upon the rich paint, but the awkward thing is that this jewel condition will probably not last for the afternoon – we have pollen from the bushes and trees, dust from the Sahara, rain showers from the Atlantic and the grit of pollution from the city. I am sure Mr Daniels knows this, but he is passionately disregardful.

He tells me he buys the latest models second-hand with low mileage and changes them about every 18 months. And he has had a parade of perfect Mercedes, BMWs and Jaguars. I am ashamed. My old Mondeo, a lovely and faultless car, was 12 years old when I sold it as a result of the jeering of Clitheroe and the sighing of Ann. Yes, it looked unfashionable and had one or two dents and scratches. When I told Mr Daniels, he gave me a look of incomprehension, as though my behaviour in retaining a cheap car so long was unimaginable.

Mr Daniels is the epitome of the car-freak. When you see him, you have to see him *and* his car; it is part of his personality. It defines him. He may be obsessive but many of the people in Amherst Street have a lesser version of the same malady (lesser in the sense that the carwash does the polishing) with their clattering diesels, big sports utility vehicles, the Chelsea tractors. The wives seem to relish these high-strutting machines, children and dogs in the back, a foot on the accelerator and a ton of NO_2 into the atmosphere. A 150 horsepower, 130 mph, four wheel drive tank to pick up the children from school? Is it fashion?

I question whether there is something deficient in me in not feeling the slightest excitement about motor cars. It's a fact that they are virtually useless around here, the most elaborate supermarket trolleys, child carriages or dog vans ever invented. The narrow streets, parked on both sides, leave a one-way channel between, which gets jammed with cars going opposite ways, workmen unloading trucks, and delivery vans with online purchases. Negotiations have to take place. Who will back up to relieve the jam? Dark looks and twisted lips and sometimes raised voices as the issue is resolved.

The car malady has Amherst Street in its grips. It is so extreme that it makes no sense.

My memory of my encounter with Carol was like a damp grey blanket draped over my head, and not a memory of the good times we had. Ann of course noticed my mood.

"What's the matter with you, Bill? You seem depressed. And yet you've been tigerish in bed. Ever since Yorkshire. I've heard a lot of endearments from you that I haven't heard in a long time."

"Must there be something wrong when a man tells his wife he loves her?" I hadn't realised how obvious I had been and Ann had made the connection with Yorkshire.

"No, but it's unusual in your case." She was looking at me in a kindly way, but I feared she would start questioning me about Yorkshire.

I had to head this off. I took her in my arms and kissed her. "You're the best wife in the world. I've been thinking about Nick. I'm a bit worried about him, that's all."

She stared at me. "Really?"

She didn't believe me. 'Really?' with a heavy look was Ann's code for, 'I don't believe you'. No, I wasn't worried about Nick. I'm exasperated by him. She knows that. So she knows I was trying to cover up. She has a rather alarming ability to read my mind. I felt I was going to get tangled up and metaphorically hang myself. I fled from the room muttering that I had something urgent to do in the potting shed.

Ann's reluctance to agree to go to Peru with me may arise from a regrettable happening which I always refer to as the *'I'll always look after you'* incident. We laugh together about it now, but I never address that phrase to Ann because it brings back a grisly memory. And it reminds me, if one ever needed reminding, that bad luck (or good) can happen in a series of unconnected events, like five blacks in a row at roulette.

On one of our wedding anniversaries, I arranged to take Ann to a country house in Yorkshire for four days. It was to be an interlude of pleasure in a place that had the reputation for both beauty and luxury. Yorkshire is a long way from London, memories of *Rose Cottage*, and I'm not a keen driver so it was bound to be a trying journey.

A chapter of accidents was about to unfold for which I suspect Ann, fair-minded as she is, holds me responsible. My thought is that a good deal of responsibility also rests on Havenhoe Manor where we were to stay and which I could not find! I drove for miles, uphill, downhill, through forest and moors, pored over maps, stopped the car and asked people, obtained conflicting advice and had to go on driving for hours.

Ann was not pleased when I disclosed I had inadvertently left my file of papers, which might have had more particular directions, at home. She sat frostily withdrawn during the latter hours of navigation. The one thing she said was "Satnav".

The car is equipped with satellite navigation. "I don't know how to work it," I said, "I haven't studied the manual yet, and I haven't got a postcode for Havenhoe." I recoil from these electronic devices as I've said. I tolerate my PC, but I am driven to distraction by the word processing functions which seem to have a life and a will of their own.

I was exhausted and frustrated when, eventually, we wound our way up the long, unmarked and secluded drive to the Manor. An extraordinary shock awaited us. The young receptionist frowned at her computer screen.

"We have no record of your booking, Mr Batley."

"That's impossible!" I asserted in a pained tone. "You have all our particulars, credit card, everything. These can't have disappeared off the face of the earth. We've come from London!"

The young woman heard this without a crease appearing in her creamy complexion. She adjusted her glasses slightly with a forefinger on the bridge and returned to the computer screen. A silence of awful imaginings fell while she consulted the one-eyed prophet.

"Oh, yes," she said finally, "Mr and Mrs Batley. You're booked in next week and the Manor is fully booked tonight."

"That cannot be!" I shouted.

Ann was eyeing me reproachfully, assuming the mistake was mine. Without my file of notes, I could only assert that the mistake was the Manor's.

The receptionist eyed me serenely. "The computer entry is for next week, Mr Batley."

"But it's not for the computer to decide this," I said. "I know the dates I booked!"

"I'm sorry," the girl said.

"Being sorry isn't enough…"

"Let me handle this, Bill," Ann said. "Let's leave the mistake about the booking until we know more, and in the meantime we need a room…" She went on in a reasonable voice to obtain a room, despite the receptionist's remark that the Manor was full.

The room was a long way away through Havenhoe's tortuous halls. When we located it, we found we were opposite a dining room where a post conference party was being held.

The loud noise was clearly audible in our room. We agreed it was intolerable and Ann volunteered to go back to the desk and change it if possible.

"You're not going to have much luck. Even this room looks as though it's under repair," I said miserably.

"You've had a difficult drive, Bill," Ann said, "Why don't you have a drink and try to relax while I sort this out?"

I should have been the one to parley with the management, but I said meekly, "Thanks, dear. I'm sorry about the mess," and when she had gone, I gratefully opened the bottle of whisky we had brought for get-ready drinks before our planned gourmet dinner.

While Ann negotiated with the reception, I helped myself too liberally to the whisky and chatted to the technician who came in unannounced to fix the air conditioning. He spread his tools out over the carpet and we talked about Iraq and Syria.

We eventually changed this room for what we were assured was the only other one available in this 'fully booked' hotel, by which time I was fogged by the whisky. The new room was small, sombre and just escaped being squalid; it was clearly an emergency bolt-hole at the ground floor rear. We were stuck. So much for four nights of luxury!

Our next thought: nourishment. We hadn't eaten for six hours. We found it was too late to get a meal at Havenhoe. I protested at the desk that no decent hotel should be unable to feed a guest. Ann shut me up, and we went by taxi to a nearby pub. I neglected the hamburger but drank half the bottle of wine I had ordered, and I am told that I fell asleep at the table. It was the strain of driving all day. To pay the bill, Ann was embarrassed by having to feel around in my trousers to get my wallet. When we are travelling, I often carry my cards and notes in what I call my penis purse. It's on a loop on my belt and sits inside my trousers at the front. She kicked me into action after disrobing me in front of the publican, and we were taxied back to Havenhoe.

When we got back to our room, Ann found that the card-key did not work. She went back to reception yet again on the understanding that I would wait outside the door. When she had gone, I was surprisingly allowed into the room by a patrolling security guard. I threw myself on the bed and passed out again.

Ann told me afterwards that she had to face a new receptionist on duty. The process of issuing another card key was apparently not a formality. Ann was escorted back to the room by another security guard. I had disappeared from the corridor. Nearby corridors were searched by Ann and the guard. At last, they went into the room. There I was, spread-eagled and unconscious.

The end of this for me was to wake in the dawn, fully clothed on the bed with an explosive headache. I had that disorientated feeling you have sometimes when you wake in a strange place. The past events were a haze. Ann lay on the carpet, with a few towels under her and a cushion to rest her head. My next thought: my wallet. Where was it? I scuffled around with my clothes. Lost! My cash and credit cards gone! I felt ill.

Ann had stirred and was watching me. I think she let me endure my discomfort in silence for two minutes or so before she said, "Your wallet is in my handbag if that's what you're looking for."

A warm fountain of appreciation for Ann seemed to come up inside me, especially, as my wallet was found. I now assumed, in my alcoholic fuzz, that my only offence was to pass out on the bed at the end of the evening. I tried to make light of it. "Well, we've had some ups and downs, but you're all right," I said, adding the fatal words: "You know I'll always look after you."

Ann choked with hysterical laughter and tears. She spent the next 15 minutes telling me exactly how I had looked after her, heavily underlined. We left the Manor that morning after breakfast with me, metaphorically, waving a threatening fist at the management.

Later, a small pleasure. At Amherst Street, I found a booking confirmation from Havenhoe Manor showing that I had made no mistake about the date of the booking. I pursued the Manor for damages with vindictive glee, but they could not give me absolution for saying to Ann, "You know I'll always look after you."

I am in serious danger. Ann apprehended me when I returned at 6 pm from the pub.

"Bill, I had a strange telephone call today."

I had a stab of guilt which the soothing effect of two pints of lager could not allay. My worst fears were roused. "What was it?"

"The caller hung up when I answered."

"Probably a wrong number," I tried to look and sound as though it was inconsequential.

"I don't know why I did it, but I got the number on call-back. And I called back." Here, Ann paused. I don't know whether my fear showed. "Yes," she continued determinedly, "the caller was a woman. She was on the line. Quite friendly. I said, 'Who is that?' and she said, 'Who are you?' I said, 'Ann Batley'. She hung up instantly."

I felt some little relief that Carol's call (I was sure it was her) revealed nothing directly against me. I tried a casual line: "The sort of silly exchange you get on this ring-back stuff, customer surveys, lawyers looking for accidents."

Ann nodded warily, "It didn't sound like a business call to me."

Maybe I had convinced her. I went upstairs to stop any further talk. I was annoyed. I was under siege from Carol. And I was under suspicion from Ann. The ridiculous thing is that this whole tangle started with my concern about Ann and Bernard Chandler. It was Ann's conduct, not mine, which was in issue.

12
Carol for Lunch

I was walking up Fulham Road yesterday. Winter weather in spring, and worse, a biting easterly wind. The shops seemed closed, huddling darkly behind their windows and few people were about. I raised my head and saw a figure lurching toward me. We could have collided. I saw his face, and he saw mine. I knew him.

"Hello, Jason," I said as we both spun round, eyes fixed on each other.

He gave a sour smile. "Bill Batley."

"The same. Just out for a constitutional."

He began to turn away.

On an impulse, I said: "What about a cup of coffee, Jason?"

He turned back. "You live your life between cups of coffee," he said, contemptuously.

I was going to say, "I'm paying," but that would have been indelicate. Instead, I said, "Well, T.S Eliot did it with coffee spoons."

"The same Batley, indeed. Always a quip. Usually inaccurate."

"Let's go in here," I persisted. We were close to a grotty looking cafe I had never entered before.

"No, I have to get on… Oh, all right then," he replied irritably.

In a moment, we were seated facing each other over a white plastic table. Jason leaned forward confrontationally. One other customer, a woman with buggy and baby, was at a distance.

I found it hard to believe that I was opposite a man, Jason Wild, whom I knew well, who had disappeared from my ken for years, until now. At one time, he had been the star of the company for whom I worked. He had been slightly my junior in joining the company (and in age) but passed me with effortless promotions. He was promotion hungry. He became a managing director and then a member of the main board. I never worked for him or him for me, but there was a period of a few years when we were associated in the workplace through cooperation between our different departments. He was a candidate for chairman of the board and was appointed by the government to head an important commission of enquiry in the City. In those days, Jason Wild was almost a giant in my eyes. And he well deserved the status.

A waitress served our coffee, and we loosened our coats. I could see Jason's spotty jersey and the bedraggled collar of his shirt. I thought he had aged more than I had. His face was lined, yellowed, roughly shaved and his grey hair was thin. But there was still a fiery light in his eyes which I could remember.

"What are you doing in this remote outpost?" I asked, a pleasantry to open a talk between two people who knew each other in many ways, but were not friends.

"I'm going to visit my daughter. She has a flat in Shottendane Road."

"I live over by Bishop's Park."

"Of course, in the exclusive, comfortable part."

"It wasn't all that exclusive or comfortable when I bought a place there."

"I'm not afraid of you, Bill."

This was a surprise gambit. "I never thought you would be. Nobody is afraid of me or ever has been."

"You know what I mean, afraid of being talked down to by a righteous prude, speaking from the sandcastle of his proper little life."

Jason Wild used to be well known for his caustic rhetoric. "I haven't done any talking, Jason, but that's how you see it is it?"

He leaned back with crushing satisfaction. "Sure. It can't be otherwise. You've played by the book. You've done everything and everybody right. You've taken no chances. You've kept your nose politely up your bosses' arses all your working life," he spoke slowly with ridicule allocated to every phrase.

This was also a refrain my friend George Cutler sang, albeit, in a kinder tone. "That about describes my working life, Jason, but I'm not going to talk down to you about yours." His canard didn't worry me because I thought most of my colleagues were more like me than him.

"Then why did you ask me to have a drink?"

Jason Wild represented something I had puzzled over with Ann many times and not only in relation to Wild. "I'm fascinated by a man who has the ability to win a high place in his career and yet recklessly throw it away. I know people do this occasionally – politicians, businessmen, judges, top public servants. I have to wonder why."

"What is this, reality TV?" he sneered.

I thought about my reply. It was likely that Jason would get up and walk out. "Well, you asked the question. The answer is idle curiosity."

He accepted this more calmly than I expected. He even showed a tinge of amusement. "Yes, it must look rather odd from your sandcastle. Still got your trim little wife? Ann, if I recall."

I was astonished that he remembered Ann's name from a few social events, years ago with him and his wife, whose name I couldn't recollect. "Sure. I mean, the same wife. I can't even claim a decent adultery let alone a divorce."

Wild didn't seem to be listening. He brooded over his cup. "More than once we were in the same party at the opera, and I'm thinking of Tosca. Do you remember?"

I couldn't remember the occasion. I sometimes dozed at the opera. I somehow knew Tosca's story. "Your memory is surprising. I can bring to mind the box at the Royal Opera House on the occasions when I was allowed to use it. Very superior."

"Do you recall what happened to Tosca?"

"Suicide? Is that what happened to you? Yes, Jason, what you did seemed to me like a kind of suicide. But frustrated love had nothing to do with it. Frustration of another kind. You were driving around King's Cross soliciting prostitutes." He was hitting me hard so I was hitting hard.

"Yes," he said. "I lost everything that *you* value, Bill. My reputation, my job, my wife and family. My kids are just beginning to see me occasionally, but I don't want your sympathy."

"You won't get my sympathy. You did this. You didn't just fuck-up. You decided, deliberately decided, to walk on the fragile edge of a cliff. Why, Jason, why throw away everything you'd achieved for the pleasure of whores?"

He scoffed, "You can't understand what I did because you are in thrall to power and position. You couldn't throw power and position away because you never had them. You only had a taste of them. You're one among 10,000 tryers."

"But you have been there, attained the dizzy heights and found it more compelling to bargain for the flesh of a hooker?"

94

He smiled contemplatively, "When you're alone in the city and you've had a line of coke, the flesh is attractive. You feel you can do anything you want."

"You never counted the likely cost?"

"It was exhilarating, the highest high you can achieve." He stood up, it seemed proudly. "Now you know the answer to your question. Retail it at your next dinner party and your guests will be bug-eyed."

He was going to walk out of the door without a further word to me.

"One moment, Jason. Let me ask you why *you* accepted my suggestion of a drink?"

"Because I wanted to satisfy myself that you are the prick I thought you were."

"And I wanted to find out if you were really smart, a sort of Nietzschean superman, or off your nut."

He raised two fingers in a rude gesture and went out of the door. I wanted to ask how his fortune had fared from the time the scandal hit the front pages of the national press ('City

Bigwig arrested for kerb-crawling'). The media had a field day and in the euphemism, Jason 'stepped down' from the company and resigned his public service post. Family problems followed. The newspapers said he had his substantial pension intact, but his high reputation was gone.

I told Ann of the meeting when I got home, including her being remembered. She said she wasn't proud of that, and I asked her if she thought what Jason did was just extreme sexual frustration maybe exacerbated by drugs.

"I think he is a clever but unbalanced man. Untrustworthy. He could just as likely have committed a chiselling fraud despite his huge salary or a huge fraud and taken off for the Caribbean."

"A lot of people felt sorry for him. He lost so much for… so little."

"It wasn't so little. Kerb-crawling is a degenerate crime and a danger to women."

That silenced me. I remembered the brightness in Jason's eyes. Was it the light of a superior intelligence or of a kind of madness?

In our household, a situation can arise which we call 'the bathroom wall' syndrome. I will explain how the phenomenon got its name. A tradesman was painting our personal bathroom to conclude the installation of a new shower cabinet. One wall, not in need of repair, was a faint mauve colour which we liked and wanted repeated in the new work. As a result of us not giving clear instructions, the new work was painted a pale yellow shade.

The shower cabinet fitting worked perfectly well, but the painted walls (we thought) clashed. There was much discussion between us about which of us had been and was now in charge of the work. The debate moved on, over a week, to whether to get the decorator back to repaint the whole bathroom, or simply get the new work done in matching paint. Heat was generated.

About a month later the subject had entirely disappeared from our agendas. We had become used to the bathroom walls. I had never been so conscious that disagreeable details often disappear when the big picture is good. Hence, 'the bathroom wall syndrome'. It has happened at other times in the house; and certainly, in our lives outside.

House-proud owners like us are always slightly obsessive about details of décor – until they fade into the background. Recently, the hole in the kitchen tiles (smashed by a falling saucepan) was such a detail. "My eye is always drawn to that mess when I go in there," Ann said at first. I patched the hole with Polyfilla and brown paint, I concede after considerable prevarication. I knew Ann's cool thanks reflected her feeling that it was still a mess. But my work did, at least for the time being, put off the talk about renewing the tiling of the whole kitchen floor. The syndrome was working!

Perhaps this is a further example of the syndrome: I lay in bed at 4:30 am yesterday, after a trip to the waterworks, wide awake, and heard the first of the day's aircraft pass over. I cuddled down and took solace from an engine howl which many years earlier disturbed and annoyed me. I wouldn't agree the planes are quieter today although that's what the Heathrow devotees assert. Whatever, the aircraft don't bother me now. More like a wasp buzzing against the window glass for a few moments. And this conclusion doesn't mean I'm in any way converted to Heathrow expansion, but the big picture here in Fulham is a good one.

It must have been three weeks or, perhaps, four after Ann intercepted the call from Carol when she called again. I had been quite resolute in my desire to sever whatever the connection was that we had made. I was disappointed to receive her call one weekday morning when I was in the potting shed. I was hoping it would never happen. I hadn't even given her my mobile number, but the number is on a label on the back of my phone, and she could have copied it when it was on a bedside cabinet. If she did that, it was an act of considerable forethought.

I burst into her opening remarks, saying, "Look, Carol, I thought we'd agreed that it was all over."

"We did, Bill, but I've missed you so much, and I only wanted to talk a little…"

"But it won't do us any good. It'll make it worse." I was conscious that I was implicitly admitting that there was something there, something that could be made worse, when perhaps I should have told her I didn't feel anything for her. The truth was, I liked her but not seeing her again wasn't going to hurt me at all.

"You probably don't understand the effect you had on me, Bill. I've been dreadfully unhappy since we parted. I haven't known what to do," she let out a sob.

In some ways, this was gratifying when I recalled my fears of a faltering performance. "You're making too much of it, Carol, and it has to end."

"Couldn't we meet just once? It would help me an awful lot. I'm feeling lost."

"It's only prolonging your pain if that's what you feel."

"At least help me, Bill. Let's meet and talk," she spoke in a distraught tone.

Although I had to put Carol off once and for all, I was worried that if I was brusque with her, she might resort to other means of harassing me. "If you insist we can certainly talk, but I've explained my position to you. I thought we were just having a bit of fun, and…"

"Meet me for lunch, on Saturday, Bill. We'll talk."

With real reluctance and feeling my day was blighted, I agreed.

The weather was brilliant on the day I met Carol in Wimbledon Village and drove her to the Depot Restaurant in Barnes. My own feelings were gloomy. I hadn't been looking forward to this meeting, but there was no way I could get out of it. If I cancelled, Carol would stay in touch with me until another date was made. Every call to the house was like an arrow that could wound Ann.

Carol looked tranquil when I met her and summery in a bright dress which showed off her figure. She filled the car with a delicate perfume.

I managed to get a table at the Depot at the back of the room, on the Thames side, where we would be able to talk. Our conversation in the car, and as we settled at the table and looked at the menu, was about everything but our 'problem'. The restaurant soon filled up with the usual confident diners, casually dressed and enthusiastically embarking on their weekend; many Hooray Henrys with louder voices that their willowy companions. Carol and I fitted in quietly but very well. I couldn't help thinking that we must obviously look like a 'couple'. But we weren't.

We ordered salads and as we were doing so, Carol said, "Bill, I'd like some wine. Today's a lovely day for a bottle of sauvignon blanc."

I looked at the waitress who grinned expectantly. To my mind, this was a day for coffee, black coffee, but what could I say in the clamorous excitement of that dining room without appearing to be mean? When the waitress had gone, I said, "Carol, we have some serious talking to do."

"We will talk seriously," she said, disarmingly.

And so the ice-bucket bearing the sauvignon blanc arrived in good time before the salads. A little of my gloom dissipated after a glass of wine, and I resolved to deal with this meeting like a kindly 'agony uncle', remaining clear, objective, serious and above the fray of argument. There was, however, the issue of *when* to advance my case. I didn't want to get to the 'this is my last word' stage in the middle of the meal. That would be counter-productive and uncivilised. I judged it best to wait and chat about other things.

The lunch passed off easily, and the wine, and I had the awkward feeling that Carol and I were at one with the rest of the diners, talking, drinking, savouring the moment. The image was shattered violently as I looked around me and noticed, not two tables away, Freddie Carmichael and his wife, Wendy, dining with an elderly woman I had also met, Wendy's mother. These three people lived in a nearby street to Amherst. All three had met Ann, and Wendy could be called a friend of hers. Horror of horrors! Wendy caught my glance and waved to me. I raised my hand in a feeble acknowledgment. They had already seen me, but I had been so engrossed with my companion that I hadn't seen them! No doubt they had plenty of time to speculate about whether I was lunching my girlfriend. Freddie turned his thick neck and grinned, I thought salaciously.

I rarely dined at the Depot, and I could have guaranteed to dine there ten times in a row without meeting anybody I knew. And yet, at this crucial meeting with Carol, this one-off event in all the world, Freddie Carmichael and his wife and mother appear.

The question was what to do. Get a check and run for the door. Sit it out and wait until the Carmichaels decamped. But they would, yes, they certainly would come over to the table and leer at us. What could I say if we chatted? How would I explain Carol's presence? I had to be up front with Carol about my embarrassment. I explained quickly. "This is not only very embarrassing, but it could be damaging, you understand?"

Carol wasn't perturbed. "It's in your mind, Bill. They don't know what we're doing here. I could be your decorator or your architect. I don't have to be your mistress."

The empty bottle of wine, now upside down in its bucket, said it all for me. Fortunately, Wendy Carmichael was unlikely to be on the phone to Ann about this; theirs wasn't that sort of relationship, but a casual meeting between Ann and Wendy in the street could lead to, "I saw Bill last Saturday at the Depot…" Trouble. Big trouble.

I decided to pay the bill and run. As we went out, I gave the Carmichaels a friendly thumbs up signal but avoided the passage passing their table. I gunned the car out of the parking lot as quickly as I could and headed back toward Wimbledon. I had gone into the restaurant with a dismal feeling. There had been a brief interval of enjoyment. Now I had come out of the meeting with more grim forebodings about my future.

In the car, I did all the talking I should have done at lunch. I did it in a harsh, almost bullying tone. That damned lunch had been worse than useless! Carol listened without saying much. When we pulled up outside her apartment, she said, "Why don't you come up, Bill? I'll give you a cup of coffee before you go home."

She said it in such a meek voice like a resigned person that I felt I could agree. I had been doing all the talking. I was depressed, down in a dark hole. And I felt I couldn't care any more – it was like the feeling I had when I started giving food away at the food bank. I nodded and placed the car on the forecourt. I followed Carol up the stairs. As I was following her, I was quite close, and I had a memory of her naked body moving in front of me. When we entered the apartment and closed the door, we jostled together in the hall, I felt her softness and I grabbed her. My hands were all over her.

We were naked in her bed in minutes without a word spoken.

13

Being or Non-Being?

I told Carol before I left her bed that this moment was absolutely the end of our connection. She didn't speak. I threw myself into my household affairs at home, chastened by my foolishness in trusting that the luncheon date would end all.

I was diverted by an unexpected and sad happening in our street. Ann met Andrew Muir at a street party a year ago when he offered her some gladioli bulbs. Andy had lived alone in a big, increasingly-dowdy home since his wife died 20 years ago. He was aged 85 and many years retired, an engineer who had patented a device used in the manufacture of pharmaceuticals. I invited him to come round for a beer occasionally or called into his house for one. He was one of the group of residents like the Fosters that I call 'the settlers'.

He had no children, and he was an only child of an only child. He had no blood relatives that he knew. His wife's family lived in Liverpool and were never close to him. He really was on his own. He had no interests outside his home that I had heard him speak of. He was too self-contained and well preserved for me to feel sorry for him, but I was interested in how he coped with his solitariness.

I found that Andy was an acquirer. He wasn't a collector because there was very little focus in his acquisitions other than that there were more stuffed predatory animals and birds than other things. He had a house full of ornate walking sticks, fountain pens, smoking pipes, Greek vases, wristwatches, watercolour landscapes, cigarette lighters, wood chisels, Swiss Army knives, wood planes and small, wood-turning lathes. He had never been a woodworker. He showed me these things with pride and at the same time I could see that there were lots of other different kinds of articles jammed in cupboards and on shelves. He had assembled many hundreds of books; and recordings of music on old vinyl discs, cassettes and CDs. All quite random from what I could see.

When I first went to his house, I sat with him in his study and he offered me a sherry. He was surrounded by his purchased trophies which spread over every wall – tigers' heads, a cheetah head, the jaws of a shark, a stuffed bald eagle. Sunk in his high-backed chair, he looked shrunken and lonely. I couldn't see him as even an imaginary big game hunter, and he didn't pretend to be one.

"You've lived with your animals since your wife died?"

"I have, Bill. Claire was and is irreplaceable in my life."

I have no doubt that Andy took pleasure in the articles that he acquired. It was the sheer quantity and irrelevant diversity of them which puzzled me. The mind simply couldn't contain this quantity at any particular moment. Many of his acquisitions had to be thrust into cupboards in the dark, although I suppose he could rove, with an ornate walking stick from the hall, to the head of a wild pig in the study, at any time he chose.

As an aside, Penny Cutler has a similar trait, or is it a complex? Clothes. George says she can't go past a dress shop without trying something on – a coat, a blouse, the latest cut of skirt. And she almost always buys. It's very expensive George says, but I gather he doesn't comment too adversely when his wife spins around before him in the bedroom in a new collection of underwear. She has two rooms in their large house entirely hung with her clothes. Many dresses have only be been worn once. Some, she has admitted to Ann, never worn at all. She laughed and told Ann the unworn ones were bought for events that never happened.

Penny is a very well-dressed and stylish woman at a very high price. Ann says it's because Penny is not really sure of herself socially and needs to feel at least as smart as her friends. This may be true in part. I think she means to outsmart her friends. But what I find curious, as with Andy, is the quantitative side. Do you really need racks of clothes to satisfy your confidence? Penny seems to be quite an intelligent woman, but on this point she has a blind spot. Andy Muir is a bright man, but he has a blind spot too. Have I a blind spot, a wacky peculiarity that I can't see? If I have, at least it's not about acquiring things.

Susan Clitheroe told me on Sunday morning that Andy had been taken to hospital early that morning. "Carried out by a couple of cheerful Australian girls," she said. I was shocked. His house was there, locked and deserted.

I guessed he had been taken to Charing Cross A&E which is only a mile away. I went there, but he had been sent on. When I explained that Andy had no relatives that he was in touch with, I was directed to the Hammersmith Heart Assessment Centre. I caught a 2:20 bus and went on the long straight, up the Fulham Palace Road, through Hammersmith and Shepherds Bush and on, along the Uxbridge Road just beyond the Westway. A short walk and I was there. The hospital is next to Wormwood Scrubs prison – an interesting juxtaposition of two places which minister to extreme illness.

I found Andy in ward A7. The hospital seemed relaxed about visiting hours. He was hooked up to a monitor on the wall registering his heart beat and blood pressure, with catheters stuck in the veins of both arms and an oxygen pipe up his nose. My arrival with no gifts was a blessing. This was not a place to bring flowers. It was a place of science with lights and bells flashing and staff moving around quickly and quietly. We chatted monosyllabically for a while as he brightened up, pleased by the visit.

"I just felt a pain in my leg about five o'clock this morning. But I knew, it was something worse. The ambulance was there in minutes."

I wanted to say he was lucky – which he was. To be here in a premier hospital. He was also unlucky. Instead, I said, "You're getting the whole works?"

"Yes, they're getting me ready for a bypass, subject to testing, testing and testing," he said.

"You'll be a new man."

"I'm not sure I want to be a new man. It's optional. I could go home with pills."

"And live on the edge of a heart attack for the rest of your life?"

"That wouldn't be so bad, Bill. My life is stale and nearly over anyway. Pffft and I'd be gone. Into a state of non-being."

"You're ready for that. Non-being?"

"Sure. There's nothing out there, you know."

"My jury is still out on that. But wouldn't it be good to have a new lease of life?"

"Those are the words of a 50-year-old. Why face the pain of months of recovery from a mighty op if you're 85? I think of Claire, my wife, who died of cancer when she was your age. It's 20 years ago. When the doctors told her that her breast cancer was inoperable, she elected six months of experimental chemotherapy. It was six months of hell. She was ill every day and dead at the end."

"You think she should have avoided the chemo and gone quietly on morphine?"

"She thought like you do. She thought the pain would be worth it. I miss her even now. I'd like to join her."

"How can you join her if death is non-being?" I said this without sounding challenging.

"Ah-ha! At least you're listening to me. I mean join her in the sense that I too leave this place, follow her path."

"Andy, I think you should look at it this way. For you, it's win-win. A reconditioned engine or an early trip into non-being. Both good."

"I like that," he said. "I haven't made up my mind yet. But it doesn't matter, does it, Bill? Nothing really matters."

A nurse came up to the bed wheeling a computer, and I moved away leaving him smiling. And I remembered Freddie Mercury's song.

I made another bus journey to the hospital to see Andy two days later. The thought of him lying there alone overcame my distaste for the journey. I was curious too about his decision for his future. It was a real life 'to be or not to be'.

On arrival at the hospital, I had to climb four floors by the back stairs, because the one lift of three that was working was clogged with patients being moved to different wards. The building is old and tortuous but ward A7 is like the inside of a rocket ship: monitors are pinging, panels are blinking with lights, nurses with computers on trolleys are moving around the ward like daleks, recording everything.

I held up the *Guardian Book of Short Stories* which I had purchased for Andy and put it on the side table. "How are you doing, Andy?" I said to the figure who had his nose, with its oxygen tubes poking out, just above the sheet.

He pushed the bedclothes down to speak. "I've been tested all day and night. Given my blood and urine to the laboratory. Had coloured ink squirted into my veins. Been X-rayed from my arse to my elbow. Everything's on hold now. I've got a urinary infection. They can't start cutting me up until I'm fit enough to play at Wimbledon."

"So you're going for the knife?"

"I haven't decided yet. The surgical team don't give their spiel with their final verdict on me until they're ready."

I was lucky enough to get a glimpse of the cardio-thoracic surgical team which was doing its rounds, five men in green operating theatre gowns, led by Kamal Dessouky, an Egyptian who must have been only five feet tall, slender but with a big pot like a pregnancy pressing behind his gown. I had picked up his name and description on the wall chart, as I passed the reception desk. His assistant was Wilson Ong, a Chinese, and the head anaesthetist was Mark Aarons a bald Englishman. The knot or clot of surgeons and their assistants moved toward Andy's bed. They took no notice of me. They took no notice of Andy either. They looked at charts and muttered between themselves. Dessouky nodded satisfaction. He seemed to survey Andy from a great distance with glassy grey eyes. He made no comment outside the group. Only Aarons stepped forward. He asked Andy how he was and pulled the sheets back. "I want to look at your veins." He ran his hand over one of Andy's legs, smiled, and said, "Good veins. We'll be taking one of those out."

Andy looked startled. He opened his mouth to speak but the knot or clot with a private life of its own, moved on.

"They don't do bedside manners," I said. "Scientists and technicians are in a different bubble."

"The nurses and the young doctors talk plenty," Andy replied. "Enough. They mentioned a three per cent risk rate."

On one visit, I had to retire to the day room while Andy gave his daily sample of blood and urine and suffered other tests. His heartbeat and blood pressure were charted and watched in every second. I went outside on the deck in the open air. I was alone and sat in the sun watching the little mice who live under the decking and come out for a few crumbs from the crisps and biscuits of the visitors. They do not affect the cleanliness of the ward which is extreme. The mice have a certain standing because relatives of theirs have contributed, in some aspect, to the perfection of the incredibly complex procedure which Andy was facing.

The deck is graced with a rather elaborate bronze water feature which looks angry at having no water. It's good that the authority which erects a hospital makes space for a few sculptures, but less easy for them to strike the right note. On the ground floor, there is a glassed-off portion of a corridor containing a big stone, quarried on the site by hard labour when it was a poorhouse shelter in the 1890s. It sits forlorn in front of a dusty mirror. The arrangement looks like the cage of a hidden reptile in a zoo.

When I went back to the ward, Andy told me he was going ahead with a quadruple bypass. "I don't know why I elected to do that," he said, "but I had an odd experience. I felt sorry for the man in the opposite bed. He was talking to his wife (I guess it was) on his mobile, and he was telling her the agonies he'd suffered. He hasn't even had the op yet, only the tests. I thought he must have been near death in the night. When he'd finished moaning to his wife, a helper was waiting to take his order for lunch. And do y'know what? He ordered a lunch like you never saw: bacon, eggs, tomatoes, sausages, chips and rolls with jam, followed by coffee and sat there scoffing it in a right good mood."

I laughed. "So you decided to live and enjoy."

"I can only lose my life, or maybe come through with a stroke, vegetabilised."

"Play the odds, Andy. Think of that big risk free area of 97 per cent."

I went home in the 2:20 bus, bouncing and jerking along in a Tower of Babel. The number of different languages being spoken was amazing, none of them English or an intelligible variant on English. The noise was deafening. People were shouting into mobile phones or across the seats to their friends. There was a happy fervour about the passengers.

I continued to visit Andy every few days. He came through the op very well, and I drove him home. "They kicked me out after six days," he said, "and demanded that I walk up the stairs on my last day!" He came home to Amherst Street with a roster of carers to look after him. On the occasions I visit, he seems happier than he was before the op – happy with his affirmation of being, rather than non-being. And I think he likes having the carers fussing around.

When I was with Andy, I always thought I was looking at what could, in all probability, happen to me: an old, sick man who has lost a beloved wife. I could foresee the loneliness.

14

I Divulge a Secret About My Love Life

George Cutler is my best friend. When I was at school, I recognised him but didn't know him. He was an outstanding sportsman a few years ahead. We met at university with a common interest in the walking club. He was studying law. We went on a number of walks and climbs together around Europe. I met Ann through him. He was romancing her, but I won that contest. George wouldn't admit that. He says Ann wasn't his type.

Although our friendship was positive, there was always an element of competition between us. We have often disagreed over 35 years but these disagreements have not ended the friendship. We communicated, even if we did not meet, by letters and emails and telephone calls. I think the essence of it was that we observed each other's lives. I watched him, and he watched me. And we still watch each other. I know him, and he knows me.

Confidentially, I regard his life as an example of how not to play it. All the wives, the children and grandchildren – these claims on your emotions, not to say your wallet. I'm sure he regards my life as mundane and boring. Nondescript. He enjoys thinking he is the paterfamilias of our friendship.

George got a good degree and was picked up by a City firm. He made a lot of money and was able to retire comfortably at 50, although I believe he was pushed like me. He now lives two blocks away from me with his third wife, Penny, 18 years younger than him, and their daughter, Budgie, aged 12. We meet for a beer or to play cards and occasionally as a foursome with our wives. Unfortunately, George has a bad leg. Our trail walking days as a pair are over.

George's house is very similar to ours. I often go there, and we sit in his garden shed which has been lined and contains easy chairs, a table and a cupboard stocked with liquor. There is no sign of any gardening implements. The doors can be opened wide, and we sun ourselves and look at the garden. This upgraded shed is a crude version of my better equipped, all-weather potting shed on the first floor, although there is no alcoholic liquor in the potting shed.

George questioned me about my recent trip to Yorkshire. He knows the area, and he has nostalgic feelings about the walks, he has done. When I had briefed him, he said, "So, terrain and food good. And what about the female contingent?"

I couldn't resist a guarded but satisfied smile. I suppose one small part of me was rather reassured by what I'd done. It was an endorsement of my virility and my continued attractiveness to women. Being in company with George, in that competitive way, the egotist in me crowded out prudence and the larger part, the regret and unease.

He guessed immediately. "Ah-ha! You sly bugger. I want to know the details."

We had always exchanged a lot of details about our lives, but they never touched on the intimacies with our wives. And these exchanges involved tacit confidence. I didn't have to worry about Penny hearing it all in pillow talk. "It was just a couple of nights. Nothing."

"What was she like?"

"Actually, a nice woman. I think. I hope."

"Better than Ann?"

"No way."

"Why, then?"

"I was annoyed by Ann paying a lot of attention to that cunt, Chandler."

"Ah, yes. The good Bernard. You told me about him. Doesn't seem like Ann's sort."

"I seriously hope not."

"So it's all over with the woman?"

"Absolutely!"

He gave me a satyr-like grin, "Are you sure you won't pop away occasionally for walkies and snuggles?"

"No chance. I wouldn't even need to troop to Cornwall or Yorkshire. She has her own place in Wimbledon." I shouldn't have mentioned Wimbledon, a confidence too far.

"Just up the road! Tempting?" He was eyeing me closely now. He could intuit my thoughts. I didn't want to admit I had actually *visited* Wimbledon, but he knew.

"It's over, George," I said as blandly as I could.

"Are you sure? Come on, admit it, you dirty, filthy man!" he guffawed.

"Look, George, it was just once. I mean that. She called me and dragooned me into lunch…"

George was shaking with mirth, "The siren calls. Your little willy stands up. The luncheon wine melts your inhibitions!"

"I'm not like you, George. Frankly, it's the opposite with me. I'm troubled about this woman calling me at home, and Ann getting involved and my marriage screwed up."

George considered this, I thought with some pleasure, schadenfreude perhaps. "Actions have consequences, my boy. You have chosen to break your faithful, almost virginal attachment to Ann. Emotional forces have been unleashed. What will happen?"

While I was contemplating this nightmare, George returned to his questioning: "Let me ask you, Bill, does Ann ever compliment you?"

"Not a lot. I think she's appreciative."

"Do you compliment her?"

"All the time. I tell her I love her, and she's the best cook I know."

"Mmm, pretty crass lies, eh?"

"Not at all. I really mean what I say."

"Bill, how many women have you had in your life?"

I shrivel up inside. "Not many."

"Come on, be a man."

That was the point. The answer would show I'm not a man. "I don't know, a few. While I was a student."

"Then Ann and this Wimbledon bird?"

"Yeah, I guess that's it, George."

"You're telling porky pies. I knew you when you were a student. The answer is two, isn't it – Ann and Wimbledon? Admit it!"

"OK, I admit it. I'm not going to ask you to boast about your own conquests."

"Two women!" he chanted, "You're practically a virgin!"

"And you're a bloody old roué!

He was too delighted to care about my riposte.

Nick called at the house on a day when Ann was at work. I deliberately arranged this, rather than invite him to come round for a bite when Ann was here. I wanted to avoid the conflagration that might occur when Ann divined my attitude.

I had also received a hurry-up telephone call from Nick after the meeting with him that I have already mentioned. I did not hurry. Unfortunately, he had formed the impression that I was indeed going to 'help'. He plainly thought that he was on a winner. He came into the house more easy and agreeable than usual – at first.

"When is the bankruptcy notice going to be heard, Nick?" I said as we settled down in the lounge.

"At the end of the month," he said. "It's a bloody fix!" he started up from his chair in a loud, bad tempered voice. He went into considerable detail about the perfidy of the people who had done this. "If I could have afforded it, I would have appealed the judgments and won," he said, flapping his hands, rising and striding round the lounge.

"Sit down, son."

Nick said that the money from me would be a loan, repayable within six months from the assets he was liquidating. He was even good enough to mention the earlier loan which would be included with interest. We had never discussed interest.

"What is the asset you are selling?"

"A factory in Croydon worth at least two million."

"Why not offer it in satisfaction of the judgements?"

"Well, it's more complicated than that, Dad. It's an asset in a fund and…" he went into a long, muddy explanation about the fund.

I could see that the hope of getting my money back would probably remain a hope. His likely tardiness about keeping his word with any precision would poison the already difficult relationship between us. It would be better to say no and face the immediate upset. However, I had to do that in a way which was as delicate as possible. I couldn't bring myself to say, as perhaps I should, "You're old enough to be looking after your own affairs."

"Son, I can't lay my hands on the kind of money you need." I had decided to adopt the sad parent role, when I should have been interrogating him about his own shortcomings.

"But you can give a guarantee," he retorted quickly.

I had seen this coming. He was right. With our mortgage-free house and my savings, I could give a guarantee. I pretended to consider it. "No, Nick," I said finally. "Your mother and I have enough for a comfortable retirement with my pension. Don't you think it unreasonable to ask us to put that at risk?"

"It wouldn't be at risk, Dad," he said heatedly.

"I'm sorry, Son. You know I understand risk."

Insurance, like bookmaking, is about risk and reward, finely tuned. Nick's 'proposition' was flimsy. And he was, as his career to date showed, if not a loser then not a big success. I would guess that Barry Macklin was much more successful financially. I would be a fool to give Nick more money or a guarantee for it.

"Why not ask Barry Macklin? He's a member of the family," I said gently.

"He's not!"

"I'm sure he'd be glad to help." I was being aggravating in saying this. I knew Nick despised Barry. And I knew the reason. Nick had charmed Barry and Jane at first meeting, but when he asked Barry to join him in business, Barry had realised that this meant making a large donation to one of Nick's funds, and Barry wisely refused. I was sure he'd refuse to help now.

"I'm not asking Macklin because he's a dumbarse."

"A dumbarse with plenty of money," I observed mildly.

"For shit's sake, Dad. I'm asking *you* to help me!" Nick was seething now and plaintive, his eyes bulging. "You've got plenty of money, Dad. Mum's told me. And you don't trust me."

Ann must have blabbed about my investments and savings accounts. "I thought this was about business, not trust," I tried to smile.

"Fuck you, you boring old dick!" he said, springing to his feet and striding to the door.

I followed him down the hall to the front door. As he was going down the path, I said, "Remember, you're my son and I love you!"

That much is true. The feeling I have for Nick is deep and subliminal, but it doesn't extend to easing him over self-created stiles at 30 years of age.

Ann was caustic when I told her this result (in an edited version) that evening. I never mentioned Nick's abusive remark. I was hurt that my son spoke to me in that way. We spray words around carelessly at times but some can strike like bullets and leave a lasting wound.

You might have thought, from Ann's reaction, that Nick was already broke and the neighbours in the street were jeering at us. "You have the money and you're heartless!" she concluded.

My plea that I was only safeguarding our marriage savings for the future was completely ineffective. I also suspected that Ann's vision of Nick, wrists and ankles tied, being committed to a bonfire which only I could extinguish, was wrong. Nick would be shopping around. I was just his first stop.

I retired from this conflict with a stony face and a firm will. I would wait to hear the bad news of Nick's bankruptcy over forthcoming weeks. Ann's words were in my ears: "The future involves safeguarding our family, not saving for vacations!"

Tragedy in Amherst Street: a workman crushed by a falling iron beam in the basement of a house at the end of the street. The property has become a crime scene with yellow ribbons staked around it.

The residents are very keen on excavating their cellars to provide basements. Some of the basements are like aircraft hangers: a place for the children to play, an en suite nanny's room, a film or TV lounge, a games room with a billiards table and, perhaps, a granny flat. Some basements are wider than the house above and extend to the boundaries. It's a tricky construction, supporting the house while the foundations are replaced and the boundaries are shored up with reinforced concrete going down 15 or more feet. There is a risk of collapse, but there is a hunger for space.

Ann and I don't need more space – we could do with less, but the Clitheroes have had their cellar excavated. I asked Jim Clitheroe why. He blathered for a while about additional bedrooms and a TV room (there are only the two of them with seven bedrooms), until I said, "It's money isn't it, Jim? You're a property developer."

"Well, yes. It's a substantial increase in the value of the house," he said, as though this had just occurred to him. "That's not a crime, is it? Why don't you do it yourself?"

Our semi-detached was a fortunate purchase in a housing market that was to go on rising for years. Will the foreign lawyers and bankers and chief executives who have colonised the streets around us, and pushed up property values, begin to go away with Brexit? Perhaps it doesn't matter. We like to talk about property values as though they are ready cash. As far as Ann and I are concerned, the cash will not be realised because, unless something cataclysmic happens, we don't intend to sell.

Ann has conjectured about what *could* be done with a large basement room. I have listened to her painting a *House and Garden* picture, with glass doors opening to the back garden, which would also be partly excavated. She would be unlikely to demand that we actually do this, but if I showed the slightest keenness, I'm sure she would be more than supportive.

I said to her, "We could put a bust of Napoleon in the garden, in the line of sight through the glass windows in the basement." I received a killing glance but that seemed to close the subject down.

I stood outside the Amherst Street house days after the fatality. The police tapes were hanging tiredly. The place had a blind, broken look, deserted after the removal of the body of the nameless foreign worker. There were stories of a prosecution and a bankrupt builder. But I knew that in a few weeks the site would come to life again: men in hard hats, skips, trucks loaded with steel girders, the digger spewing out soil from below. Space is money.

When the weather is fine, Jane and I take the baby to Bishop's Park. We thread our way through the baby carriages, puppies, scooters and bikes and have a cup of coffee in the cafe. On this particular day, Jane wasn't her bouncy, loquacious self. I didn't enquire why. I was quite happy. I like these outings. When we sat down in the café with our coffees in front of us and the baby was happily dozing, Jane squared up to me.

"What have you been doing, Dad?" she said, ominously.

She eyed me as though I was guilty of something disreputable. I searched my recent 'doings' and came back to only one thing – Carol. I found it hard to believe that Jane could know anything about Carol. I thought it must be something else and I responded innocently. "Only buying a multi-pack of dishwasher tablets."

"Mum is terribly upset and worried."

Oh, no! Ann has been talking, exposing her suppositions. "Worried about what?" I said with feigned surprise.

"You know! This woman!"

I scalded my lips with the coffee, trying to get thinking time. Admit or deny? "What woman? There is no woman," I retorted. I expect I sounded as convincing as Bill Clinton. I could feel my cheeks reddening.

"How could you, Dad? You've done exactly the opposite of what I advised you to do."

Denial was going to get me nowhere. "You advised me to head off Bernard Chandler. I couldn't do it, Jane. Your mother is set in her Bernard Chandler operations, whatever they amount to."

"I said, take Mum for a decent holiday. So you go off with another woman!"

"It isn't like that at all, Jane. I love your mother…"

"This isn't the way to go, Dad. It's childish, almost spiteful."

"What has Mum said to you?"

"She says the woman has been ringing the house."

I blurted, "But that's all it amounts to, Jane. A mistake!"

"No. You were in Yorkshire with a woman. Mum knows. She knows you. She can tell from your behaviour. It's more than a call on the telephone."

I feel as though I have been stripped naked. I haven't said a word, but all is known. I try a counter-attack. "What does your mother think of Bernard?"

"She likes and admires him, but she isn't in love. But it's like I said, you have to get on the case."

"Did you point out to her that her antics with Chandler may have encouraged this?"

"She's not in bed with Bernard. She says so and I believe her. Otherwise, her attitude to your gallivanting might be different."

"Fair enough. But does she admit she's a cause of this… gallivanting as you call it?"

"Not in the least. She says her relationship with Bernard is public and low key. Women can have men friends, Dad."

"Certainly, but does the reverse apply?" I said miserably, but thinking I had made a smart reply.

"Not on walking holidays with a snuggy little bed waiting at the hotel after a few drinks."

I stumbled into that one! I was beaten. "I never intended anything to happen, Jane. I went for a walk…" I should never have said this.

"And a predatory woman was lying in wait… Get real, Dad."

A predatory woman? I've been mauled by tigers in my own house.

15

Daughter Jane's Revelation

I have to mention what you could call, in relation to the British male, an abnormality of mine. I live near Craven Cottage – the home of Fulham Football Club. When people know that they always ask, "Are you a supporter?" My answer is, "Not exactly." By which I mean that I don't mind the club being there and doing what it does. The truth is that I occasionally watch Match of the Day on BBC television and agree that football deserves to be described as 'the beautiful game' – that is forgetting the shadows that can accompany a very big business. It's fascinating entertainment. I don't support any club. I'll leave it at that.

I have been to Craven Cottage twice in the 20 years we have lived in Amherst Street. Ann bought me the first ticket as a birthday present. I bought the second myself to see whether the fervour of the crowd and the noise was as demented, as I remembered from my first visit. It was. Apart from yelling and incomprehensible chanting, the fans were jumping up and down on the planking in the stands. It was deafening. And you couldn't really see all of the game from one seat. A television view, I found, is better. I've made an unmanly admission: I should be going to the game, smelling the sweaty strip and enduring the meaningless clamour.

Amherst Street changes on match day. It is closed by the local authority. Crowds, sometimes as many as 20,000 (Premier League), move through the streets surrounding Craven Cottage, munching hot dogs and sipping from cans of beer. This is not disturbing. The mobs add a bit of spectacle to the quiet streets. Removing the odd empty beer can from my fence after the game is easy. The farmyard smell of the piles of turd on the road from the police horses is a striking change from diesel exhaust. It's odd that the police horses don't have bum bags like carriage horses.

As the enthusiasts stride through the surrounding streets in their dark, grungy clothes and the odd coloured woolly hat, I can feel their barely suppressed excitement; their loud declamations as they speculate about the forthcoming game, and the sheer lung power of the chanters. This is a parade of mostly men between 20 and 60, revelling in the prospect of the game. The police are everywhere; it's a free entrance for them. At home, in the potting shed, I occasionally hear the very distant roar of the crowd when there is a score. And when the wind is right, I can hear the same noise from Chelsea. It's a pleasant sound, communal enjoyment – at that distance.

While I am thinking about sport, I should mention another of my oddities. I was having a beer with friends in the Brown Cow – my local – recently when I won the raffle of a ticket to a Six Nations game at Twickenham. I explained I was 'tied up' on the match day and gave the ticket to a friend. It was a white lie.

I started my career in insurance in an office full of rugby enthusiasts. They would criticize past games, reconstruct the teams that should have been played in their opinion, bet on forthcoming games, predict outcomes, savage referees and managers and argue furiously amongst themselves about positional play. At lunchtimes, rugby was often the sole subject of conversation – unless we were on the brink of an international crisis. A number of this group of pundits were senior to me, and I had to be grateful that I was invited to sit with them. That involved listening, nodding agreement and squirming inside.

I saw what the game does to men's bodies. I looked with amazement at the coloured pictures in the newspapers – huge hulks with bullet heads, black eyes, squashed noses and ears like blobs of pastry. And then there are those unfortunate players who have the sense knocked out of their heads. Concussion is not good for you. The head boy at my school, an exceptional half back, went on to graduate from Sandhurst. He also continued playing the game at which he excelled. He became a promising lieutenant but had to retire after two years with a mental breakdown which he told me was caused by repeated concussion. When I met him after retirement, he was half the man he could have been.

Nick, my son, has no fear of physical injury, or perhaps no imagination. He participates in dangerous sports like climbing, and off-piste skiing without a qualm. He was captain of the first 15 at his school. He used to taunt me with, "The queue's getting longer, Dad," as the season wore on, referring to the line of injured boys who, as rugby players, had the privilege of being served first at meals. The Six Nations tournament makes me think of the Romans watching animal baiting. Why would tolerably civilised people ever want to do this? I know women play rugby football now and perhaps this heralds either a gentler game or a new era of female monsters.

I have begun to relish my visits to Jane a little less. The subjects of 'that woman' and Bernard Chandler keep coming up. Jane isn't a nagger, but there is an elephant in the room. I try to counter by asking questions about Benedict and Barry. I have inadvertently strayed into territory where there is a dangerous sensitivity. For example, I asked on a recent walk in Bishops' Park, "Is Benny going to have a daddy?"

"Barry has signed the birth certificate," was the ready answer.

"Are you two going to get hitched?" I know I'm pressing on a nerve here, but I take a chance. As her father, it's a permissible question and I do think about Jane's future.

"We're thinking about it."

"Security for the child?"

"Would marriage make a difference, Dad?"

"I suppose not, if Barry wanted to duck out." Jane has never precisely articulated her view. She obviously feels more free without the status of marriage. Since I believe that Benedict apart, her relationship with Barry, is her number one concern, her lukewarm approach to marriage can't be at the expense of her relationship with him.

"And what's so great about marriage? Look at you and Mum."

She had steered us back to the Carol-Bernard situation. "Don't write us off," I persist. "I love your Mum. Chandler is only a passing breeze."

"And you're girlfriend isn't?"

"I don't have a girlfriend." I'm going to maintain this position unflinchingly.

She pulls a face which says, "That's improbable."

"I met a woman on a walk and OK we walked and talked together and that's all. Please, Jane."

"Oh, Dad, you're such an unconvincing liar. How did the woman get your telephone number if you didn't give it to her."

"I swear I never gave it to her," I said very heavily.

"No, I realise you actually didn't need to. You only had to ring *her*!"

"I only rang her to tell her to stop bothering me." I had gone an inch too far again. I didn't need to say this, and I realised I shouldn't have. Jane has her mother's forensic skills. She'll extort a confession from me and get me to sign it! I have to stop digging a pit for myself with lies.

"You look as though you're in shock, Dad. And I'll tell you something else about Bernard Chandler. It won't break any confidences with Mum. It's what I know myself from Daphne Chandler." Jane went to school with Daphne.

Now, I really am in shock. I'm going to have to endure something awful. "OK," I say as calmly as I can.

"Bernard Chandler and his wife are planning to part."

Oh, hell. *The Mrs Chandler factor.* I'd never thought about that. "Because of her husband's attention to Ann?"

"I expect so, but I don't know. Daphne didn't want to elaborate."

"Yes, he's hunting for fresh meat," I said disdainfully.

"Mum could be interested, Dad."

"You mean more interested if he's leaving his wife?"

"Sure. It's a wakeup call for you."

"What shall we do, Jane? What can we do?" My voice went up a few tones consistent with the awareness that we had taken our seats in the crowded café. I'm perturbed and confused.

"I can't do anything, but you can take Mum away for a while. And there's something else," she put her coffee cup down deliberately and patted the child's blanket protectively.

It was going to get worse.

"When you were away with your girlfriend, I called at home to deliver a plant Mum wanted at about 7 pm."

"Oh, no!" I could see it all before she explained.

She went on grimly. "I didn't get any answer to my knock so I used my own key and went inside. Chandler was there…"

"Oh, shit!" Of course he was there – fucking my wife!

"I got to the dining room door when Mum, who had half-heard me, was getting up from the table. They were having dinner. Chandler, smug as you like, had his table-napkin tucked into his collar, his wine-glass half empty…"

The image heated my blood a little, but wasn't as bad as I expected. "What did Ann say?"

"She said they were having dinner and talking over school stuff. I shoved the plant pot into her hands and fled out of the front door."

"Did she get the message that you were upset?"

"Must have. I haven't seen her since."

"Where to *after* dinner I wonder? Not to the matrimonial bedroom I hope. The spare room is usually made up."

"Dad, I can't understand whether you're just saying that to suggest you're tough, or whether Mum getting laid in the spare room is better than using your bed."

Actually, it would be worse for me, screwing in the matrimonial bed, a kind of ultimate 'up yours' to our sex life. But I wasn't going to dispute these points with Jane.

Something of an Ice Age had followed my rejection of Nick's 'proposal'. I waited to hear the news of the bankruptcy which I knew would come from Ann.

On a recent night when we were dining, she said, "I heard from Nick today."

"And?" I was quite composed in the silence that followed.

"Nick says he is in the clear. The petition or whatever it is, is not going to be heard. It's been dismissed."

I was relieved. "Good. I thought he might have had a number of ways out."

She paused and I thought more criticism would come. "I realise you know more about business than I do, Bill," she said, reaching for my hand across the table. "And I understand you acted in our personal interest."

This was high praise indeed. I refilled our wine glasses zestfully. And then I thought, with a shiver, what if I *had* guaranteed the payment for Nick out of love for Ann and her concept of family?

16

I Am an Anarchist

I have worked dutifully at the food bank for some months, but I have become bored and restive. It is very mournful work. The helpers are mournful. They are neatly dressed and clean middle class people who frown all the time, mostly ladies of about 50 or 60. They take themselves very seriously. Pullen himself hardly appears but when he does, he strides down the alleys of shelves mouthing imprecations like "Move briskly now", "Keep talk to a minimum", "This isn't a social centre".

Our customers are of a wide variety of ages, sexes, classes, colours and ethnicity. They are also in a variety of conditions, from dirty, untidy or drunk, to newly washed, smelling of shower-gel and stylishly dressed. Most have smartphones. When in the food bank, they tend to behave as if they had been invited into Aladdin's Cave. They cannot believe the largesse.

For a while, I adopted Pullen's military attitudes with my customers, pushing a basic bag into their basket with cursory enquiries about them, shoving them along, picking up optional items while babbling a version of the rules. I noticed that many were wary of me, a few were anxious that they might not get what they needed. There were also plenty who had a sense of entitlement, or thinly veiled rage and some with a cunning eye who were playing a game.

To relieve my apathy, I began to spend more time with the patrons, to talk to them about their many and varied troubles. I felt I was looking at people, for the most part, who were telling me their story from the bottom of a dark cess-pit into which I could only imagine falling. In their talk, they revealed some of the horrors that were in the pit: murder, rape, starvation and disease and the destruction of their families (with some hyperbole, I suppose). Some contended their benefit hadn't come through, others that they had been maltreated by their landlord and thrown out on the street. All had a story of deprivation, injustice, violence or ill health. None admitted that they were incompetent, though many were. They seldom ascribed their fate to bad luck at the betting shop or the bingo hall, excess alcohol or drugs, but it could have been. They usually found somebody to blame. Some were genuinely needy and some were at a low point which they would rise from with a little help. Some were mentally defective.

When I had checked them in, I began to say, "You are in a bad way. Who is to blame?" if they hadn't already told me. I received and could compile, a long and incredibly varied list from President Assad of Syria, or some other foreign potentate, to ISIS, Al-Qaeda, the British police, MI5, people smugglers, British colonial asset strippers, the NHS, the Tories and the Prime Minister. Only one or two were prepared to admit that their plight was their own fault. When I asked about their families, I got guarded replies. Plainly a lot of their families didn't want them. But some didn't want their families or that's what they said.

After the first few weeks, Pullen required me to spend some time checking the documentation which established the claimant's rights. If anyone came to the bank without the requisite forms signed by a doctor or other responsible person, he or she had to be sent away. "They can't walk in here because they want free groceries," Pullen said. There were unpleasant scenes when I had to try to explain the formalities, but I never sent people away empty handed if they had come without the necessary papers.

If Pullen wasn't around, I decided to let in those who hadn't got the signed form or hadn't completed it properly or who had obviously forged it. I began to hand out more groceries than the rules allowed. Some of the other helpers noticed. One said, cynically, "You're a bleeding heart, aren't you?" I didn't deny it but I didn't feel I was 'doing good;. What I thought was, 'What the hell! These people have had a shitty deal, and I'm not going to give them another one!' The fact that some of them had caused their own problem didn't make the deal any less shitty. People don't self-destruct for fun.

I began to tell people when to call in. The number of people who came on spec began to increase during my shift. Some of them were rogues who were on to a good thing. I knew it. I didn't care, because I thought that even the rogues were at the bottom of the pit, ruined lives. I felt a sense of exhilaration as I filled their bags, and the exhilaration increased the more supplies I could pile on to them, a mad solution in a mad world.

The stocks of food in the bank began to fall rapidly on my shift, but they could easily be rebuilt. It was only a matter of time before Pullen became aware of what I was doing. Most of the volunteers whom I met knew and didn't care. Those who did care rebuked me, but I took no notice. A quiet word would have passed to Pullen. And my paperwork didn't square either with the stock or the authorisation requirements. An appearance by Pullen was thus foretold.

He came glowering out of the shadows on a night when I was surrounded by a group of young Romanians or gypsies. I don't know the difference. They all denied being gypsies. Why? Is it the rusting trucks, empty oil drums and piles of trash on the grass?

Pullen had been watching me and he shouted, "Stop, Batley. Cease and desist or I will summon the police!" The two woman volunteers present were white-faced. "Get these men out of here unless they have papers!" he commanded me.

The men had no papers. They gathered the goods they had been given and made ready to leave silently.

Pullen shouted, "You men, stop! Hand back those bags unless you have papers!"

The men looked at each other, uncertain. One pointed to me. "He gave us."

I stood woodenly by. The men shrugged, grinned and slipped out of the door with their provisions.

"Batley," Pullen said, his eyes circling the room as though looking for support, but there were only the two distraught women. "You are an anarchist!"

I felt quite easy. "Just practising."

"You are also a very insolent man."

I didn't have to take insults from Pullen but I was fascinated by his dark, boiling face and shuddering jaw.

"You have broken every guideline and rule. You have wasted probably hundreds of pounds worth of provisions. You don't understand that there are limits to what we can provide."

"I do understand very well that there are limits. I haven't wasted anything."

"You should be prosecuted...for criminal waste!"

I began to move toward the door.

"You are dismissed, Batley. Never come here again. I shall write to your referees about your disgraceful conduct!"

I turned at the door and waved goodbye to the two women who were still transfixed. I felt quite light-hearted, as I walked to the bus stop.

Another small drama awaited me. I hauled myself upstairs on the 2:20 bus in Uxbridge Road and noticed one of the men I had served at the food bank sitting at the rear of the compartment. On the seat beside him, he had one of the brown paper bags I had filled with food. He was about 20, tall, thin and swarthy with black stubble on his face. We had momentary eye contact. I took a seat six or so rows in front of him and so with my back to him.

When the bus had travelled one stop, an inspector got on. He came down the cab checking passes. He was a very tall West

Indian. He wore a white shirt and black tie. After he had passed me, checking passes, I heard the sound of raised voices from the seats behind me. I turned round to look. It was my 'customer' who had apparently slipped in the rear door at a stop and had no pass. He was nevertheless able to loudly defend himself. He abused the inspector in almost indecipherable words, except for the obscenities.

On an impulse, I turned and raising my voice said, "I'll pay the fare."

The inspector ignored me. The volume of the altercation mounted. The driver, who would have seen what was happening on his closed circuit television, stopped the bus. I heard a loud cry. I turned round again. My 'customer' bolted past me, a knife in his hand and down the stairs to the lower deck without his bag of food. The inspector was on the floor on his back. His shirt was saturated with blood, groceries scattered around him. The man ran out the rear door and disappeared into the crowd.

I realised that my performance at the food bank would not play well with Ann or Susan Clitheroe and decided to reveal all. First, I told Ann about the incident on the bus omitting my misguided interference in it.

"I suppose some of these migrants are on a knife-edge," Ann said sympathetically. "He may not have had any money."

"Knife-edge is right. That is what he used."

We were having a late supper together that evening. I thought that in a way this was a scene which set the volatile events at the food bank at a distance. We could contemplate it from the comfort and security of our chairs. I had poured a glass of red wine. We were taking our first sip. In that pleasant pause, I said, "Ann, I'm an anarchist."

"You're certainly pretty untidy around the house, Bill."

"In the view of former stationmaster Herr JD Pullen."

"Pullen? At the food bank? What's gone wrong, Bill?"

"I was fired today."

Ann's eyes opened wide and unbelieving. "My God! What happened?"

"Pullen says I broke the rules and gave food away to people who weren't entitled."

"Is that true?"

"Yes, if you take the rules literally."

"But why, Bill. Why?" Ann's voice rose with this entreaty.

"I don't know... I felt the people I saw should have the food."

"But you have to have rules..."

"I interpreted the rules liberally..."

Ann gave me a perplexed look and after a moment said, "You *are* an anarchist. Wait till Susan hears about this."

"Pullen is going to write to her. You could get in a word first."

"What the hell can I say, Bill? My husband had a rush of blood to the head and started giving away food?"

"All right. I'll just bear the shame and ignominy," I said, knowing Ann would make a very good case in my favour with Susan.

I decided to face Ann with Jane's vision of Chandler with his napkin tucked under his chin, at our dining room table, drinking our wine. It was a nauseating picture. Jane was right. I needed to move positively against Chandler. I steeled myself to do this and it took several days as I waited for the right moment. I chose Saturday morning in bed. I exerted myself to bring us both a cup of tea at 8:30 am. Ann was just waking up and rather pleased at my gesture.

We propped ourselves on the pillows and had a few inconsequential words about what we were doing that day and I began, "Darling, something is troubling me and I'd like to talk to you about it."

'Darling' is not a special word of affection in our house; it's rather worn, as likely to be used for 'Darling, could you clean up that puddle on the floor?' as anything more intimate, but Ann seemed to sense a problem and turned to me seriously, putting her iPad on the side table. "What is it?"

"Bernard Chandler."

"Oh, that. Are you trying to even the score after that woman's call?"

"I'm wondering why he was here for dinner when I was away. He has his own domestic arrangements, doesn't he?"

She flinched at this confrontation, but only momentarily. "He's separating from his wife."

"That doesn't explain it. This isn't a cafeteria."

"Jane's been talking to you. She shouldn't have done that. She should mind her own business."

"It is her business and mine. She's worried about you. And I am too, Ann." I saw Ann's confidence wilt a little.

"There's nothing to worry about. I'll talk to her," she said, picking up her iPad again.

"Sorry, dear, but you can't brush this off as something to do with Jane. Dinner with wine, in proximity to the matrimonial bedroom when your husband is away? Chandler isn't a needy man who has had hard luck and needs a snack and some advice. He's an appallingly arrogant, hirsute creep who prances around this house as though he'll shortly own it."

"Bernard's never been in this bed, Bill. That's for sure. Give me a little credit for delicacy."

"In the guest room, perhaps? I'd rather give you a credit for chastity than delicacy."

Ann recoiled and didn't answer, but I felt I'd made a serious point. She *was* over the odds in having him here. She wasn't going to gratify me with an assertion that she had *never* slept with Chandler. So like her. Saving some leverage for herself. I guessed that on balance she probably hadn't slept with him, but you can never be sure.

Afterwards, I thought, why are we so devious? I could have said: "Have you ever slept with Chandler?" The truth is that I didn't really want to know. I was apprehensive about knowing. It would be hurtful. What happens between the sheets is a complete chapter known only to the participants, and I would prefer it was left that way. This might explain the vagueness in our various discussions. I'm sure that Ann doesn't want to know about me definitively, either. I will certainly deny screwing 'that woman' until I am beyond my dying day.

Judi and Mike Levitt had lunch with us today. They were just short of two hours late in arriving at Amherst Street and didn't call to alert us.

We had a pleasant time. Ann, knowing the likelihood of their lateness, had allowed them an extra hour in her scheduling. You could say that they were only an hour late, as far as we were concerned. They came up the path with flowers and wine and a smiling apology. After drinks, we didn't start the meal until four pm. When they had gone at around 7 pm, Ann said: "They are charming but incorrigible."

"You could apply that line of Philip Larkin's about what mums and dads do to children," I said. "They fuck you up. They don't mean to, but they do."

"Mike and Judi are nice. They're just very laid back. Remember Cabo St Lucas?" Ann asked.

I remembered it only too well, as I helped clear the clutter of dishes from the dining room. Cabo St Lucas is a town off the southern tip of Baja California, Mexico, described as 'where the desert meets the sea'. It has white cliffs and long white beaches. Since the 1980s, it has developed rapidly as a resort. When we arrived by cruise liner, Judi and Mike were occupying a vacation house several miles up the peninsula. We had arranged to meet them. Mike had promised drinks and lunch at a restaurant on the coast. Mindful of the Levitt's tardiness, we had to be sure we were returned to our ship in time. It was due to depart at midnight with all passengers aboard by 11 pm.

"Tell Mike the ship leaves at nine," Ann said.

I agreed, "I'll be quite strict with him about time."

We had a 20-minute journey to shore by tender from our ship. We came ashore at a marina full of luxury yachts at 9:30 am. In a temperature of 90 degrees, we walked the hardly bearable boardwalk around the marina, crowded with twee shops which had almost no customers other than our fellow passengers. I was hoping that we wouldn't have to sit it out and wait for Mike and Judi but they were there as promised, sprawled on chairs under the awning in front of a bar. After the greetings, Mike said, "Let's have a marguerita before we start." We went inside where it was cool and the drink, which took a long time to come, was soothing and well worth waiting for.

I questioned Mike about his plans. "It'll take an hour or so, maybe a little more. The food is classy Mexican. I've never tasted better."

"What is there to see around here?" Ann asked.

"Not much, unless you like looking at condominiums," Judi said. "Or dinky old Catholic churches."

Cabot St Lucas was one of those places where you need a good book unless you golf or fish or are happy by the pool.

"The fishing is good," Mike insisted.

I noticed that it was after 11 am when we started our journey in Mike's four wheel drive Land Rover. I slipped into a kind of coma, assisted by the marguerita, as we jolted along hard white roads, pitted with hollows, or melting patches of tar macadam. We stopped and bought fruit at a roadside stall. Along the road we passed many collections of white high-rise apartments in the distance, a few green oases, a golf course. Eventually, I knew I would have to have a serious word with Mike.

"Do you know this area, Mike?"

"Not this particular part. Our place is further inland."

"So how are you finding your way?"

"I guess, I've kinda lost it. I mean, all we have to do is press on and I'm pretty sure we'll come to Santa Ana. I know the way from there."

"Uh-huh." I turned to Ann. She pulled a face. Mike saw her in the rear vision mirror.

"Come on, Ann," he said, "It's not that bad. Look, we'll stop at Santa Ana if you like. Put something in your tummy and a drink in your hand. How about that?"

"Let's do that, Mike," Judi said.

"OK, but we're not going to get anything half decent. It's better to hang out for our target."

"I think we should stop as Judi said." The vibration from the road made my head buzz and I wanted some relief.

Another 20 minutes and we arrived at the hamlet of Santa Ana. We stopped at the market beside the highway, blistering and deserted in the sun. Behind the stalls was a bar-restaurant, and we went into the dark interior. Mike, whose Spanish was good, talked to the proprietor. Cold beers appeared.

"The only thing here worth having is tacos and black beans. I've ordered a plate to keep starvation at bay," he said.

We were the only customers but the tacos and beans took half an hour and two more rounds of beer to arrive, by which time I was tapping my feet and looking at my watch.

"Take it easy, Bill. You're on holiday," Mark said.

Mark and Judi tucked into their food. In fact Judi, who particularly liked black beans, ate half of Mike's as well. Ann and I picked at our plates. "It's slop," I whispered to Ann.

Before Judi had finished her, or rather Mike's helping, I had to speak up, "Mark, we've been on the road for four hours already including stops. Are you sure we're going to find this restaurant?"

"Oh, sure. Not far now. I must admit the distance has surprised me a bit. However, You'll love it. A really sophisticated place."

"Can we get an idea how long it's going to take?"

"Half an hour maybe."

We collapsed into the Land Rover, and I was soon shaken into an insensible state – beer and road noise and an arid landscape. More than an hour had passed when Ann tugged at my arm and pointed at her watch.

I took a deep breath and tapped Mike, who was humming to music on the car radio, on the shoulder. "Sorry old boy, but I've a feeling we aren't going to get to this restaurant."

"What's the matter Bill, aren't you hungry?"

"Yes, I'm bloody starving! I haven't had anything to eat or drink except a cup of coffee on the ship, a marguerita, three or was it four beers, and a mess of black beans, all day."

"Calm down, my friend, we'll be there shortly. You'll love it and thank me."

"No, Mike. I accept your good intentions, but no." Hunger had made me very bad-tempered but I concealed it.

Mike threw the car on to the loose gravel at the side of the road and hit the brakes hard. We rested in a cloud of dust. "What the fuck shall we do!" he shouted.

"Turn around and go back now," I said. "We're lost on these God-forsaken roads. We have a ship to catch."

A silence fell. Judi spoke very quietly. "Mike, do as Bill asks."

"You're crazy, Bill, fucking crazy. No way we're going to miss your boat. Ann, what do you say? Lovely food just around the corner."

"Better go back, Mike. We're just anxious about the ship."

Mike swirled the SUV around in another cloud and we were heading in the return direction on the deserted road. Mike drove fast, and we travelled in silence. Even the car radio didn't dare to speak. It was an hour before we were in territory near Cabo St Lucas and Mike stopped outside a development of shops and condominiums around a large shopping mall, branded 'Club Escobedo'. A few cars were scattered over acres of car park.

"I think we ought to offer our guests at least a sandwich to stop the hunger pangs."

"Mike, that's a lovely thought, but we have to be back by 9 pm," Ann said. "And it's eight now."

"No, Ann. You've got it wrong. The last tender goes at 10:30," Mike said. "I know because in an idle moment this morning, before you came ashore, I asked the cruise staff on the quay."

I knew Mike was right about the timing, but I was still doubtful whether we could get to the quay in time and take in the Escobedo. I admit that I was thinking of the delicious meal I could have aboard the vessel if we got a tender sooner. "We don't want to trespass on your good nature, Mike. You have a long way to drive tonight, and…"

Ann said, brightly: "We seem to have got some extra time. Let's do it, Bill."

Mike and Judi cheered, and he drove across the lot and parked near the entrance. When we stepped into the cathedral-like marble lobby, I found the Escobedo was a centre for a casino, a swimming pool and a gym as well as shops selling high fashion. I parleyed with the cashier as a gesture to show Mike I really was willing. I wasn't. I had to buy tickets for entrance which seemed very expensive, but they covered all the activities of the centre, including a meal.

"We came in for a sandwich and you're paying for a four course meal," Mike said.

"The point is, I'm paying, Mike."

"I won't be wanting a swim, but thanks for your generosity," Mike said, his feelings apparently still crushed.

We went into the dining room which was clean, modern and comfortable. Only a handful of diners were spread about. We chose the table we wanted. Nobody appeared in the room. After five minutes, Mike got up from the table and pushed through the servery doors. He came back to the table. "Now we will have some action."

A girl appeared and distributed menus a few minutes later. There were many items on the menu. Study was required.

After a while, confused trying to translate so many items into recognisable dishes, I said: "Mike, can I suggest you order a small snack for each of us. No black beans or tacos. A pastie sort of thing, you know, a burrito is it?"

"Will do," he said, but it seemed to take a long time for the waitress to come back to us. Mike had to go into the kitchen again. After some further delay, and a long conversation in

Spanish, the order was taken. Beers were served and we settled down to wait.

When I calculated that we had been in the restaurant for over an hour, I said, "Mike, we're going to have to go."

"Don't be silly," he said. "You have until 10:30 pm and it's only 9:30 now. Tons of time. This is Mexico."

"But we don't know how long it's going to take to get from here to the marina."

"Fifteen minutes, I swear it."

I looked at Ann. She was tense. "Mike and Judi, you've been very kind and things haven't gone as planned. Ann and I are uneasy. It's not fun. I have to insist that you take us back to the marina now. I do insist."

"I'm very sorry," Judi said. "Mike, we must go *now*. I did so much want us all to have a good time..."

"It's been wonderful just seeing you," Ann said.

Mike's complaint to management on the way out produced two free vouchers. He was wrong about the short return journey. He wasn't sure of the way and we weren't on the quay until 10:15. Quick goodbyes and we were in the tender. I was ravenously hungry and weak. The restaurants were closed when we went aboard and we had to make do with coffee and cookies, and when we had clambered into bed, double whiskies. "What a fuck-up!" I said. "Was there anything that did not go wrong?"

"Only Mike and Judi's good humour," Ann said.

The next day, I had a friendly email from Mike which said, *By the way guys, we had a bang up meal at the Escobedo with those tickets you left in the car before we drove home.*

17

Mrs Chandler Appears

I came out of our gate this morning with Rex, paused for a moment on the footpath and a large wolf-like husky about 30 feet away spotted us. It came lolloping towards us, snout curled back over snarling teeth. I stepped back inside the gate with Rex and shut it. The dog reared up on the gate yelping, baring its red mouth and looking ferocious. The dog-walker came along the footpath, grinning. "He's harmless," he said as if it was amusing and I was a coward. He walked on. I had no chance to speak.

A dog, the kind of dog I have, a fox terrier becomes part of the family, and I go through the often awkward and inconvenient routine of looking after it or him – I prefer him – feeding, walking, treatment by a vet if necessary, kennels when we go away, without thinking. I don't begrudge the attention I give the animal, which craves it. When I feel alone, the company is warming. The walking is exercise. The picking up is not pleasant.

Amherst Street and environs is big dog territory and a territory of big dogs. This is city. Greater London. Nevertheless, it seems that everybody has a dog, often more than one. It's incongruous. In nearby Bishop's Park, there is strife between the dog-walkers and the mothers of young children, who object to their little darling being smeared, or those who can't find a clean space to spread out a groundsheet for a picnic. The local council allocates dog exercise areas, but the dog-walkers don't seem to keep to them. Dog-walking is like bicycling, speed limits and taxes. Yes, there are rules but many don't follow them.

There appear to be three kinds of dog-walkers: those who don't pick up, those who do, and those who do but regard it as their right to litter and discard the bag then and there. Fouling notices are posted and re-posted in Amhurst Street, but it doesn't make much difference. I don't necessarily blame our residents. Numbers of people from beyond walk their dogs though these streets perhaps on the way to Bishop's Park. It is strange that people have to be told – and reminded – that they mustn't drop shit in the street. OK, it is a small minority of people, not dogs, but they do make a big stink.

Given a probably selfish love of animals, I wonder what prompts people to keep fierce and large dogs which belong either in the country or on an industrial estate. There are plenty of these animals around here. It may be over-concern for security, but I think it's also to create a self-image of strength. Does a person need to cultivate a Bill Sykes image? These owners are one with their dogs, just as Mr Daniels and his car are inseparable. Actually, dog-owners, particularly this variety, tend to look and waddle like their dogs. The facial similarity can be uncanny. I seldom see a pretty girl with a bull terrier unless she's a paid dog-walker.

I was reading the *Guardian* after breakfast this Saturday morning and answered a knock on the front door. A fifty-ish woman was there with short, tousled blond hair and unhappy creases around the corners of her mouth. She seemed uneasy. More creases appeared on her face when she saw me. "I called to see Mrs Batley," she said.

"She's out, shopping, can I help?"

She didn't refuse my offer but showed doubt. The lines faded a little. "Are you Mr Batley?"

When I nodded, she hesitated for a few seconds, bit her lip and then said, "I'm Thelma Chandler."

I was sure that Ann had never met Thelma Chandler. Mrs Chandler was making a cold call, plunging into what was likely to be inhospitable territory. It must be important. It would take some nerve. "Bernard's wife? Please come in," I said pleasantly.

Plainly, she was on a mission related to her marriage and in a slightly embarrassed way, I was glad to meet her. I could see that I might have the opportunity to interpose myself between her and Ann. I could learn much.

Ann had taken the car to the supermarket as usual on a Saturday morning. She would be away for at least two hours. She likes to shop at her own pace, without me lounging about with a supermarket trolley and suggesting unacceptable purchases.

Mrs Chandler entered nervously, but I put her at ease. "Ann will be home soon," I said as I led her into the lounge and gestured toward an easy chair. "I'll make a cup of tea."

"I'm not sure whether I should stay." She looked around the room. "You have a lovely home, Mr Batley."

"Home is what it's about, isn't it? Your husband and my wife," I said thoughtfully.

The heavy lines had returned around her mouth. "Yes." Her blue eyes were reddened and brimming. I thought she could see that we two had something to discuss, never mind what she intended to say to Ann.

"Come into the kitchen while I exercise my domestic skills."

I made the tea quickly and silently except for exchanging first names. We trouped back into the lounge. "What has Bernard said or done about this, Thelma?" It was sufficient to be very vague.

She sat on the couch, straight-backed. She drew a deep breath, but I believed I had won some of her confidence. "He told me some time ago that he thought we should part. He said we weren't getting on well enough. I was very upset. Recently, he told me he'd met another woman."

144

"What do you think he meant when he said he'd *met* another woman?"

"I don't know. I asked him how far it had gone. He said he and the woman, your wife I think, were fond of each other. I asked him who the woman was and he said somebody he met at school – work. I guessed it was your wife, because he's mentioned her quite often in the past."

"What was stopping him leaving you when he first mentioned parting?"

"Money, I guess. We have a jointly owned home.

"What do you want to happen, Thelma?"

"I want him back!"

"Can you tell me more about your marriage?" I asked, realising this was an intimate question to ask a stranger, but in a way we weren't strangers. And despite my vague words she understood. She was looking at me as a possible ally.

She sat quietly, sphinx-like for several moments, breathing hard. "It's nothing really and it's my fault. I wasn't as sympathetic as I could have been when Bernard more or less stopped loving me. I thought he'd gone off me..."

"You mean he started off to make love and... didn't finish?"

"She nodded her head hesitantly. "But I don't want to talk about it. I suppose I was upset and I thought all sorts of wrong things."

"He had a problem?"

"I didn't understand. I wasn't sympathetic enough."

"I know how these things can go. They seem to get more and more important..."

"Yes, exactly and it degenerated into arguments. I should have understood. I can make it up to him, I'm sure. And you, Mr Batley…"

"What about me?"

"Bernard said that the woman he fancied had a husband who'd gone off with another woman."

"I haven't gone off with anybody, and I don't intend to, Thelma."

"It's so good hear that… What is the problem with your marriage, Mr Batley – Bill?"

I couldn't refuse to answer, although I would have liked to. "I think it's your husband hanging around my wife." I certainly wasn't going to discuss my sexual capacity. Anyway, it was irrelevant. Chandler *was* the problem.

But at the same time I knew that in a shadowy way, I had been listening to my own story. Not erectile dysfunction in my case, I believe, but uncertainties about my performance, uncertainties probably leading to diffidence and strain in the marriage bond. Perhaps there were thousands or tens of thousands of husbands like me – and Bernard. The fact that Bernard was affected, the very pistol of virility, with all his head hair, made me feel less alone.

I chatted to Thelma, not an unattractive woman, with hardly a pause until I heard Ann come in. "In here, dear, with a guest," I called mysteriously from the lounge.

Thelma and I made a falsely comfortable tableaux when Ann entered the room. Ann realised something was wrong and looked puzzled.

"Do you know Thelma Chandler, darling?"

"*What*?" Ann said, in what was almost a squawk. She showed a momentary flash of panic in her expression but recovered instantly.

"Thelma's come to see us about Bernard," I said in a tone which befitted the local parson.

Ann sat down reluctantly on the edge of the most distant armchair, her arms huddled protectively around her. She didn't speak.

"I came to ask you, Mrs Batley if you would...let Bernard go."

"I haven't got hold of him," Ann said coldly.

"You're not going away with him?"

"Certainly, not."

"But he told me..."

"I'm not responsible for what he told you, Mrs Chandler," Ann said with asperity.

I marvelled at the way the meeting was airing ambiguities and euphemisms. The question of who was fucking who would never be answered. I hoped, however, that I would learn more from the dialogue between these two, but I didn't get the chance.

"Bill, do you mind leaving us so I can talk to Mrs Chandler, woman to woman. She came here to see me."

Thelma was nodding agreement to this move.

"Very well," I said, standing up, disappointed and eyeing them both grimly. "But I hope you'll remember that I have an interest in this matter."

"What's your interest, Bill?" Ann asked sharply as though my claim was surprising.

"I love my wife, and I've no intention of leaving her."

This was received stonily by Ann, and with a grateful nod from Thelma. Had I lost all my credibility with my wife? I left the room. What I was aiming for was a one-all draw which might rescue my marriage. Ann held Carol against me, and I held Chandler against her. That should make us even.

Ann and Thelma spent about 20 minutes together. When Thelma had gone, I curbed my impulse to rush to find out from Ann what they had said (and decided). I buried myself in some filing in the potting shed (I don't trust the computer. You can lose computer files. I prefer hard copy files). An hour later, I surfaced bursting with curiosity. I found Ann in the kitchen, calmly making sandwiches for lunch.

What did you tell Thelma, dear?"

"What I said when she was here. I don't intend to run away with anybody," Ann delivered these lines quite matter-of-factly.

I thought the situation called for at least a little passion. "Neither do I, my sweet," I said, putting my arms around her from behind and drawing her close.

"You better stop that if you want your lunch."

"It'll be a fine sandwich, but I can think of better things."

Ann dropped the knife and turned round. We kissed and went upstairs silently. Odd how talking with Thelma had warmed her toward me, the female protecting her nest. But as I have said, the female is the great unknown to me.

Afterwards, when the haze of satisfaction had passed and we were stirring, thinking of getting out of bed and having lunch, I decided to get my shot in against Chandler. "I was sorry to hear about Chandler. I'm sure Thelma told you…"

"What do you mean, Bill? She never told me anything about Bernard, other than wanting another chance with him."

"Their marriage problem, erectile dysfunction." It may have been a low blow. Although Ann appeared firm about our marriage, I had to take every step to buttress my position.

Ann curled her lips dismissively, "Oh, fooey," she said. "You have that at times, yourself, Bill. It's in your head." She was unconcerned.

"Darling, why are you able to dismiss Chandler's erectile dysfunction as fooey? Do you have personal experience which proves otherwise?"

Ann laughed, "You're so jealous, Bill. No, I don't have personal experience. Erectile dysfunction is fooey."

I was heartened to hear her view. For a moment. Did she really imply she hadn't been to bed with Chandler, full-stop? Or did she mean that she hadn't had an erectile dysfunction experience with Chandler? My instinct was to clarify this and to challenge her on whether I really ever had erectile dysfunction, *the medical problem,* although I knew it might make me delve into situations which could make me wince with embarrassment. But I was left gasping my questions in the air when she sprang out of bed and disappeared into her walk-in wardrobe.

I've watched Jim Clitheroe's tactics for a long time. He calls us when his wife is away, asking if we'd like a drink. Ann always invites him round. She's a very good cook, unlike Susan Clitheroe. Jim knows this. He comes ostensibly for a drink, but hangs on knowing we must dine soon. And Ann has to ask him to stay. She's very agreeable about this, but I complain to her afterwards about reciprocity. If he really wants to have a drink, why not ask us to go to his place or at least bring a bottle? If this only happened once or twice, you would say that my attitude is as mean as his. But it's always the way.

I have noticed that Jane's friends, and perhaps many young people like them are ready with their credit card for what they have ordered. Restaurants don't mind taking several cards for a shared meal. However, if you have good friends who take it in turns to pay, you have to be honourable about taking your turn. Where does that leave me with the Clitheroes?

In this, they're like a guy who sometimes drinks with us at the pub. He's always last to buy his round, and then, only when he gets an elbow in his ribs and a nod toward an empty glass. But we tolerate him. Ann and I agree that our neighbourliness and friendship with the Clitheroes is worth more than the cost of a few dinners.

Ann, counselling perfection, says, "Just don't put yourself in a position where Jim can knife you." I nod wisely, but it isn't so easy. However, I resolve to swallow the curmudgeonly Jim Clitheroe with all his warts.

Last week, he pulled his best trick yet. A dinner engagement at a local restaurant and an implicit understanding that it was Jim's turn to flash his credit card. We had a good time. Both Ann and I enjoy the Clitheroe's company. Jim's a good raconteur. However, having read my notes on my last dinner encounter with them, I ensured that I let myself go on king prawns to start, fillet steak with pepper sauce followed by crepe suzette.

We sat talking afterwards, finishing off the wine.

"What do you think of it?" Clitheroe asked me.

"The wine? It's OK," I said with marked lack of enthusiasm, remembering our previous encounter when I foolishly asked this question. The truth was that even I could tell that the wine was very good.

"Oh?" he said, tossing his head and raising his voice, "You must have rubber taste buds. That's brilliant cabernet sauvignon."

When the glasses were nearly empty, Ann muttered that we should be going and gave me the 'get the bill' glance. I made no move to ask for the bill. To my well-disguised consternation, neither did Clitheroe. Battle lines were being drawn.

Susan said, "Darling, did you tell Bill what happened today…in the laundry?"

I didn't know what bearing this could have on paying for the dinner. I simply drummed my fingers on the table impatiently.

"Oh, yes, Bill," Clitheroe said, with a grin, as though it had slipped his mind. "I should have mentioned it before. One of life's little accidents. Susan put my credit card in the washing machine this morning. And of course we had one of those mild disagreements afterwards about whose obligation it was to go through the pockets of my jeans – you see?"

I didn't see at all. What I did see was culpable negligence about neighbourly priorities, and a sneaky desire to avoid payment. My mind raced for a way of heading this off, but there was none. Only a stern rearguard action was possible.

I leaned back genially, "Jim, old buddy," I said, "I'll accept readies any day. Out with your wallet and fill my hat. Do you want to contribute, Susan? All donations welcome."

I heard Ann exhale, too astounded to put a word in.

Jim was disconcerted too. "I'm afraid I haven't got that much on me," he said, producing his wallet and then tucking it away.

"Show!" I said, "You haven't even looked yet, mate. Show!" I banged the table affably.

Jim was shamed into producing his wallet. He opened it cautiously, and I leaned across and got my fingertips on the protruding notes, extracting them gently. Four twenties. Not much on a bill which we all knew would be over two hundred.

My manner exuded amusement and charm, but I was fuming. I paid for the meal, pocketing the cash. We all took a taxi together. We're neighbours. I huddled silently in the dark of the cab when we arrived at our address. Susan and Ann quibbled in a friendly way, each trying to pay the fare. I said, as jovially as I could, "Let Susan do this one, Ann." Susan did.

I couldn't see the faces of the Clitheroes' in the darkness as we alighted. Only Susan said goodnight and thanks.

When we were inside our front door, Ann exploded. "You're a rude, penny-pinching bastard!" she said. "You don't deserve to have friends!"

I retorted: "I'm not sure I want a friend who is as mean as Jim Clitheroe."

"It wasn't his fault!"

"Do you seriously, *seriously* believe that knowing in advance that he hadn't a card, he couldn't have organised payment?" I spoke very contemptuously.

Ann responded to my tone of voice. She stood silent for a moment. Then a little dimple in her cheek showed as it does when she's amused. She stepped up to my chest. She slid her palms up over my shoulders and pulled my head down. She kissed me passionately. She said, "No, I fucking well believe he could have paid! He can be a shit!"

We had good sex that night.

18

Bernard Chandler with a
Glass of Milk

Cyril Bow is a man of many causes. A feisty 70, he lives with his quiet and uncontroversial wife, Edna, in my street. She is a friend of Ann's, and he is a long time campaigner against the plane trees which line both sides of the street. The politics of pollarding the planes say something about us all. Ann has forbidden me from mentioning the trees when Cyril and Edna are in the house. But as we have just had a close vote on how to cut the trees, I did mention them when they were here this afternoon having a cup of tea with Ann.

"Disappointed about the tree vote, Cyril?"

"You know my views, Bill…" he replied.

"Oh, Bill, please don't go into that now," Ann said.

"I only want to understand…"

"It's fine, Ann. I don't mind," Cyril said. "In fact, I like talking about the plane trees. It's therapeutic. They're a bloody nuisance in I-don't-have-to-tell-you-how-many ways!"

"Tell me one way, Cyril," I asked.

"The birds shit on the cars."

"Ah, yes, the cars. Your cruiser goes through the carwash, what, once a week?"

"Bill, please…" Ann said.

"Have you ever cleaned bird shit off the windscreen, Bill?" Cyril asked. His slight tremor was agitated and created a rattling sound with the empty teacup as he replaced it on the saucer.

"Don't you like trees?" I said.

"Not here. I'd cut the whole damn lot down!"

I remember my mother's almost pathological irritation at falling leaves as she swept them up. She felt the same as Cyril.

The plane trees are not a rarity in this neighbourhood but not every street has them. When they have not been pruned for a while, they rear up to the height of the houses that is over three floors. In summer, they can form a canopy over the street. They are more than a hundred years old. The trunks are two feet in diameter with a lumpy brown-yellow bark like an abstract painting by Monet. They are planted on the footpath and encroach upon it, narrowing the way and prizing the paving slabs up. The trees are a magnet for dog-walkers, because dogs like to sniff and raise a leg where their friends have been. And worse. You could say that in autumn the fall of leaves lights the way in gold. Or you could say that in autumn, the leaves come down in a deluge which fills gardens and gutters and blocks the drains.

Not surprisingly, after more than a century of being, the planes are controversial. There are those who say they are beautiful, add value to the street, provide useful shade in summer and make a contribution to de-toxifying the polluted London air. The Cyril Bow faction argue that the trees are a nuisance as they are obstructing the footpath, a dog lavatory and an unwarranted expense for us council taxpayers for their care and the leaf clean-up.

Every three years or so when a prune is heralded by the local authority, the pro and anti factions emerge. The anti-planers restrict their case to pollarding because government policy wisely supports tree-lined streets, rather than brick canyons. Pollarding involves amputation of branches to such a low level that the tree is stunted and reshaped. The antis contend this is cheaper in the long run, produces less leaves, makes the planes more manageable and less intrusive.

The pro group concedes the need for pruning, but being liberals who are prepared to overlook the constriction of the paths and the occasional dog-dirt, they plead for moderation, beauty and the green environment.

Covert discussions take place between neighbours who are preparing to engage in a secret vote to decide the issue (convened by the local authority), but embarrassed to reveal openly whether they are pro or anti, except for factional leaders like Cyril. Emails are exchanged. As the day approaches for the local authority to register the vote, passionate letters are pushed through mailboxes and addressed to the councillors of the Palace Ward.

After the campaigning, another victory this year for the pro-planers. But the antis won the vote with 60 percent! Fortunately, the council requires a 'consensus' of the whole street, which they interpret on turnout. But the danger sign is there, the austere anti-planers are advancing with their chainsaws.

I came in yesterday, Saturday morning, from walking Rex, and there, sitting in the kitchen, was Bernard Chandler. He was wearing a shiny leather jacket and a floral scarf, clearly passing through on his way somewhere. He had a glass of milk in front of him.

"Helped yourself, have you?" I said as I let the dog out of the back door.

He smiled comfortably, rippling his thick moustache and beard. "No, Ann got it for me. Do you object?"

"Too late now," I said, moving my hand tiredly to thrust away the notion.

"Sensible attitude," Bernard said, judgmentally.

"Thanks for that, Bernard. What are you doing here, anyway?"

"I called for Ann. We're going to a meeting this afternoon. She's gone upstairs."

"What is it? The AGM of the Beaver Protection Society?"

"No, as a matter of fact it's a seminar on autism in children."

Bernard looked completely relaxed. He had a small, self-satisfied smile beneath the fur. I took a chair at the table opposite to him. I leaned toward him trying to look cheerful. "Are you talking to Thelma these days?" I enquired in a low voice.

His arrogant ease dissipated. "What do you mean? You don't know Thelma."

Obviously, Thelma had not disclosed our meeting. I had Chandler at a disadvantage, and I decided to capitalise on it. "Oh, yes I do," I replied gently. "I know Thelma. Hasn't she told you what she told me?"

Chandler's pink, wet lips curled angrily in their furry aperture. "I don't know what you're talking about, Batley. Has Thelma been here?"

"Indeed, she has. I had a talk to her about your marriage."

Chandler's eyes narrowed suspiciously while he considered what this could imply. "What about you own marriage?" he snarled.

It was my turn to be self-satisfied. I beamed at him. "That wasn't the subject, Bernard. The subject was *your*…" Here, I hesitated to give my words more weight and contrived an intimate tone. "Your personal inadequacies."

"This is intolerable," Chandler said, pushing the glass of milk away and rising from the chair.

"Drink your milk like a good boy, Bernard. It's good for your willy."

"Batley, you are a…"

Just then, Ann came in with her briefcase and fleece. "Bill, I thought you were out for the morning, I've written you a note about your lunch."

"No, just walking Rex." I spoke lightly.

"Bernard and I are only going to…"

"Let's *go*, Ann! This minute! Chandler boomed in his fruity voice.

"Yes, bloody well go!" I said, carelessly. Ordering *my* wife about in *my* house!

Ann was startled. Chandler looked dark-faced. My stiff expression must have showed. She frowned, glared at each of us and decided on a diplomatic withdrawal. She went out of the front door with Chandler. I went into the lounge. Chandler's car was in front of the house. I watched. They couldn't see me through the curtains. They didn't drive off immediately. They talked.

I could see Chandler's leonine head jerking about. His fists appeared to be pounding the steering wheel. They were not talking. They were arguing. He would naturally want to know about Thelma's visit and why Ann hadn't told him. If she or Thelma had told him, he would have been prepared for me.

I waited perhaps another minute and then I saw the obviously peeved Chandler throw his head back against the headrest in frustration. The passenger side door opened and Ann got out. She was crying. She held her scarf up to her face and hurried back to the house. She ran upstairs.

I went up to the potting shed reflecting that I was gutless in not telling Bernard candidly to keep away from Ann. But how to do that without sounding slightly ridiculous escaped me, especially when they worked together. Now, by chance, I had sparked a minor explosion which I thought might not do my quest any harm.

An hour later, Ann hunted me down in the potting shed. She had changed her clothes to the more relaxed slacks and sweater she wears around the house and looked completely composed which was a good sign. She sat in the easy chair. I swung my office chair round to face her. It's a slightly higher level chair. A good position for me to conduct a meeting.

"What happened to your autism class?" I asked.

"You upset Bernard, he was furious and I couldn't go with him."

I feigned surprise. "I never said much to him, dear."

"Why was he so angry then?"

Obviously, he thought Thelma might have spilled the beans to me about his sexual inadequacies but I decided to play dumb. "I can't imagine."

"What exactly did you say, Bill?"

"I said Thelma and I talked about his personal inadequacies. Those, specifically, were the words I used.*"

Ann considered this. I thought she appreciated that what I had said was ambiguous and vague. "You should never have mentioned anything at all. It was underhand. It's not going to help his relationship with his wife. He'll be even more angry with her."

"Sorry, but I was dealing with a creep who fancies my wife. All's fair, you know." I thought Ann at least fancied being fancied. Why not?

"I was taken completely by surprise, Bill. His wife hadn't told him she was here. He found out from you and then from me. Outside. In the car. It was a body blow. His wife talking to *you* of all people."

"*Me* of all people? What did you say?"

"I said I didn't know anything about his personal life with Thelma other than he had already told me. I said Thelma had never mentioned anything like that to me. And then, he wanted to know why I hadn't at least told him that she came to see us. I said I thought it was best to forget it."

"How did he take it?"

"It was a terrible blow to his pride. He's a friend, Bill, and he accused me of disloyalty."

19

She Takes My Hand
in Parson's Green

I had a phone call this week from a woman with a pleasant voice. It was a relief to rule out Carol Spencer, although she has a pleasant voice.

"Mr Batley, it's Virginia Biggs. Are you well?"

"Ah, Ms Biggs, I often think of you as I pen my thoughts. Yes, I'm fine."

"I'm glad to hear you're keeping the notebook. Are you noticing progress?"

I hadn't the least idea in which direction I was progressing, if at all, but I wasn't going to be a spoil-sport. "Absolutely! Lots of progress."

"Fabulous, I'd like to get some feedback on the situation since we met. I have some forms…would you mind?"

"Not at all. Send them to me." Feedback is something every business seems to want these days. The negative feedback may find its way into the trash, the positive is likely to go on the internet. When I've had a bad deal, and I get a feedback form – usually on the internet – I start to fill it in with ferocity]

but on the internet, you can't see how many pages of detailed questions are asked. And they go on and on, and I usually flag before finishing and hit the delete button.

"Perfect. What are you doing these days, Mr Batley?"

"Well, at the moment I'm sitting in my potting shed…" I cast around for a constructive answer. The truth is I'm like one of the Seven Dwarfs, busy doing nothing, but subject to the concerns mentioned in this notebook, I'm very happy.

She laughed. "Perfect! I'm so glad you have your potting shed. It's a good place."

"I'm considering my options." I didn't want to go into the saga of the food bank.

Ms Biggs was too much the diplomat to press. "Perfect. Here's something to consider along with your options. I thought it might be up your street. An appointment on the board of a national charity dealing with drug rehab. It's a voluntary post on National Drugfree."

Ms Biggs' employers are also purveyors of human resources with a bottomless well of redundant executives to place. "Sounds interesting," I said cautiously. It also sounded as though I would need to get very involved and give up a lot of time.

"You'd be one of six directors. There are two executive directors, two psychiatrists and two other directors (including you) all from Footsie 100 companies. Your knowledge of commercial practice would be very valuable in a charity like this, Mr Batley."

"It might also be very useful for me to have a tame psychiatrist to refer to."

"I'm sure you have no need of that, Mr Batley. The chairman, by the way, is Rebecca Stallworthy."

She said the name as though it ought to be familiar to me, but it wasn't. I asked for a day or two to think it over. I have come to enjoy my reflections in the potting shed and I wouldn't want to reduce them too much.

When I told Ann, she was enthusiastic. So was Susan Clitheroe. Jim Clitheroe sniffed. He said, "It's better than being a grocer, I suppose. You'll probably be fired more quickly. Ha–

ha–ha!" My friend, George Cutler, said, "Go for it, Bill. You may get the occasional sniff." With these endorsements, I notified Ms Biggs and received a pile of forms. I went to a meeting with Rebecca Stallworthy, MBE (whom I had learned was a very notable do-gooder).

I met her at the down at heel head office of Drugfree, south of the river, in Southwark. I already knew that this was a country wide organisation with a number of rehab houses, not in great financial shape. Rebecca Stallworthy (call me Becky) was very informal. She was a well built and untidy, hoarse voiced woman of about 60. She lolled back in her chair and smoothed her wild, grey hair ineffectually.

We chatted quite inconsequentially for a time (nothing about Drugfree) and she said, "I think you'll do very nicely, Bill," as if she was choosing a game sausage from The Parson's Nose. We arranged a date when I would meet the board and they would vote on my membership afterwards.

That seemed to me to conclude the formal part, so I said, "Is there anything you want, especially from me, Becky." I was thinking of my particular commercial experience which she knew about from my CV.

"I want your loyalty."

"You mean my vote."

"Yes. It doesn't always get that tense, but I have four horses which want to pull in different directions – at times. I have to manage them. I can run this outfit perfectly well, but I need support, brains, lateral thinking. That's where you come in. I also like to know in advance what the others are thinking." She flashed her eyes at me meaningfully.

I felt I was being recruited as a spy and an ally rather than an independent director, but I assumed she'd talked to all of the other four like this. It sounded interesting. "OK, Becky, I'm all yours."

She loaded me with papers about Drugfree, gave me a winning smile and I departed.

I let Ann calm herself after her row with Chandler, which I hoped would end their close friendship, if that was all it was. On Sunday, I suggested we go out for a walk after lunch and find somewhere for a cup of coffee. I was thinking it might be easier to talk about Chandler in public rather than at home. Although, when I considered the conversations we had about Carol, Chandler and Thelma, and even the confrontations with Chandler and Thelma, I marvelled at how we all evaded the point. A man from Mars might have thought we were talking in code. And I suppose we were. But we communicated. We deciphered the code and understood. We each had a secret code-key which we did not disclose and that left room for different understandings about what was actually happening.

Ann looked melancholic, but she accepted and we had a brisk walk to Parson's Green. The weather was undecided, scudding cloud yes, a sprinkle of rain and a sun determined to shine. We got a good table in Le Pain Quotidiene, quiet, in a corner where the laptop nerds sit for half a day. The light was cutting in through the glass windows, and a child on a scooter was riding up and down the aisles between the tables. We ordered big bowls of black coffee which warmed our palms as we drank. Ann had hardly said a word to me. I didn't know what to expect.

"I'm sorry Bernard upset you yesterday morning," I said as Ann concentrated on cutting the slice of chocolate gateau which we decided to share.

"You upset me too, Bill, talking to him like that."

"I've been meaning to tell you I can't stand Bernard, and I'd prefer you didn't invite him into the house."

"He's a friend and colleague who has taught me a lot, and I value the friendship."

"Is that all it is?"

She considered, looked me straight in the eye. "Yes, it is."

In the calm of her reply I found something disturbing, as though she wasn't quite convinced herself, or wistfully wished it was more. Or was she playing a card? "He evidently has a bad temper," I said.

"No, Bill, you needled him. What you did say made him so …You told him you knew about his problem. And that was very hurtful."

"Is that what he said I said? I never mentioned erectile dysfunction. It's his own guilt feelings."

"You should never have said what you said. It was a very nasty blow."

"I think I was entitled to say that. I told the truth. This big tomcat licking its chops and drinking my milk in my kitchen and probably having an affair with my wife! Men have killed for less."

Ann had tears on her cheeks but I felt I had to press her. "You say that Chandler is a platonic friend. But Thelma told me that Chandler said he was in love with you and that you were going off together. That's the Chandler side of this. Is that a lie?"

"I can't account for that, Bill. Maybe, with his wife, Bernard is trying to cover his deficiencies…"

"His sexual deficiencies…yes," I added, keeping the triumphalism out of my voice.

"All right, Bill. You don't believe me. Here's something from your side. I had another telephone call from that woman. I recognised the number. She said, 'Is that Mrs Batley?' I said, 'Yes, who is speaking?' She said, 'Carol Spencer. I'd like to talk to you.' I said, 'No, Carol. I have calls every week from women my husband has been pestering and propositioning!' I hung up on her."

"You said that?" I was burning with wrath at Carol's intrusion, but rather pleased at Ann's response to Carol in its defensive thrust – apart from the pestering business.

"Look, Bill, I'll make an agreement with you. If you call this woman and tell her clearly that it's all over and stick to it, I'll promise not to invite Bernard to the house and not to go to camps and conferences with him."

I felt that was an unexpectedly generous offer. "And you'll tell him that any funny ideas he might have had about a future for the pair of you are out, finally and definitively out," I added.

"Yes, Bill…" Her voice became very faint. "I'm really very happy with our marriage."

I had scored a draw! I reached over and put my hand gently on her shoulder. "I'll be very happy and relieved to do what you ask, dearest. I don't want to lose you."

I could have gone into defensive mode, arguing that my relationship with Carol couldn't be over because it had never begun, but my native caution stopped me. Better to let Carol fade into the mist rather than try to disparage her – and face Ann's interrogation. We walked back to Amherst Street, hand in hand and went straight to bed. It did however occur to me that her agreement to tell Chandler to drop his ideas about their future showed that *he* did have such ideas and *she* must have had them too.

I have made a terrible mistake, really two or three mistakes. It started when I agreed to look after my neighbour's dog while she went on a vacation to Japan. Elinor, a divorcee of many years had two grown children and lived alone in five bedroomed home in our street. I knew the dog, a very gentle, old golden retriever. He would just stand still and look at the footpath when Elinor stopped to have a chat with me. Rex, if he happened to be present, ignored Percy. So I had no reason to think that the two dogs in the same household were incompatible.

"I usually send Percy to kennels, but he's so poorly now that it would be too disruptive," Elinor said. I believe she saw me as a sympathetic soul and a dog-lover without thinking of the task she was imposing on me. Equally, I never thought too much about it when I made the promise.

Percy was accommodated without any fuss in an old kennel of Rex's which I had failed to send to the tip. This was placed in the doorway of our garden shed, now almost empty, which itself hid behind a clump of laurel bushes. Percy was assured of a warm bed and Elinor approved the arrangement. Rex was in a porch adjoining the rear of the house.

Elinor arrived with a bag of medications and a list of Percy's dining requirements when she delivered him. The list was quite strict. Percy was to have a portion of cooked beefsteak ('not too fatty') cut into cubes, three times a week, and a portion of roast chicken ('with bones removed') twice a week, plus the usual dogfood. He was also to have certain pills and potions from the medicine bag at his twice daily meals.

It was an onerous undertaking, but I rose to it. "I'll have to hire a chef. Will Percy share fillet mignon with us, Elinor?"

"I know he's a bit spoiled, Bill, but he's so lovely." She flourished a handful of banknotes.

"Put those away and take us for lunch at the Riverside Café when you come back."

Thus, the deal was sealed. Elinor flew abroad, and I cooked for and walked my new charge with Rex. I faithfully administered his food, pills and medicines for several days. Then early one evening when I had fed Percy his roast chicken and was adding a few thoughts to this notebook in the potting shed, I heard a loud noise in the back garden; it was a combination of Rex's hysterical barking and Percy's deep, chesty bowfing.

Ann called me from the foot of the stairs: "Bill, I think the dogs are fighting."

I ran downstairs and through the kitchen into the back garden. The row continued unabated behind the laurel hedges. When I was outside the shed, I could see Rex with Percy's empty bowl between his forelegs, and Percy cringing back in the shadowy interior, blood running from lacerations on his muzzle, trying to protect himself with wheezy woofs. I grabbed Rex by the collar, dragged him across the garden and locked him in the porch. Then I tried to comfort Percy, at least to examine his wounds but he wouldn't let me near him. When I went inside the house, Ann said: "Did you notice that Rex hasn't touched his food."

"No, he hasn't. He's eaten Percy's."

"Jealousy, I expect. You've made such a fuss of Percy."

"I've tried to comply with Elinor's orders."

"What are you going to do now, Bill? We have a civil war in the garden."

"Nothing. I'm going to have a gin-and-tonic. I'll think about it in the morning."

I awoke in the morning with the dogs on my mind. Did this mean that I had to do separate dog-walks? Did it mean I had to lock up Rex at Percy's mealtime? I threw on a few clothes and went down to let Rex out. He wagged his tail, excitedly preparing for a walk. Then I locked him up, noticing that his bowl was still full. He had dined well last night at Percy's expense. I walked across the garden toward Percy's kennel.

"Come on, old Percy," I said. I wasn't greeted by the usual mewling.

I looked inside the kennel but Percy wasn't there. I had the sudden fear that he had run away. Then I looked more carefully into the darker reaches of the shed. There were some old sacks on the floor at the back. Percy was lying on them.

"Come on, boy. Come on, Percy," I said, as I stepped inside, but Percy didn't stir. I stood over him. There was something in the way he was lying, eyes closed, utterly flat on his side, which alarmed me. I poked him with the toe of my foot. He didn't move. His eyes remained closed. I poked him harder. No sign. I touched his furry belly. He was cold. He wasn't merely very sick, he was dead. I ran back to the house and upstairs. Ann was just getting out of bed.

"What on earth's the matter, Bill? she said, startled.

"It's Percy. He's dead."

"Oh, shit. That will kill Elinor."

"What am I going to do? What will I say? Elinor has another week of her trip. Do I call her or keep quiet?"

"I think you'll have to ring her. You can't face her with no Percy virtually the minute she's expecting to be reunited. She loves Percy like a child. And you'll have to tell her the truth."

"Sure, but what is the truth?"

"That Percy was mauled by Rex and died of… shock."

Ann tracked down Elinor's hotel in Kyoto through her travel agent, and I prepared to make an early evening call, her time. I hoped I didn't need to get into detail. It would look as though I had been careless, as though I didn't understand my own dog. I felt an utter fool and Elinor was going to be very hurt.

I reached Elinor easily and revealed that I had bad news. When I said Percy was dead, she uttered a faint cry but nothing else.

I waited. "Are you there, Elinor? I need to get your instructions about what to do with…Percy. I can fix everything if you want…"

"No, Bill," she said in a diminished voice. "I'll give you my vet's address. He's been a friend for years. Take Percy to him and let him deal with everything."

Elinor heard me out while I tried to explain how sorry I was to break into her vacation. She said nothing, but I came away thinking that I had at least avoided the grisly details and that they would fade as the days went by.

When I told Ann, she said: "Fine so far, but how are you going to deliver Percy? The address is North London. I don't suppose the vet has a pickup service for dog's bodies."

"I'll have to think about it. I've checked the online map and the surgery is in a busy street. Parking will be impossible. Even public parking is blocks away. But the underground is close... I'll take that."

"Get somebody to do it for you, Bill."

"Who? Explain that to a carrier? He'll refuse. No, I'll do it myself. Then, I'll know it's done properly. I owe it to Percy and Elinor."

In this good spirit, I got down to the details of Percy's funeral cortege. I hadn't realised what a big and overweight dog he was until I had the problem of carrying him. I talked it over with Ann. We agreed that as a bundle, Percy would be awkward. I had to admit he was just about at the limit of what I could lift and wrapping him up in brown paper or a big plastic bag would be awkward. And how would I manage on the underground? Then, Ann produced a suitcase.

"But that's the big one you use when we go on long trips," I said.

"We have to make the sacrifice for Percy."

It seemed to me that she was too ready with self-sacrifice. "You're not saying that our long trips are at an end?"

"No, Bill. I'm not saying that. I want one of those new model hard plastic suitcases when we go again, one with four little wheels."

"I suppose we owe Percy this donation of a perfectly good suitcase."

The case *was* too fine as a funeral casket, but above all I wanted to get Percy on his way. Wrapped in old towels and with smelly liquids dripping from his orifices, he was laid in the suitcase which I had lined with plastic in case of leaks and smells. I hope I felt rather than looked shamefaced, as I dragged the bag on its two wheels the short distance to the underground. I nearly busted myself trying to heft the case up the steps at Putney Bridge and a fellow passenger came to my assistance. At one point in the task, I think he took the full weight. "Watcha got in here, mate. The weekend shopping?" he joked.

I smiled and thanked him. "A bit of computer stuff," I said.

I boarded the train for Upminster and placed the case in the space near the door where there were already two other cases. The compartment was crowded and I was lucky to get a seat nearby, but not with the case in my view. The less I saw of it, the better. I was bound for Angel on the Northern line which meant I would have to change at Monument, itself a long step. I read the Metro newspaper which somebody had discarded on a seat.

When we were approaching the station, I went to the door area where I had left the case, but I couldn't see it. Other cases and bags were there but not mine. I thought, at first, that I must be confused about where I placed it. The train was braking to stop. I walked quickly to the two nearest exits, but no suitcase. The doors were open. I couldn't get off without the case. The doors closed. I was on my way to Tower Hill. I walked the whole of the open train but I couldn't find my case.

At Aldgate East, I got off the train and changed platforms to return home. I called Ann.

"You'll never believe it but somebody's stolen the case off the tube. I mean, I had to leave the bloody thing near the door!"

"Oh, Bill," she laughed, "what a surprise for the thief."

"Never mind the goddam thief, I called the vet's office earlier and told them Elinor had asked me to deliver Percy and they're expecting Percy to arrive."

Ann remained highly amused and hardly serious, but persuaded me to tell the vet what happened. "It wasn't your fault, Bill."

"No, it wasn't. And I never killed Percy, either. But I will look to Elinor like a suspect in both cases."

I was resigned to being viewed as incompetent and returned home thinking of the emollient explanation I would have to make to Elinor and her vet. When I was watching the news at 7 pm on Channel 4, sitting happily with my drink, Percy almost forgotten, a breaking news item came up about a hoax bomb scare at Victoria underground station. The station was cleared for two hours while the police bomb squad ascertained that the contents of a suitcase abandoned on the concourse were not explosive. The suitcase contained a dead dog.

"Oh, God," I cried, spilling my drink. "That's Percy!"

Ann had a slight smile. "You don't know. We're not involved anyway, Bill."

"Are you sure you removed your name from the suitcase?"

She considered this. "I can't be sure. I didn't think that having my name on it mattered very much."

"The police are going to be looking for the owner of the case. They'll want to press a shedload of charges, like wasting police time and causing something or other in a public place. Hell, Ann!"

"They may not find us, but should we tell them. Call them now?"

"We'll be interrogated – or I will – all night. If we hadn't seen the newscast, we wouldn't have known... so it's quite reasonable to leave it until tomorrow."

"Are you quite sure, Bill?"

"Sure," I said, confidently, though I had no confidence at all as I helped myself to another drink.

20

I Venture to Wimbledon

Ann and I had just gone to bed. The day's events were heavily on my mind, as I switched off the lamps. After a few moments there was a very loud banging of our door knocker and a continuous buzz on the doorbell. I sat up in a cold sweat.

"It can only be one thing, Ann – the police."

"My name must have been on the case. I'm so sorry, Bill."

"Not to worry," I said, very worried indeed. I put a dressing gown on and hurried downstairs.

"What's the noise about?" I said in an outraged householder voice without waiting to examine the men confronting me; a leader in plain clothes and two uniformed officers behind him. In the street, there were three or four police cars with lights flashing.

"Is Ann Batley here?" the plain-clothes barked.

I stood firmly, full in the doorway. "Ann Batley is my wife and you'd better explain to me what's going on and show some ID."

"Can't you recognise a police uniform?"

"You're not in uniform. Who are you?"

Plain-clothes drew a card from his pocket and handed it to me. He was Detective-Sergeant Martin Duckett of the Bomb Squad. "A suitcase which we believe belongs to your wife was found at Victoria underground station today in suspicious circumstances."

"Come in and sit down, and I'll get my wife. Sorry, but I don't think we have room for the rest of your detachment." I shut the door emphatically on the cops at the gate.

Duckett and the two uniforms perched uncomfortably on the edge of their easy chairs.

When Ann came down, she admitted the suitcase must be hers. She said she last saw it at the front door this morning. I took up the story, including the demise of Percy and explained my ill-fated journey. The three officers looked bemused. DS Duckett said he would like to ask me a few questions.

"Did you report the theft to the police, Mr Batley?"

"No, I didn't… I was too distressed at losing Percy. I would have done that tomorrow." I looked at my watch. "Today."

His eyes narrowed suspiciously. "Did you report the theft to the police when you became aware of the news reports about a hoax bomb?"

"No. I don't pay much attention to news reports. I read the papers in the weekend."

Ann looked at me pointedly. DS Duckett noticed this. "So you didn't know about the bomb hoax?"

I hesitated. "Only when it was too late in the day to do anything."

"So you did know about the bomb hoax but did nothing?"

I looked at Ann, feeling I was saying this for her. "Yes."

"And you knew full well that a suitcase with a dead dog in it could only be yours?"

"I thought it somewhat likely."

174

He shook his head as though I was a hopeless case. "It looks as though you could have got off the train at Victoria, dropped the case, and boarded a later train to get yourself some closed circuit alibi pictures."

"No, why the hell would I do that? Please call the vet later today. He was expecting Percy. Percy's corpse."

DS Duckett looked frustrated. The only thing that would have satisfied him was being able to handcuff us and lead us away to the cells. "We'll do that, Mr Batley. There's been a marked lack of candour in what you've told us, and if and when we interview you both again it will be under caution."

Ann and I went to bed very unhappy. "It's like the sword of Damocles," Ann said, "We don't know what's going to happen."

"I'm sorry, dear. Another horrible mess I've got myself into."

"I know you meant well," she said, putting her arm around me.

Mr Bhatta has gone. His shop is closed. A board is nailed over the door. A grey curtain hangs like a rag in the window. I peered inside through the dusty pane. The space is empty. I had never realised how dirty the shop was. Mr Bhatta's presence illuminated it and my eyes, at least, couldn't discern the grot. The footpath outside was littered with empty cardboard boxes and trash. I never had a chance to see him at the end. He will have gone on his smiling way.

Mr Bhatta has reminded me that *everything* is changing and the change goes on in every millisecond of the day, both to people, the whole universe and all the matter in it. Mr Bhatta disappears. So while change and hence the uncertainty of life is no surprise, it actually is a surprise. Will the train be on time? Will my good health hold? Will the police prosecute me about the disposal of Percy? Mr Bhatta's solution is acceptance. I haven't gone beyond struggling with the anxieties which claw at me at times like angry cats.

I had to keep my promise to Ann, and I rang Carol at her flat in Wimbledon. I felt betrayed by my own weakness on my visit there, and I was determined to be flint-hard this time. When she came on the line, I was ready with my spiel. I didn't intend to leave any time for pauses, but she gushed when she heard my voice: "Oh, Bill! So wonderful to hear from you!"

I felt like a rat and I tried to say my piece in one breath: "Carol, we mustn't meet again. Please don't ring me at home." More of my wheedling.

"Bill, I'd like to see you. Couldn't we meet here at my place?"

"No, Carol. I've just said what I have to say. There would be no point in meeting."

"You don't seem to understand about how I feel. Surely, we can meet so that I can explain?"

I felt like saying that it didn't matter whether I understood or not, but however staunch I was, I had to be careful of her feelings. "I think I do understand, Carol, just as you understand my feelings."

"It's all about you, isn't it, Bill. I don't really come into it," she said, miserably.

It *was* pretty much all about me and at this moment, going the wrong way. "Not at all. I just felt it was best for both of us to talk on the telephone, but if you want to meet…" I had no sooner said this than I realised it was risky.

"Let's have lunch in the Village on Saturday, Bill."

Another lunch! "Carol, that wouldn't be…appropriate." I could see it, a bottle of wine and tears. I had to use some of the steel that Jane said I ought to have. "I suggest Starbucks in Wimbledon at 11." Clear and decisive. Starbucks would be full of laptoppers, college kids with their books and birds of passage who had missed their breakfast.

Carol hesitated, but she accepted. "I look forward to seeing you, Bill. It's important to me."

I was in a quandary whether to tell Ann of the meeting. She was likely to be unsympathetic about me ministering to Carol's hurt feelings with a visit. I decided on silence and invented a meeting with one of my poker playing pals.

It was a windy winter day with white clouds scudding across the sky and a threat of showers in the air. I was late getting to Wimbledon and aimed to drive past Starbucks before I parked. I saw Carol on the curb, surrounded by bags of groceries and looking saturated and gloomy. I pulled over out of the traffic and lowered the passenger window. "Sorry to be late. Go inside. Get a seat and I'll park and be there in a moment," I said.

"Oh, Bill, let me get rid of these bags and put something dry on first. Drop me at my place, please."

I was stationary on a double yellow line and hindering a car trying to get out behind me. It was the decent thing to do. "Sure, get in," I said, reluctantly. She heaved her bags on to the back seat and slid in the front. This was unexpected, but I didn't think it was a ploy.

Carol's apartment was several blocks away, a conversion in an old house. Her place was on the first floor, up a flight of narrow stairs. She said there was space to park on the forecourt as a guest. I had to help her with the bags, because it would have required at least two trips upstairs. "I don't know why you get more that you can carry," I growled.

"I do all the shopping in one hit and take a cab."

I worked out that rain or not she was going to ask me to take her to her flat. It annoyed me. When I had put the last of the bags in the kitchen, she asked me to stay for a drink. I could see her. She was across the hall in the bedroom, shedding her wet clothes. Foolishly, I went to the bedroom door.

"Come in, Bill. We hardly need to be shy."

I didn't move but she came up and slipped her arms around me. She had a thin slip on. "I'll go back to the car while you finish off here," I said.

"Let's make love, Bill, one more time," she whispered.

I don't know how I did it, but I said, "No," and gently unwrapped her arms.

Fortunately, because I was feeling torn, the door buzzer rang and kept on ringing urgently. Carol picked up the remote and asked who it was. I couldn't hear the reply, but she said, "I'll come down. Just a moment."

I said, "I'll go down too. It's all over, Carol."

Carol looked flustered, troubled. "No, Bill, I want you to stay here until this person's gone. Let me deal with it. Please."

There was something peculiar about this caller that made her frown. I went to the top of the stairs to listen while she went down to the door. I couldn't hear the conversation. The man's voice was raised, curt. He wasn't a doorstep fish vendor. Carol's voice was low but urgent. She had only opened the door a little. She was telling him to go away, that was the gist of what I heard. He was protesting. Eventually, she shut the door on him and came upstairs looking drawn.

"Now it's all about you," I said, with a touch of sarcasm.

"It's nothing, Bill, nothing." She came close to me.

I put my hands on her shoulders and eased her away. "I'm not surprised you've got a man chasing you, Carol. It's not nothing. I wish you luck. It's time for me to go."

"No, please, Bill. I love you. That man is nothing to me. You're making assumptions. I was hoping we'd...I want to love you one more time."

Thoughts of one final lovemaking which had passed through me like an electric current a few moments ago, were gone. The idea of another man groping around her repelled me. I was icy. "No, Carol. I'm going. Try to think of the brief time we had as a good time in the past. Don't get in touch. Please don't ring my home."

"Wait, Bill. You shouldn't go down while he's there... He's impulsive. He was watching us come back from the shops. He knew you were up here."

I thought she might be trying to delay me. I felt nervous about Mr X. Then, I decided I was being a whelp. She was at the head of the stairs, sobbing, as I went downstairs.

"Bill!" she cried.

I went out of the door without speaking and closed it on her sobs. If the man was there, I didn't see him.

I'm critical about computers and the internet, but there is one facility they have which can be very helpful: providing a record of the past. How many criminals have been entrapped by their old emails or the use of a credit card? My experience of this record facility is rather more trivial.

Ann wanted to go to a forthcoming Modigliani exhibition at the Royal Academy, and she bought two tickets long before, on a visit to the Tate Modern with a friend. She paid in cash. When the day came, we had lunch at the café downstairs and presented ourselves at the entrance to the gallery.

"You have the tickets, Bill."

I realised all too clearly then, that I did not have them. "I forgot. I'm sorry. I assumed you had them."

Ann had an expression of disbelief tinged with distaste. "You couldn't forget! But they were on your desk, in that pile of stuff... I didn't want to ask you if you had them. It sounds naggy."

I didn't take this easily. I had a sinking, worthless feeling. "It's my fault entirely. I usually remember. You didn't need to remind me and you never do. But on this occasion, I thought that you had the tickets. I don't know why."

"Let's go down to the ticket office and talk to them," she said, bravely accepting my folly.

We waited in a queue for a while. Our accounts woman, Yasmin, by her badge, received Ann's explanation stonily. "Were the tickets posted out to you? We'll have your address on record."

When Ann told her she paid cash over the counter, Yasmin said: "Pity. At least, if you'd paid by card we'd have an entry. I don't think I can help you."

"You mean we'll have to pay again?" Ann asked.

"I can't think of anything else," Yasmin said with a bland expression.

I drew Ann aside and stepped up to the desk. "I think you *can* actually help us, Yasmin."

Her black eyes rested on me. She didn't speak. I did this in a good natured way; it doesn't help to lose your rag. "Could I ask you if we look like the kind of people who would concoct a story to get free entrance?"

"I can't make judgements like that," Yasmin said, now fixing her eyes upon her computer screen, dismissing us.

"What you mean is that you don't have the authority to make that judgement." I paused, for effect more than anything, drawing a few notes from my wallet. "However, I think I better talk to your manager before I pay again."

Yasmin disappeared though a door behind her and in half a minute or so a younger woman in a bright dress emerged. 'Valerie, supervisor.' She had a carefully fixed smile. "I understand the problem," she said.

"I would like to know, before we pay again, Valerie, if we look like a couple of crooks, trying to get into the show for nothing?"

The supervisor paused and actually looked at us both. With amusement she said, "No, of course you don't. But we have to have a few rules, you know. However, on this occasion, we'll issue duplicate tickets."

Ann sighed her thanks.

"All this trouble for *not* using a credit card or buying online!" I said, hyped up by the exasperation I was concealing.

Ann gave me a bitter sweet smile. "I won't remind you of your mistake, Bill."

At least, the show was brilliant.

Ann came home from school yesterday looking worried. Her cheeks were white, her eyes large. I went into the kitchen where she was making a cup of tea.

"What's the trouble, dear? A narrow miss in the car?"

"Nothing like that, Bill. It's school."

"Is it about your promotion?"

She nodded. Ann wants to step up to deputy head teacher. I'd rather see her as a part time supply teacher, and then we could spend more time together, but I don't want to stand in her way. Retirement, or part-time retirement is good, but not if you feel wasted. Ann seems to have a lot left to give. She'd make a fine deputy head, or head.

"Yes. The promotion's off."

"But I thought the headmaster told you that he wanted you."

"He did. He said he welcomed the appointment. But he made it clear that it was subject to formalities."

"Like checking your criminal record?"

"The union has said that they don't think they could work with me."

I paused for a moment to take in this extraordinary statement – and then the penny dropped. "Oh, God! Bernard Chandler is the union rep! I remember him boasting to me in this very room about his authority as the rep. Sort of power behind the throne stuff. Headmaster a glove puppet – all that. I thought it was crap."

"No, it's Bernard. And he wasn't joking in what he told you."

"It's pure bloody malice, Ann!"

"He's been humiliated, Bill, by you and Thelma in front of me."

I had fired the bullet. Words that kill and maim. "Humiliated or not, I didn't think he was nasty enough to do this," I said.

"Well he has. And that's the end of the story."

"But it's a groundless lie, about the union..." I protested. "Chandler has been your best pal up to a few days ago."

"The head is afraid of the union. He won't take me if the union oppose it."

"But you can oppose this. It's an injustice... Surely, you raised this with the head and the governors."

"I did. I told the head that Bernard Chandler's attitude arose out of personal issues. He said that was something he couldn't go into. Apparently the chairman of the governors, whom Bernard had approached, had been in touch with him.

"What a vindictive creep. You don't want to fight?"

"No, Bill. I'll leave. Relationships at the school would be messed up even if I was able to get the appointment."

"Walk out after all you've done?"

"There are plenty of jobs. And the head will give me a good reference. I heard of one post the other day, at the Temple Court School, in the Palace Road," she said, with a sad smile.

I might have encouraged Ann to fight this outrageous act of Chandler's, but I decided I liked the idea of her leaving the Castleton School. She'd be out of Chandler's orbit.

"What a total turd the man is! Let's go into the other room, and I'll make us a whisky and dry."

As we consoled ourselves with a drink I thought, at the same time, that I had achieved a desired objective. Chandler was going from our lives. Ann would leave Castleton. But I have to accept my share of blame for the brutal process. Ann was wounded and her career blighted – unintended consequences. But in three months' time, I was sure that it would all look different, much better.

21

Another of Nick's Surprises

I came home one evening from a film at about 6 pm, and Nick was there with Ann. I was surprised. He doesn't pay casual visits. Sometimes, he is out of touch for months. There was a girl too – a Nordic looking girl, slim, tall, about 25. Her long, straight, blond hair looked natural. Her long, straight, tanned legs were shown off by a leather mini-skirt and pink boots. She looked alert and happy. I particularly noticed that she had a fashion watch on her wrist, with a big coloured face, heavy in gold. I guessed it didn't come off a market stall.

Ann did the introduction. "Darling, this is Linda Pascal, Nick's fiancée." Nick stood there grinning as though he'd accomplished a rather clever move.

Now, I saw the ring on Linda's finger. Three diamonds, not huge, but not small, gleaming intrusively. I don't know precious stones, but I do know that Nick doesn't do gifts by half (even the occasional gifts he has given me in the past). Cartier or Tiffany's must be very pleased. All this so soon after averting bankruptcy.

As I was greeting Linda, I was thinking she looked like a rich chick – a trust fund baby. Her warm smile, her ease, the grace of her movement, all seemed to me to testify to a privileged upbringing, and she had scarcely spoken a word yet. The name Pascal rang a bell too, a big family in the pharmaceuticals industry, although there were lots of families of that name.

Nick hadn't told Ann or me that he was getting engaged. It was irritating that our lack of parental togetherness with him, in this age of communication, would be evident to Linda. But no matter. It was simply a fact. He had arrived at the door, I gather, without even calling Ann ten minutes before. This was pure Nick, surprise, or shock if he could get it.

I retrieved a bottle of Champagne from the cellar, and after toasting the health of the pair, we stood around the lounge chatting. When Ann and Linda were engrossed, Nick drew me away to talk.

"Bill..." he prefers to address me like this when feeling expansive, "I'm going to let you and Ann have a statement shortly covering that 30,000. You can let me know whether you want it to stay with me or withdraw it."

He made it sound like a regular investment. I'll 'withdraw' it like a shot if I get the opportunity. Ann has always told me to forget this debt. I thought that the sum due to us, even at a small rate of interest, would be a lot beyond the original sum. I made agreeable sounds.

"Have you any plans to tie the knot tighter?" I asked.

"Oh, we're working that out right now," he replied, evasively.

The happy couple declined to stay for a meal or to let us take them out for one, and departed about an hour later.

"Nice of Nick to get in touch with us on this," I said to Ann after I had closed the door.

"He's just a wild boy," she said, always ready with an excuse.

"He's supposed to be a man," I countered and sighed, "At least, the bride's family pay for the wedding."

"No, Bill, times have changed. Often both sides contribute, or the couple pay themselves. Don't be an old scrooge."

"I feel a bit sore at us being treated as an incidental."

"Nick doesn't mean anything by it. He's always been careless about courtesies."

"That's not all he's careless about."

Ann and I finished what was left in the bottle of Champagne and moved to the red wine while she prepared dinner. She was obviously pleased. We agreed Linda was a 'nice girl'. In fact, you might choose her for your son if you were looking at a shelf of opportunities on the face of it. As a pair, they were well matched physically – handsome and up-to-the-minute stylish.

Ann cast a few shadows. "She seems to have left a posh school and wiled her time away at art school. She doesn't work."

"Obviously, doesn't need to. She'll be good with the home décor and produce beautiful children."

"And there's something else. She's Jewish. Her parents want Nick to convert."

"As long as he doesn't join Al-Qaeda or ISIS, I don't care."

"If he does convert, it'll be a formality because he's not religious."

I didn't want to worry Ann, but I thought that from my knowledge of Nick, he would not accept pressure from anybody, including Linda's parents. He had a Luddite streak. It wouldn't matter if he was killing the golden goose. He lacked the diplomatic skills necessary to extricate himself from the Pascal parents with good feeling. But we would see.

Ann has started her new job at the Temple Court School and is enthusiastic about it. She seems to have accepted my part in this as unintended as far as her career is concerned. I don't know whether she harbours any feelings of loss about Chandler as a friend or lover. I expect she does, but we don't go there for good reason as I've said.

Ann told me that George was at the Temple Court Sport's Day with Penny and Budgie. Ann had been drafted as an organiser and official on this occasion. George tried to run in the parents' egg and spoon race, but after half a dozen paces his gammy leg let him down and he had to drop out. The race was won by a trim, dark haired father. George was left alone in the field with his silver hair blowing in the wind and a look of agony on his face. While the children were mobbing their dads on the finish line, Budgie, hands on hips, not really understanding, was remonstrating with her father.

"George trying to pretend he's 35," Ann said.

"He certainly looks a lot older than that."

Ann flashed one of her I-can-read-your-mind glances at me. "You may look a lot younger than him, Bill, but you don't have four children, two ex-wives, a new wife 18 years your junior and a bad leg."

"George has a lot of spirit, but he's trying to swim against the tide."

Ann suddenly changed the subject: "I heard something awful about Bernard from a colleague at Castleton School today. Chandler nearly came before the court, charged with assaulting Thelma Chandler."

"What do you mean, nearly?" It was an unbelievable volte face for a scholarly schoolteacher and an arrogant man, very much in control of his life.

"Apparently Thelma withdrew the charge before his appearance," Ann said.

"Like many battered women."

"You see what you did?" she said, sadly.

It was another unintended consequence as far as I was concerned. Suppose I hadn't met Thelma. I could have been walking the dog and all this might never have happened. But the Ann-Chandler relationship would still have been threatening me. Where would it have ended, in this event? I wasn't going to throw this back at Ann. You can never know what the precise consequences of your acts will be. "Will Chandler's job be OK?" I asked placidly.

"Oh, yes. But not his pride. The assault will only be known by a few of the teachers, and I doubt whether they will even want to talk about it."

"I'm sorry for Thelma. She came to us trying to salvage her marriage, not to destroy her husband."

Ann shook her head in a silent gesture which said, "I don't understand."

"Erectile dysfunction, once raised was the germ," I said.

"You sound rather self-satisfied, Bill. The master psychologist, manipulating people."

I apologised but didn't go on to try to justify myself because there is a slight disconnect between Ann and me on this. When Thelma told me about her marriage problem, I think she believed she could explain it as not all that serious, and take the blame as a result of her lack of sympathy. What she didn't realise, at the same time, was that she was dealing with dynamite. An erection is the very essence of masculinity, but vital as it was and is to Chandler, and to me, neither Thelma or Ann treated it as all that serious. It could be that women see this problem in a different way. Perhaps, women aren't wedded to the image of vigorous sex that men pride themselves on delivering. That's a comforting thought as I get older.

22

George and the Nanny

Ann came home from Waitrose with the shopping this morning saying she had bumped into George. "Really he is ridiculous," she said, "hobbling around, pretending he is perfectly at ease and getting irritated with the staff, when in fact he's lost. He was in a check jacket with a handkerchief spilling out of his top pocket and very tight jeans, talking on his smartphone to Penny." Ann is a good mimic and she got George's loud, plummy tones: "Darling, was it Cheddar or Wensleydale you wanted."

"No man over 40 ought to wear jeans, Bill. Mind you," she said, "it's not only George. Saturday is the day when the dads, especially the older ones, whom you might guess have second, or even third wives, like George, are sent out with the kids and the shopping list. The dads seem to want to prove that they are expert at this, and it can be handled in a trice. And of course, at the same time, dad is talking loudly to junior, usually about the geography of the upper Amazon, or anything else entirely unconnected with the shopping. This loud conversation shows that junior is smart and well-educated like his dad. Or, like George, dad is on his smartphone to his wife enquiring about varieties of cheese, while junior obstructs other shoppers with the supermarket trolley."

"It must have made you sorry you didn't marry George. Think of it, darling, you'd be driving his Jag to get the shopping."

"I love George, as one of your friends, because he's an interesting man, but when I knew him years ago, I recognised him as a rake and he always has been. I wouldn't be driving his Jag today. I'd have been relegated as ex-wife number one."

Ann was referring to the seismic upheavals caused by his three marriages. We were very close to ground zero because of our friendship with George. I was his confidant through all of this, never his counsellor. I think he appreciated that I wasn't judgmental. I couldn't bring myself to get involved in the dark business where hearts are confused with obligations, because I knew I had no answers. I could work out what I might have done if it had been my life, but my solution wouldn't fit his.

George's affair with the children's nanny which led to his divorce from his first wife, involved Ann because George wanted Ann and me to accept Lisa, the nanny, as his girlfriend in a social way and have them in our home. At the time, they were being treated as lepers by many of George's friends. The association with us was precious to George.

"Shall we invite George and Lisa to dinner one night, get them out of that dingy flat?" (George's bolt-hole between marriages). I said this to Ann after George had hinted his leprosy to me. I didn't expect Ann to leap at the suggestion, but I was taken aback by the vehemence of her reply.

Her words were chilly and immediate: "I won't have Lisa in the house, Bill. I have always thought of her as a very capable and decent person until now, but Joyce Cutler is a personal friend. She's the victim of an act of treachery and deceit and a monstrous breach of trust by the pair of them."

The difficulty was that Ann knew the whole sorry story from Joyce Cutler. From that point of view, what Ann said was right. I knew the story from George's viewpoint which was different: arguments, excessive drinking, Joyce's flirtations with other men and George's with other women. A melt-down on both sides.

I have no doubt that George thought I was in agreement with him, that what he did was understandable. This was because I was uncritical. I simply listened to him. I actually thought that screwing your nanny was like shitting in your own bed, even though the marriage might have been on its last legs, but I never said so.

George didn't have to do this. He was a handsome man who could have found women outside his home, but he also had something of the satyr about him. He revelled in the wickedness, crawling into the nanny's bed and covertly having her while they were in the same house as Joyce. He hadn't the slightest conscience about it. And Lisa was visibly a tasty plum of young womanhood.

Out of friendship for George, I tried to persuade Ann, "Come on, dear. That's a bit high and mighty. You know Joyce is no angel. Their marriage has been a mess for a long time."

"Bill, what I said is final. I will not associate with Lisa. George is your friend. You take him and Lisa out if you want to. Your liberal ideas are so liberal that at times they embrace the illiberal, the chaotic."

"Ann, we have to accept the Lisa, Joyce, George triangle."

"Maybe, but I don't have to entertain Lisa and I won't."

"Would you entertain George, solo?"

"Not without telling him what I thought. And I'd prefer not to have him here while Lisa is an item."

That was it. End of story. Later that day, I said to Ann that I understood her view. However, when I told George flatly that Ann wouldn't have it, he jeered, "Ah, the righteous lady! Thank God you married her, Bill, not me!"

So George went into purdah (but not as far as I was concerned) until the George-Lisa meteor burned out a few months later, and George found himself other women – and wives.

Becky packed me off to Enfield, north London to see one of Drugfree's rehabilitation houses. I went on the tube and bus. Featherstone House was a large, old, detached property, formerly a grand home, now forgotten in a back street. The big front garden had neat lawns, shrubs and flower beds. The front of the house was partly scaffolded and at least five painters were at work.

One of them put down his brush and greeted me, and when I said I was from the London HQ, he led me through the front door, down the hall, to a man at a desk in an office. He was like an automaton, programmed to conduct the guest. He never responded to my cheery greetings.

The manager, Des Hannam, was forty-ish, with a pallid complexion, a pony tail and long, not too clean fingernails. He sat me down and plied me with coffee. He didn't actually say I was a nuisance, but I felt I might be. When I commented that everything seemed very orderly out front, he explained that the inmates were organised in teams which compete for points in performing the household chores, including cooking and cleaning. "It's about planning your time and using it to best effect."

Memories of Ms Biggs and of my own struggle, not so much with planning, but with the execution of plans. "Cheap labour," I said, which sounded critical but wasn't intended to be.

Des wasn't fussed. "We teach them that any labour has dignity. We do lectures, based on the psychology of an addict, films, gym classes, quizzes and personal counselling. And some educational and vocational courses. As well as trying to help them get a job when they're discharged."

I talked with some of the inmates – ones who had been nominated to talk to me. They seemed to stir out of listlessness and come alive and some were even enthusiastic.

"It's good for them to know that they have to perform socially with you," Des said.

Then, he guided me on a tour of the kitchens and bedrooms and the common rooms which were temporarily vacant. It was all plain, comfortable and clean. When we reached the back veranda and I was eyeing the neat plot of healthy looking vegetables, I said, "Do you get any cures?"

He wasn't perturbed by the question. I had heard talk at a board meeting about the drop-out rate. "It depends on how long they stay. The longer, the more likely the cure."

"What *is* a cure?"

"A cure is when you have a rational understanding that going through *another* cure would be a hell like throwing yourself off the edge of the Grand Canyon into the Colorado rapids." Des smiled at me for the first time. "Get it?"

Becky had told me that Des was a reformed heroin addict and that they often made excellent managers because they knew. His eyes bulged slightly and were very bright. He seemed utterly focussed on what he was doing.

"I do, yes," I said. "So a week in a Swiss clinic won't do it?"

"Not if you're a hard drug addict. You need to put in time so when you look back, as you will, you understand more readily that you don't want to go back. Time is part of the cure."

"What about other drugs?"

"You can smoke cannabis for as long as you're privileged to live. It's a choice between having your brains blown away and cancer."

"So, what percentage of cures?"

Des was back to his taciturn self. "The local authorities don't have the money for 12 months care. We have to take people for shorter terms and often it doesn't work. Better than nothing, but it doesn't really work. We track outcomes."

I had expected a snap percentage, but I didn't think he was being evasive. "Money," I asked, "What about the rich kids who can afford it?"

"They don't come to a place like this, local authority funded. But I'll bet if you looked at their outcomes, you would find the same. Their problem isn't money. The problem those guys have is giving up a year of their precious lives."

After I had talked to some of the patients here, young men from 20 to 30, I had the feeling that they didn't have any lives outside the house that weren't in ruins. It made me think, but only for a moment, that I lived in an impregnable castle, surrounded by my agreeable little life. I did live an agreeable little life, but it wasn't impregnable. Change, perhaps sudden change was waiting.

All had been quiet about the engagement and wedding for a month. I thought, perhaps, Nick and Linda had decided to put their wedding aside for a while, but about a month after their visit to us, Ann told me of a telephone conversation she had with Nick.

"He told me that he and Linda were making their own arrangements for the wedding. Apparently, he fell out with Linda's father."

"That's Nick. I imagine he told Pascal, a millionaire businessman and a knight of the realm, that he was a big cunt."

"I don't know precisely what he said to Sir Arthur, but Nick's not going to convert and Linda is quite happy with that. She doesn't get on with her father or with her stepmother who is a year younger than she is. And she's not really religious."

"I think I get the picture. This little couple are on their own. Disowned by the bride's family."

"Nick said he will have to pay for the wedding because Linda doesn't have any savings. In fact, he said that she's maxed out her credit card."

"It's all on her wrist and back."

I interpreted Nick's call to Ann as advance notice of a claim, rather than a request, for a large sum of money to pay for the wedding, but I limited my comment to, "We'll have to see how events develop."

"We'll have to make a contribution, Bill."

"Ann, dearest, if we are making a contribution, who else might be?"

"Oh, God, you're not going to be difficult about money on your son's *marriage,* are you?"

"*Contribution* is the wrong word. We'll be asked to pick up the tab."

"And we should!"

I wish Ann would regard me as a wise guardian of our funds rather than a skinflint – a guardian, trying to protect us against a reckless and improvident man who should not be leaning on his parents at the age of 30. Nick had shifted his target from me to Ann. He had softened her up knowing she would influence me. Good tactics on his part.

23

Carol's Last Stand

Nick has called Ann and said that he and Linda are making plans for the wedding, but he's a bit short of cash, and he'd like to talk it over.

"I can translate that from his language to ours pretty easily," I said to Ann when she told me.

"There's no need," Ann said.

"You mean he's already told you how much he wants?"

"We didn't discuss any details. I just know it's difficult for him."

"Well, what's it to be, a gift or a loan (non-repayable) of course?"

"Bill, please don't humiliate him."

"I'm glad you recognise that he could be humiliated. He *should* feel humiliated without a word said from me."

"I know, that's why we've got to help out."

"Barry Macklin would have too much pride to do this."

"Barry's parents are not able to do what we can do."

"Ann, my dearest, we should not be doing this. Nick is supposed to be a grownup, but he doesn't act like one. He cuts a figure as an investment banker doing big deals but actually he's greedy and he lives beyond his means. Look at his car. A Porsche."

"Bill, he's a young man."

"There's a disrespect for us in what he's doing. He never had a second thought about asking us to ante up three quarters of a million on the threat of his bankruptcy. He knows the kind of money we have and yet he was prepared to do that...and give us a lot of tosh about a *loan*."

"You wisely steered us out of that, Bill. Let's forget it. We have a family wedding coming up."

"Linda seems a very nice girl from what little I've seen of her," I said, "but Nick wants to live with her like a billionaire entrepreneur. He doesn't have to do that. He's a poseur and I'm afraid, on the evidence so far, a loser."

"That's too harsh, Bill. We're talking of a wedding. You're blowing it up into something it isn't."

"He should be having 30 guests at a local hotel. That's more in keeping with his means, but no. He will want the party of the year."

"You only get married once, hopefully, Bill. Let them do what they think is appropriate."

"The bill he presents to us will be outrageous. I know it will. It'll take no account of Nick's means. He'll want to present himself, especially to Linda's tribe, as the big man."

"Let's meet and talk about it, Bill. And remember, it's not a subject to be mean about. We have to remember the kind of girl Linda is, and the style of life they live."

"I don't mind remembering their lifestyle, but I don't want to finance it."

Ann closed her eyes in desperation. Was I being mean? I agreed with Ann that we must talk about it in a civilised way with Nick, but I remained resolute.

Ann arranged for Nick to call one night after dinner. I had pointedly rejected Ann's suggestion of having the happy pair to dinner. I told her I wanted Nick to call on his own, and I wanted her to remain present. "He won't explode so readily if you're there," I said.

"*Please*, go easy, Bill."

Nick arrived full of cheer, immaculately suited. He's charismatic. He's a person that you would notice in a crowded room. He radiates a kind of electric current which makes people turn toward him. He can't stand, ignored, in a corner. He soon gathers an audience. He's never boring, and he has charm. It's a wonderful quality, and I would say his greatest asset (I'm a total contrast as his parent). The problem is that charisma is a starter of business, but not a finisher. Charisma isn't necessary to analyse balance sheets and evaluate risks. And that may be Nick's trouble. He's a starter, not a finisher. When I say 'starter', I mean he's not merely a man with bright ideas. He can attract a loyal team around him. He can do all the complicated things about setting up a business. He can literally start it, but in my experience he never seems to finish or get the details right.

We three seated ourselves in the lounge, drinks declined by agreement and polite enquiries having been made about Linda. I made sure I sat where I could look at Nick squarely. I wanted to box him in. I didn't want him striding about the room waving his arms and making speeches – as he prefers to do.

I cut to the action. "How much do you want, son?"

"I think 35,000 would do it, Dad," he said, leaning back with a generous look, as though in some way this was being kind to us. "You can't be too precise with weddings."

I was shocked at this bold play. I could feel the ice forming around my heart. I forced a smile. I glanced at Ann. Her expression was blank, which I interpreted as surprise at least, if not shock. "Could we say no more than 35,000?"

"If you wish, Dad," he replied, tolerantly, raising his hands in supplication.

"Have you costed any specific items?"

"Not precisely, Dad, no," his tone was a little less smooth.

"You didn't pluck that number out of the sky. Could you give us the ball park figures?"

"Shall I detail the wedding breakfast menu?" he said tartly.

This rapid change of tone was a warning sign. Nick had a very short fuse. I knew that if I said he had a bloody cheek, as I should, he would abuse me and stalk off with the slamming of doors. That might solve the problem for me, but my main consideration was Ann. I don't think she would forgive me. She had a lot at stake: her motherly and family feelings, the desire for peace in the family, and her own social sense of how the marriage might look to our friends. I would have to capitulate.

I pulled a difficult smile. "No, just tell us about the variety of soup you're planning."

"Mum, he said, turning abruptly to Ann and raising his voice. "Do I have to take this crap from Dad?

Ann startled me. She stood up and put her hand affectionately on Nick's shoulder. "I'm going to make a cup of tea. You boys fix it up."

Nick's appeal to his mother had been dismissed, and he was now at my mercy. He sank back in his chair visibly deflated, his lips tight, his eyes narrowed. I think concern and anger were fighting each other in him. Concern kept him in his chair. Anger would have him flouncing out of the door.

A long and chilly silence followed Ann's departure. I was in no hurry. I eyed a tiny crack in the plaster ceiling. I thought that if Nick could manage on 20,000, he would probably ask for 35,000. Why not? It was consistent with his view of the Bank of Mum & Dad. I also thought that Ann wouldn't like it if I stipulated a loan. She would have said families don't do that. It had to be a gift. But the difference didn't matter to me, because the money would never be repaid.

I said, "All right, Nick. 15,000." I made no qualifications.

Nick appeared to struggle with himself whether to continue with his original claim, or bargain, but remained silent. I found his reaction incredible. Not the faintest flutter of thanks. There seemed to be no limit to his sense of entitlement.

Ann brought in a tray of tea cups.

"We've settled on 15,000, dear," I said, not for a moment thinking this would end the negotiations.

Ann astonished me again by readily accepting the reduction without waiting for Nick's acceptance or complaint. "That sounds sensible," she said briskly. "Now, let's talk about other things."

Nick had watched her carefully. He must have known the bargaining was over.

I was working in the potting shed last Saturday morning when Ann came in with the mail. When I say 'working', I was making an entry in this notebook. The mail usually consists of pitches from estate agents, offers on health insurance and holiday brochures. And of course, banks statements because I am not (yet) with the paperless. This morning, one particular letter stood out before any were opened. I could see that Ann was looking at it curiously as she placed it on top of the small pile at my elbow.

The envelope was cream of quality paper and addressed by hand in round, flowing characters written with a broad nibbed ink pen. As soon as I saw it, I ran through, in my mind the people who might address me like this. Not many.

"That looks interesting, Bill."

I pretended to be engaged in my own writing because I feared the letter might be from Carol. If I opened it in front of Ann, who knows what would be revealed? I had not heard anything from Carol since I abruptly left her apartment following the scene with her man friend. I hoped never to hear from her again. "I'll get around to it," I said, trying to appear preoccupied.

Ann and I are open with each other but equally respect an area of privacy. For example, I have no idea how much she has in the bank, although, I expect that if I asked her she would tell me readily, and I never see her correspondence with friends unless she shows me a particular email or letter. On this occasion, she never said anything more and left the room.

I opened the letter with some trepidation. My worst anticipation was realised. The letter was from Carol: *Dear Bill, You were completely wrong in concluding that the man bothering me on your visit to the flat was a boyfriend of mine. If you had only waited and allowed me the opportunity to explain! I won't go into it in this letter. You and I were going to talk that morning and for me it wasn't merely that I was looking forward to it, but needing that talk to bring me to some kind of closure and calm. After you left the flat, I thought for a time that I would be able to forget but I can't. The end of our affair seemed to me so brutal and so wrong, after an experience that was so beautiful. All I ask is that you meet with me and have that talk. Yours, Carol.*

What could I say to Ann about this? I was sure that her curiosity had been stirred by the letter and it was likely that she would ask me later what it was about. If I showed her the letter, it would be evident that I had been to Carol's flat. Questions were inevitable. Where was the flat? How often had I been there? The letter referred to an experience 'so beautiful' – no more poisonous phrase could be introduced into my relationship with Ann. The whole effect of the letter upon Ann would be to cast me as a liar and deceiver.

If, on the contrary, I concealed the letter and made up a story about it, the likelihood was that I would trip up on my own falsehoods, not be believed and give the impression that the dalliance was continuing.

The problem seemed to be insoluble. And what was I to do about Carol? See her? Have that talk? Become entrapped again in some unimaginable way? Her very act in writing to me was like a smouldering explosive, because it could raise questions without the envelope being opened. Carol's so-called love for me now had a tinge of the malign. Any letter she wrote to the house, especially one as flagrantly feminine as this, would in all likelihood be seen by Ann before it reached me.

I felt I was cornered. I formed a desperate plan. I went down to the kitchen. Ann was arranging some flowers in a vase. "Would you come up to the study, please, now," I said. "I want you to witness a telephone conversation I'm going to have."

"What's the matter, Bill? You look pale." She looked serious herself. She must have guessed that I had been upset by the letter.

"I'm angry," I said. I didn't attempt to explain myself and she didn't ask.

She followed me upstairs. When we were settled, I keyed Carol's number. Her soft and youthful voice answered almost immediately. "It's Bill Batley here," I said firmly in a loud voice.

"Oh, Bill how good…"

I interrupted: "I've got your letter. I asked you not to get in touch with me…"

"I had to write, Bill…"

I interrupted again: "Let's get some facts straight. When I called you to ask you not to get in touch with me…"

"I had to see you…"

"You insisted on meeting. I suggested Starbucks."

"Bill, don't go on like this…"

"You were waiting outside Starbucks on the day with piles of groceries in the rain."

"I was wet through…"

"I agreed to drive you home. I couldn't do anything else."

"Yes…"

"When I left your flat, I repeated what I had made perfectly clear on more than one previous occasion – that I didn't want to hear from you again."

"You were so wrong about the caller at the flat, Bill."

"I don't care about your private life, Carol. I don't even know you. And you don't know me!"

Carol squealed. I looked at Ann, who had a sickly stare. She would have heard the squeal, but Carol's part of the dialogue would have been virtually inaudible.

I broke into Carol's sobs: "Let this be our last contact, Carol. No more letters and calls!" I switched the phone off.

Ann looked stunned.

"Do you want to see this wretched letter?" I asked her.

She was still for a moment. She had tears on her cheeks. She shook her head negatively and went out of the door.

It was a bruising encounter for both women but my plan had worked. I felt a sense of relief. It was a Houdini-like feat to get out of this impasse. The letter, which I destroyed, had been dealt with. Most important of all, the word 'beautiful' would not sully Anne's memory of my transgression. And perhaps my credentials as a steadfast husband who kept his word had been slightly improved.

Jane called me a few days ago and asked if I would speak to Barry. She said he had a business problem. He was very upset that one of his partners had let him down. I was hesitant.

"You know about contracts and things, Dad. It would just be a preliminary chat to point him in the right direction. I've told him I would speak to you. I think he'd appreciate it."

"Jane, when families get involved in business it doesn't always work out."

"I'm glad you think of Barry as family, Dad, but you're always so diffident about...*everything*!"

"There aren't many certainties, sweetheart, but OK, OK."

I walked to Jane's flat that night after dinner, as arranged. She offered tea or coffee which I refused and she disappeared. Barry was sitting at the dining room table which had been cleared, with a thick file and a laptop in front of him. He was wearing a white shirt and a skewed tie. Barry wears a suit to work because he sees government officers, architects, potential buyers and property speculators every day.

"Thanks for coming, Bill," he said, running his fingers through his untidy fair hair. "I've been screwed."

He explained that he had made a deal with a friend, John Randall, which involved sharing the cost of purchase of farmland near York. They had no planning permission and intended to hold the land, in the hope that they could get planning approval in future. They would share the ensuing development costs.

"Randall, the rat, unexpectedly *got* planning approval and now says my contribution was a temporary loan – which he will repay! Everything is in the name of one of his companies."

"No written agreement?"

"Because Randall was a friend, Bill, and I trusted him and the deal moved very quickly."

"Your word against his," I said. "With legal help you may get through, but I wouldn't bet on it. No emails?"

"I trusted this guy, Bill. I've known him for five years. I've done deals with him. I liked him. Jane and I have been out with him and his wife. Jane is friendly with her. And this is a big deal – for me, anyway. Maybe 90 quality homes." Barry's face was red. His lips quivered.

He was wounded about being duped, and he'd lost a valuable opportunity, but he'd get his capital and interest back. I thought he wasn't going to lose much – unless he decided to litigate and lost. "It's unpleasant, Barry. You've wagered hundreds of thousands of pounds on the word of a partner."

"But Randall was *a friend,* Bill. Where are you in this world if you can't trust a friend?"

"It doesn't matter if he's your blood brother or your father or your mother for that matter. Business and friendship, business and family are like oil and water, they don't mix."

His brow puckered. He didn't accept what I said. "You can't go to a friend with a piece of paper and say, 'Sorry mate, but unless you sign this first I can't be involved.' It's a mingy, pin-pricking attitude.'"

"It doesn't have to be as crass as you make it sound, Barry. You can say, 'I have to document the details. My bank and auditors will require it.'"

"I want people around me that I can trust."

"Sure. Get friendly people around you by all means, but always ask yourself, 'Am I adequately protected?' People are basically selfish, Barry. And when they feel there's an opportunity to make money, it's hard to resist. And maybe there was a misunderstanding."

"No misunderstanding. Hell, I'm not in business as a moneylender."

Barry had wilted, his indignation now a small residue of irritation. "It seems a lousy view of humans that you can't trust them."

"I wouldn't put it that way. You can and should trust people in lots of ways, but in business *you* have to be self-protective. Don't leave it to somebody else. How else would all the lawyers make a living?"

"No deals on a handshake?"

"Never."

"Bill, I've made a lot of money on a handshake."

"You're an honest guy. It's the other guy. You only need to come unstitched once and you find yourself like this."

"Do you think I should sue the bastard?"

"If it's your word against his, it's less than a 50-50 chance. If you lose, you could pay a mountain of costs. Get legal advice. Rattle your sword a little. But don't sue unless your lawyer can give you an odds-on chance of a win."

Jane came into the room. "Can I get you guys a drink?" When she saw Barry's expression, she frowned. "What have you been saying?"

"Only that some humans are greedy bastards," Barry said. "And I have to give more support to the legal profession!"

"Oh, Dad! You didn't…you're such a cynic."

"Bill's right. Let's have extra-large whisky-and-sodas."

24

Becky Passes Me a Poison Chalice

Becky has given me a rather curious mission. Before the last board meeting, she asked me to stay behind when the meeting was over. I thought, perhaps, she was going to reprimand me for some offence which I might have unknowingly committed. Instead, she said, "Bill, I want you to have a word with Nestor McComb. Some of the girls in the office say he's been manhandling them."

"You mean sexual assaults, Becky."

"No, no, no. I mean silly touching, you know, joking."

"Sexual assaults."

"All right, Bill. Sexual assaults."

Nestor was a fellow board member and a psychiatrist. As far as I knew, he was a complete oddball if his views were to be taken seriously.

"Why me?"

"You've had experience of this kind of situation with your own staff. Right?" I nodded and she continued, "And it's better man to man."

I wasn't necessarily certain that it was better man to man, but I said, "What do you want me to say to him?"

"You know better than I do. Just warn him."

"His job could be in issue on this kind of allegation."

"I know. If he decides to go, that would be a good thing. He's just window dressing. But I don't want to offend the Broadly Hospital where he works. We have to have a case against him that will keep him quiet."

"And you want me to get the 'evidence'?"

Becky was sprawling in her high-backed chairman's chair at the head of the board table. Now, she leaned forward with her elbows on her papers and her fingers in her straggling hair. "Exactly, Bill."

I was slightly suspicious. Nestor was a vocal opponent of Becky's scheme to shorten rehab times to make them more saleable. The Broadly Hospital were in a treatment partnership with us. Nestor had argued at the meeting that Broadly wouldn't continue the partnership on Becky's terms. This was one of Nestor's more sensible positions.

"Tell me who the girls are, Becky. I mean, are they on the brink of going to the police? "

"I think that should remain confidential at the moment."

"You're sending me into battle with a wooden gun, Becky. Nestor is going to ask me what the girls say. And he's going to ask for my authority and where you fit in. When he knows I can't tell him anything, he's going to tell me to eff-off. Why don't you see him yourself. You'll strike terror into his heart."

"He'll say I'm just trying to get rid of him."

"And it sound as if you are, Becky. I would have to meet the girls and talk to them. I need to know how serious their complaints are. If it's a police matter, I can't touch it. It should be reported immediately. If it's bothersome misconduct which isn't an assault or indecency, you can get statements from the girls in writing, give Nestor a hearing, reprimand or even dismiss him. But you may end up with a costly lawsuit."

"You're not prepared to help me?"

I was fairly sure now that Becky was trying to keep the lid on public sexual harassment complaints and prepared to appease the girls by sacrificing the expendable Nestor. She didn't want me to speak to the girls because I would then learn about the extent of the harassment and she couldn't be sure of what I would do. "I'm sorry, but I can't help unless I talk to the girls."

"You're not on my side, Bill."

"There aren't any sides."

"I can't stand disloyalty."

Becky was an extremely competent CEO, but she was a model of a kind of executive behaviour with which I was familiar. You can't work in a big company without meeting this model, the bully-boy type, like Jason Wild. The reaction to an awkward road block is emotional hustling, rather than logical thought, and dissent is disloyalty.

She didn't look at me but out of the window. Her expression suggested I had made a bad smell. She dismissed me by her silence. Becky was a very stiff-necked and wilful lady. I thought she would find one of the other directors soft enough to push around.

In one of our conversations in his garden shed, George talked about his leg and what a pain it was, both actually and figuratively.

"It's not life-threatening, but it points to the fact that it's hard to keep up with Penny and Budgie."

"The age difference is beginning to tell?"

"I hate to admit it, but yes. Penny is 38, and I'm 58. I've got two kids only a few years younger than her and Budgie is 12."

"That's a big gap, but a lot of guys on their second and third marriages are in the same boat."

"That doesn't make it any easier. There are strains. She's a young woman. She wants to travel, go yachting, go skiing, go clubbing. Shit, the last thing I want to do is go to a nightclub – now."

I didn't feel sympathetic. "You can get some ear defenders."

"Very funny."

"You're a thoughtful man, George. You must have realised this would happen when you married Penny. She was about 21."

"She was. And scrumptious. I couldn't resist her."

"Your penis was doing the planning."

"Not at all," he said gruffly. "Not at all. She was – is – a clever and interesting person. I loved her for many things." His narrowed eyes glared at me.

"Many things. Really?" This was an Ann-ism which could hit hard.

"Yes, *Reee*-ally, Batley…you dope!"

"But you loved her cunt more than anything else."

"All right! I did – and still do I'm glad to say!"

"And she couldn't resist a handsome older man with plenty of money. She bought it too."

"That's a valid point, Bill. Only it doesn't level the playing field. I'm the one who can't play."

"What will happen?"

"Penny and I are like that," he held up a hand with crossed fingers. "I suppose we'll go on until she's pushing me around in a chair in my dotage."

"Maybe she'll hit the high spots on her own eventually." I could see from his downcast expression that George didn't like this suggestion. It stirred the Othello in him.

He threw back the remains of his gin-and-tonic as though it was sour. "Maybe."

"Even a quasi-virgin like me can appreciate that she's a beautiful woman." I was amused and I couldn't miss an opportunity to torment him. "She does amateur dramatics now. We've all seen her. There must be leading men around somewhere."

"I'll close the bar if you go on like this, Bill."

"I'm only joking. You know that. I'm sure Penny is as steadfast as they come."

I believed Penny was a happy wife, and I'm sure she was very close to George but I wasn't joking. And George knew he was facing some problem years. How does a man of nearly 60 relate to a 30-something-year-old wife? Ann and I had discussed George's fate, looking at how it might be as the years advanced: George alone at home in his chair with a rug around his legs, aged 75; Penny, aged 55, at a dance studio learning the Argentine Tango.

Sophie Greer one of our neighbours was at home when I returned after walking Rex on Sunday morning. I never noticed anything very different in the line of cars parked in the street outside, but after I had gone inside and greeted Sophie – a bright 'hello' suffices – Ann said, "Did you see Sophie's new car, Bill?"

The street is always lined with vehicles which would illuminate any car dealer's yard. Bentley, Tesler, Porsche, they are all there. Naturally, I didn't notice Sophie's car.

"My attention was entirely taken by the leaves on the windscreen of my Honda," I said.

Sophie, a 40-year-old Danish woman with bloodshot whites around her big blue eyes was silent, with her mouth slightly open and a rapt look of happiness on her pale face. She was waiting for Ann to explain.

"It's a Mercedes coupe thingy," Ann said.

Sophie's husband was a City lawyer too busy to socialise or even talk, but Sophie made up for that. He was well able to provide for his wife's ever changing taste in cars. "Sounds exciting," I said, "Is it a V8?"

She gave a small frown and said, "I'm not sure, but it's lovely."

"Petrol or diesel?"

"I know what they say about diesel, but would one more teeny weeny car matter? I don't know what it runs on, Bill. I didn't ask."

"Have you shown it to George and Penny? They are connoisseurs," Ann said.

"Not yet," Sophie said, "I don't get my personalised number plate on the car until Friday."

25

A Lose-Lose Game with Becky

One of Ann's sisters, Vicki, who is five years older than her, has had cosmetic surgery on her face. It wasn't too bad a face either. Similar to Ann's but Ann is more attractive. Ann doesn't have any of those lines around her mouth which tend to make it look like an old leather purse and her eyes aren't droopy. Vicki did have those signs of ageing but not in a marked way. I thought she looked well for her age – before the operation. Afterwards, her face looked to me to have acquired a tension in the skin, although admittedly the mouth lines weren't there. Her eyes seemed more wide open but not necessarily more attractive. I've seen other women whom I know have had cosmetic surgery, who have the same signs of tightness in the face, as though a new mask of skin, slightly too small in size has been fitted.

"However," Ann said when we talked about it, "Vicki feels better. That's the main thing."

I agreed, "Maybe she'll catch another man, although she could quite easily have done that before the op."

"Sure, but it's all about how you feel inside, Bill."

Vicki had had a deeply unhappy experience. Her husband, Derek, had died in a car accident. A wild, coked-up kid without a driving licence had driven into Derek's car head on and killed him, but escaped with scratches himself. Chance! The kid got away, and being a kid received what Vicki felt was an inadequate reformatory sentence. She carried the cross of justice denied.

If Derek had been killed in a storm or drowned in a flood, Vicki wouldn't have the justice problem. It's really sheer hatred and malice toward the human being who did this to her and her husband. That's what she feels. And yet, that youth was like a storm or a flood – unknown to Derek and Vicki, an unknown force coming out of the darkness to strike them. I asked Vicki if she could see it like that. Ill luck, but not something to arouse feelings of malice in her. Those malicious feelings were having a devastating effect on her. She was like a person in a continuing state of shock. Yes, some of her feeling was the hurt of loss, but much was the desire for vengeance – in the name of justice.

"I've tried with forgiveness," she said, "but when I think of that little snot running around scot free …"

Becky rang me at home on the day following our meeting; "Bill," she said in a caressing tone, "I've thought it over. I've had a word with the girls and they'll talk to you."

I was disappointed and suspicious. "Do you really want them to talk – to anybody?'"

"I'd prefer it if they didn't complain outside the company. I know. You know. But we have to call out this…thing," she said, hastily. "I don't want to cover it up but publicity means scandal which will affect the sponsors, and affect my reputation. You can't blame me for being cautious."

"You're thinking that if I talk to Nestor, he'll back out of the board quietly without risking his professional standing?"

"Exactly, Bill."

"He may feel that would be an admission of guilt."

"I think he's cautious and gutless. He'll quit."

I decided not to pursue my thoughts any further with Becky. I was in this now on my own terms and I had to give it a go. I couldn't help feeling that my efforts were was going to end badly. She made a time for me to go to the Drugfree HQ to meet the girls. I told Ann casually at lunch in the weekend that I had been recruited as an emissary by Becky.

"I know you've done this stuff before, Bill," she said, with a resigned sigh.

"You don't seem to have a lot of confidence in me."

"You're going to shut the whole thing down on behalf of Drugfree."

"Not at all," I replied sharply, "I'm going to open it out in a fair manner." I suppose I was thinking of how I could muffle it, but I realised Ann was right. There had been enough scandals involving important and trusted institutions for me to accept that cover-ups do more damage than transparency – but when you're part of an institution, the first thing you think of is, 'How can we protect the institution?'.

"You're going to be the judge whether a slap on the bottom is a police matter or just a bit of laddish fun?" she said sceptically.

"I won't be judging. I'll be saying that the girls should see the police or somebody outside Drugfree, if they have any doubts at all, and particularly I'll be pointing out that if they feel they are under pressure not to talk, they should talk." I was talking big, but I knew that sexual complaints were fraught not just with emotional complexities but with conflicting loyalties. Do you want to tell your mother that a great family friend has put his hand on you?

She looked at me carefully and said, "I believe you, Bill. So Becky has the wrong emissary."

"Possibly yes, if her intention is to keep things quiet."

"But this would be a new departure for you. You've spent a lot of time in your career, doing what you call 'protecting the company's interests'. Remember, you've talked to me about your activities. This comes naturally to you. Becky knows that without being told."

"You say it comes naturally to me as though it's a flaw, but give a little weight to history: I mean I don't fault the present impulse to eradicate harassment, but in the 1950s we had *Guys and Dolls,* macho, sexist and loaded with tits and bums. Your mother loved it. It exemplified a kind of culture. Maybe wrong? We're on a journey, Ann."

Ann was quietly giving me the 'really?' look. Not a serious person.

It was a fair cop. I had smothered complaints about sexual harassment in the past as director of human resources. I would argue that the results were fair. If there was anything serious in the complaints, our girls were paid off generously on a promise of no publicity. Was this so wrong? Yes, probably. But was there a 'right' way to do these cases?

"What are you going to do about the psychiatrist?"

"I'm damned if I know. Ask him to identify *my* complex."

"You could have his professional life in your hands, Bill. It's no joke."

With Ann's words in my mind I kept the date to see the girls, Colette and Veronica. I glanced at their personal files before the meeting. We recognised each other from the few times I had visited the office, which had a staff of ten. We went into a small interview room with cups of coffee. The girls were about 20. The white girl, Colette, was an accounts clerk, the black girl, Veronica, was a committee clerk. They were competent people. They were tense. Their attitude toward me was one of suspicion.

"Do you want to have a chat about this?" I asked, dropping my chummy smile.

"Not until we know where you're coming from," Colette said.

"I don't know," I said. "I don't know anything. When I do, I'll tell you what I think."

"You'll lean on us," Veronica said.

"To do what, do you think?"

"Shut up and go away," Veronica said.

"What makes you think that Becky wants your complaints buried?"

"Becky has said this is a slur on Drugfree," Colette said.

"We'll lose our jobs if we complain openly," Veronica said. "I enjoy my job."

"Maybe we'll lose them anyway," Colette added.

I could see that the sexual abuse allegations against Nestor were a malignant fact that would swill around poisonously in the relationship between Becky, Nestor and them, each party unsure of how the relationship would progress.

The way I saw it then was that everybody was going to lose.

I got to work. "Summarise for me in your own words, where he put his hands and what he said. And how often? Have another member of staff to join us if you want."

The girls looked at each other and agreed without speaking. "We don't need a chaperone," Colette said

I jotted their talk down. They explained that there was quite a lot of touching and sexy commentary from Nestor. It had become almost habitual. He took no notice of their admonitions, laughed when they rebuked him. This had never happened when they were both together with him in the same room. He usually smelt of alcoholic liquor.

"Do you want to go to the police or an outside adviser?"

Veronica said no and Colette said maybe. They were serious and thoughtful.

"The newspapers?"

They both grinned and said maybe.

I could see various ways to go, but no way that would satisfy all parties. I wished I had backed out when Becky called me. I thought about it for a moment. The girls watched me carefully, but the suspicious air had lifted.

"Look, there's only one thing I can do for you personally and that is to guarantee that Dr McComb will not approach either of you again. If that doesn't satisfy you, and you want to go further it's up to you. In the unlikely event that he does approach you, you must get in touch with me, and I will raise the issue with the board. It's over to you."

They looked at each other and brightened, nodding their heads slowly as they considered this, and we ended the meeting.

I met Nestor by arrangement in a pub near the Drugfree office the next day. "I want to talk about Colette and Veronica," I said as I tabled pints of lager. I wasn't genial.

Nestor was taken aback. I had said on the phone that it was board business – which it was. His broad, usually, amiable face with prominent light blue eyes, creased. Nestor's usual manner radiated interest in everything around him, but not so much as interest in himself. He had slicked back fair hair and at 50, always sportily dressed, would be a presentable alpha male to most women. He didn't reply to me.

"The two girls have complained about your sexual approaches."

"Colette, Veronica…I don't even know them. They're just people in the office. I've never approached them sexually. I absolutely deny this."

"Nestor, you don't have to justify yourself to me and we don't have to discuss this thing, but I want to you to listen to what I say because your practicing certificate may depend on it. Don't approach the girls again for any purpose. If you do, I will report you to the board. Understood?"

"No, I bloody well don't understand," he said, reddening. "Who set you up as judge and jury anyway, Batley!"

I took a long pull on the lager. "Stay cool, man. I'm not judging you. All I'm doing is warning you. That, and no more."

Nestor pushed his fingers through his hair, seeming to recover some of his professional equanimity. "Look, Bill, I'll tell you, I've joked around with those girls. It didn't mean a damn thing. They laughed and enjoyed it."

"I can't add a word to what I've already said, Nestor."

He wiped his face with his hand. "You're not prepared to hear me."

I shook my head negatively and took another draught. "No."

"Fuck you," he said, walking off, his beer untouched.

As I had an appointment to meet Ann in town, a little time and *The Times,* I sat reading in my armchair and finished Nestor's beer.

I met Becky the next day at the office. We settled in her room for my report with cups of tea and shortbreads, my written report on the desk before us.

"Just skip the paper work and tell me, Bill."

The initial cordiality began to wane in her expression as I recounted my story although she said nothing.

"Is Nestor going to resign?" she asked finally.

"I don't know. We didn't talk about it."

"But surely you hinted…"

"No."

"The girls, what are they going to do? Are they happy if Nestor stops his shenanigan?"

"I have no idea."

"You encouraged them to go to the police?"

"I told them it was their option."

"Bill, it strikes me that you have put your toe, but only your toe, in this mess and stirred it."

"On the contrary, Becky. I put my heart into it. And my considerable skills," I smiled.

"This isn't funny, Bill. You screwed up."

"Let's wait and see," I said, rising and departing with an agreeable wave of the hand. I reflected that nobody was pleased, not the girls, Nestor or Becky – or me. It was a lose-lose situation, but the girls wouldn't be troubled further. I was sure of that.

26

Shock – My Niece a Rough Sleeper

Our last holiday, before the dawn of the age of 'No more holidays abroad' had to be cancelled. My widowed mother was seriously ill with pneumonia and likely to die. She did die a month later. I made an insurance claim for a large sum of money; the trip had been fully paid. The claim was perfectly in order according to the policy, with medical certificates and receipts. I knew this much, although I never had any dealings with this insurance company before. I waited for a cheque in settlement. It never came.

I say the cheque never came. When you're expecting, the brain nags, 'Oh, yes. That cheque'. Look at it another way. I had just won a bet in effect. I bet the premium, a relatively small sum, that the insurance company would take the risk of my losses if I couldn't, for specified reasons, start the vacation. The insurance company bet that cancelling was an unlikely event. The odds are loaded in favour of the insurer, who usually pockets all the premiums, but sadly my mother became gravely ill and later died. I had filed a claim for 20 times the premium (the cost of the vacation). I had won the bet.

After a month, I rang the company, penetrated a battery of automated commands and finally spoke to an actual person. She offered to refer it to a colleague who would check up. I waited and waited on the telephone line which went dead after ten minutes.

I was quietly steaming, as I looked at the website. It was cleverly arranged to deal with everything, especially payment to the company of premiums and charges – everything, except payment of claims. I had to resort to the old quill pen. I knew my letter would rest in an in-tray in customer services for an indefinite time, so I copied it to the chief executive by special delivery i.e., to be signed for by the recipient.

Fourteen days later, I received an acknowledgment, an apology and no cheque; I was informed that because of the amount in issue, the papers had been referred to a more senior level.

"But it's now two months since you had the papers," I protested (by letter, email and telephone). Having worked in the insurance industry (not that this insurer would know) I felt shunned. This was what it was like to be an ordinary guy on the outside and subject to all the dirty tricks.

When I was on the point of launching a complaint to the Ombudsman, a draft for the full amount was paid into my account accompanied by a polite letter. No apology. However, the small flame which had been burning at the back of my mind after the first month was reduced to a flickering candle. It had taken nearly four months. My claim was so simple that it could have been concluded by a competent clerk in ten or 20 minutes. Reluctant payment is not something my former employer would have admitted, but it certainly saves money. And if you're a hopeful recipient, it's the most uncomfortable kind of annoyance.

Ann joined the Fulham Play-reading Group a few years ago and in a way I was glad to see her take a step away from school-out-of-school activities. She likes to have a lot in her timetable and she was to find out how much. She was invited by the chairman, Charles Bolland, not only to join, but after a year, to become a member of the committee (deputy chair, no less). It seemed very flattering. The committee and meetings didn't take a lot of time, and Ann enjoyed them at first. The chair and committee were returned annually to their positions by a docile, ageing membership.

Occasionally, Ann mentioned that the committee meetings were tea parties because there was nothing to do. "Charles positively won't allow us to do anything except set up the chairs in the hall, serve the afternoon tea and clean up the kitchen. The agenda for meetings, the choice of guest speakers and fund-raising plans he does himself *and* the menu for the annual dinner. If there's any decision to be made, he makes it and tells us in a manner which says 'It's all done and dusted and you needn't concern yourself with it'."

One day Ann surprised me by saying, "Do you know how long Charlie Bolland has been chair of the club?"

"Twenty years," I replied airily, thinking that would be well over the mark.

"Wrong," she said. "More."

"Not thirty years," I replied, surprised.

"Not quite. 29 years, actually."

"My God. He owns the club."

"You've put your finger on it. It's *his* club!" Ann said hotly.

I couldn't resist a laugh. "Like Robert Mugabe who used to own Zimbabwe," and I could have added like the chair of many clubs and charities, not to mention family businesses, big and small.

"People want to hang on, Bill."

"Charles is possibly a reasonable man in other respects, but he can't see that he's making you guys into servants. It's a partial blindness."

I had thought about this when I was employed because 'hanging on' in a post wasn't uncommon. Although I wasn't at the very top of my company, I was at a higher altitude than most. I could look down the slope of the pyramid of employees below me. It sometimes gave me vertigo to realise that I hadn't much idea of what sort of figure I was cutting, or what those below me were really thinking about me. And they had to think about me occasionally because I was telling them what to do. I suppose my self-interest bred the confidence which held me steady in my post, but I thought as time passed, that I was increasingly more isolated and it must have affected my assessment of what was going on.

"Does Charles lack insight?" I asked.

"He's as blind as a bat. He has a very bad temper and rejects any suggestion for change from the committee. He has a way of rebutting helpful, well-meant suggestions or new ideas too. Sort of, 'Don't worry dear, it's all done,' or 'Let's think about it for next year.' And we know of so many things that could be done to improve the club."

"What does the constitution say about how long a chair can serve?"

"I don't know. Nobody on the committee knows. The constitution has been lost, forgotten and mislaid over time."

I speculated that the document probably specified five years. I had the picture of this small club floating along with its seething but outwardly quiescent management and its partially sighted patriarch. I had met Charles fleetingly in the street when Ann was with him. One day he was outside the community hall where the meetings were held. I had just helped Ann inside the hall with her bags and papers for the meeting. He was alone at the side of the building, a short pudding of a man, over 75, a retired surveyor. His round face suddenly became a mass of painful lines as though he was having a fit. It was a paroxysm of what, agony, temper? He didn't notice me as I drove away.

I encouraged Ann, over a period, to let Charles know the committee's views. This became a revolt, headed by another member of the committee, but was supported by them all, with the request that he stand down. Ann told me that events came to a head after a meeting. Faced with demand that the committee's proposals for the club be accepted or accept their mass resignation, Charles tore off his chairman's enamel badge, threw it on the floor, stamped his feet like a petulant child and ran shouting from the hall.

"It's hard to believe but it happened, Bill."

"Regicide is painful. Who will be King (or Queen?)"

With a frustrated smile, Ann said, "I can't back out, can I?"

"The club is yours, my dear, for the next 29 years."

At lunch on Saturday, Ann told me that her sister Vicki's daughter, Lisa, was sleeping rough. It was one of those unexpected revelations which catch you off balance for a moment because it goes against everything you expect. I knew Vicki was having trouble with her daughter, but no more. The tragedy of the loss of Lisa's father in a car crash two years ago might explain part of it. The Hursts had been a stable family. Lisa was 18, an only child with a solid school record and as I knew her, a competent girl whom I thought would follow a path like Jane: university, a professional job, probably a nurse or social worker.

"It hasn't happened overnight," Ann said, "and I think Vicki has been in denial about it. First, there was conflict with Vicki at home, not about anything much as far as Vicki's told me, except Lisa wanting to go clubbing. And she's dropped her studies. Drinking. Then leaving home. The rest is out of sight as far as Vicki is concerned, ending under a tent in the park with a bloke."

"Have you just learned this?"

"Yes. I think Vicki was too ashamed, too overcome by the failure of her own life to help Lisa or to talk about it."

"Has Lisa had a mental breakdown?"

"Not in clinical terms, but I suppose the real answer to that is, yes."

"It's a big slide from Vicki's good household to …the park. Which park?"

"Fulham Palace."

"Right over the road in the bosom of the Church."

"Bill…"

"I'll go and see her."

"Will you? Bring her back here. Please … I couldn't bear to see my lovely niece like that…in the park."

"That's not like you, Ann."

"You go first, Bill and when Lisa has her own room somewhere, I'll go to see her. I've already checked with Social Services. They're on the job. There's a community-worker doing what she can."

"Imagine how your sister feels."

"Vicki's distraught and unable to deal with it. Like a mental block."

I thought Ann, too, was sickened. Lisa's was a steep and horrifying descent into misery. I remembered my customers at the food bank, whom I saw as talking to me from a deep pit. Now Lisa was in that pit.

I managed, with some difficulty, to get Lisa's community worker, Kay, on the phone. A busy person. No, she hadn't actually visited Lisa's tent in Fulham Palace Gardens. She was working with a charity helper who had told her about it. Yes, Lisa was with a man. She had interviewed Lisa at a soup kitchen.

"I didn't succeed in getting Lisa interested in taking shelter, Mr Batley."

"Why, do you think? Is the Palace so good?"

"It happens. You'd think anybody sleeping rough would want a roof. But no, it doesn't work that way. In Lisa's case, she just doesn't want to engage with other people. Her father's death has shaken up the home. She's lost confidence."

"She's drinking?"

"And taking drugs. She was pretty stunned when I saw her. But you're her uncle and she might listen to you. At present I can't help her, except by getting beside her at times, because she's adamant that she doesn't want what I'm offering. She looked awful when I last saw her. I'm worried about the winter weather. The combination of drink, drugs and cold can be lethal."

I promised to report back and walked over to the Palace the next morning, Tuesday, at about nine with Rex. It was a clear, cold, sunny day. There was nobody about. I know the Palace grounds well. I thought a rough sleeper would go for somewhere near the corner where the wall of the almshouses joins the fence of the public allotments. The trees and bushes are thick; I combed through them and saw a flash of blue. It was a small tent. As we approached, Rex started to bark which was no bad thing. There was a vague stirring inside the tent as I reached it. Should I pull back the flap and look in? Or identify myself in a loud voice? I didn't even know if Lisa was inside.

"Hello, Lisa. Bill Batley here. I've…come to see you." Rex added a collection of throaty barks.

"Piss off, mate!" was the reply in a thick, phlegmy man's voice.

"I'm looking for Lisa Hurst."

"She ain't here!"

A chillingly white hand pulled the flap aside and Lisa's face appeared, bruised and hollow-cheeked. Her bleary eyes took a moment to focus on me. "Uncle Bill," she croaked.

"Hi Lisa… You all right?"

"Sure as hell, all right." She let the flap close.

"Lisa, I can get you a place to stay…"

"Don't bother."

I was crashing into the lives of these two, but Lisa's reaction seemed to me to be so obtuse, I said, "Why not?"

"Doan't wan'it."

"You'll kill yourself out here."

"'M already dead."

"Piss orff, man!" The male voice again.

"I wanna stay with Danny," Lisa whined.

"OK, Lisa… I'll go now. I'll see you soon."

No answer from the tent. Rex and I picked our way through the bushes to the path. A stern looking man was waiting on the path wearing a fleece lettered 'Fulham Palace Gardens'.

"You can't bring a dog in here," he said with an emphatic frown.

"I know," I said, "but I was looking for somebody… Somebody who's lost. What are you going to do about the couple over there in the tent?"

"Call the police. They're trespassers."

"One of them is my niece."

"Well, you better get her out of here."

"I can't do anything. Not at the moment."

"What do you expect the Palace to do? Grant them a tenancy?"

"Nothing as charitable as that from the Bishop's Palace. Not even a bowl of soup."

"You should be the one with the soup, sir."

He had out-gunned me. I walked away.

"And don't bring you dog in here again," he shouted.

As I neared the Palace gate, a yellow and blue police car was smoothing up the drive. When Rex and I were outside, I called Kay. "What can we do?" I asked.

"I'm afraid there's nothing much you can do, Mr Batley, unless you can persuade her."

"She needs medical attention."

"The police will remove her from the Gardens, but they'll have to release her – that's assuming she's sober and thinking for herself, or maybe take her to A&E."

"Some doubt about sobriety, but you'll be seeing her?"

"I'll try to catch up with her today," she said matter-of-factly. No commitment.

Kay sounded sympathetic. I supposed she had other cases like this and she couldn't cry over all of them. She promised to ring me.

Later, I tracked Lisa's course through Kay. I met Lisa myself, twice, at a mobile café where she and Danny went for charity food. Danny was about forty (Kay told me). He looked older. Emaciated, bearded, dirty, with thin head hair. He smelled. He never spoke to me although I addressed him in a friendly way. He remained at Lisa's shoulder, glowering.

I remembered Lisa's remark about being dead and that is how she looked. She was hollow chested, her face grey and her clothes and hair filthy. She, too, smelled.

"Would you like to come home with me and get a shower," I said on the second occasion.

"Worried about my toilet, Uncle Bill?"

"Ann would like to see you."

"Then get her along to this freak show! Any amount of well-dressed people here trying to sort out the friends and relatives they've fucked up."

I'm not usually short of a word, but I couldn't reply to this bit of R D Laing. I pulled out my wallet and held the contents, several 20-pound-notes out to her. She reached quickly, took them and stuffed them into her pocket without emotion or comment.

"Are you absolutely sure you don't want to go into a shelter or room or something. I could help."

"Uncle Bill, take me off your guest list. I don't want to see you any more, geddit?"

I came away from the mobile café annoyed with myself for being inept – but I had no idea how to deal with Lisa's remoteness. She was in the pit, but unlike my food bank customers who were clawing to get out, the normal impulse, she was walling herself in.

I followed her, through Kay, over the ensuing weeks, sleep-outs in different parks, arrest by the police leading to sobering up in an accident and emergency ward, counselling by Kay and other professionals, all to no avail.

Ann took a call from Kay one bitterly cold and wet March Monday morning. Ann had a day off and we were still in bed at nine am. Lying next to Ann in the bed, I could hear Kay's tense voice on the phone: "I'm very sorry Mrs Batley but Lisa Hurst died last night. I'm calling because Lisa's mother was naturally distraught when I spoke to her and you might like to see if she's all right."

"Lisa's dead," Ann said, turning to me as though it was something that didn't make sense.

I took the phone from her. "Kay, what happened?"

"It's like I said, Mr Batley, the weather tips the scale. Last night, the police were out removing every rough sleeper that we could locate and taking them to shelter. I thought we would pick up Lisa and Danny, but we couldn't find them. Lisa was ill but she walked out of A&E yesterday morning. They were tucked away in a park in Camden as far as I know. Danny dialled 111 in the early hours of the morning when he knew Lisa was in desperate trouble but it was too late."

I thanked Kay. Ann called her sister who wasn't answering. She left a message: "I'll come right over."

When we were on our feet, Ann said, "I've changed my mind. I can't face Vicki right away this morning. She's insulated herself psychologically from Paula's problems. I need a bit of space to get the feel of all this."

"Do you want me to go? Will she be OK for a couple of hours?"

"You mean…?"

"Yeah. That's what I mean."

"Vicki will survive, I'm sure of it."

We didn't talk much or follow our usual routine that morning. We didn't have breakfast. We put on our raincoats and walked along the Thames, a harsh scene in many shades of grey.

When we were having a coffee at the Blue Boat, I thought, how can an apparently healthy young person pass up all this life that we have?

When the telephone rings in the small hours of the morning in an otherwise tranquil household, it's disturbing. Not merely the noise and being awakened, but the awful question: *why?* which flares in the mind. It happened to us recently. The telephone is on Ann's side of the bed, which reflects the fact that she receives far more calls than I do. And so she took the receiver, but I'm sure we were both equally unnerved.

Ann had a moment's incomprehension identifying the caller, and then she said, "Oh, Alice! You're all right, aren't you?"

231

Alice Jenner is our 18-year-old niece, the daughter of Ann's oldest sister, Faith. I meet her occasionally. She's very self-possessed, a good conversationalist and studying politics at university (Nottingham). Alice is not a person I would expect to call us at 3 am. I was anxious to hear from Ann as she replaced the phone and relaxed on the pillow.

"You'll never guess, Bill. She's locked out of the family house. Faith and Martin are away and she's staying there on her own with a girl-friend. She's been out to a party and they can't get in because the lock on the front door has jammed."

"So she's coming over here from Putney?"

"Yes, with her girlfriend, in an Uber."

We both went downstairs when we heard a rap on the door knocker. Alice was in the doorway smiling, clutching a little handbag. "It's so good of you," she said.

It was a cold night and Alice seemed to me to have hardly any clothes on, just a very short skirt and a wisp of transparent silk across her chest. "Come in before you die of exposure," I said.

"I'm not cold. It's limo to bar, you know, Uncle Bill," she said.

She was followed by her equally scantily dressed friend, Sandy, who seemed to be all bare legs – and out of the shadows behind Sandy lurched two uneasy-looking boys. Hurried introductions took place in the hall as I welcomed the four, betraying no sign of the surprise I felt at their presence. Ann, too, showed no surprise.

Ann went upstairs with the girls. The boys, who were silent and sober, I took to the conservatory where there were couches. I promised that blankets would arrive shortly.

When Ann had provided the bedding and settled the team down, she crawled into bed.

"Did you know about the boys?" I asked.

"Alice never mentioned them or Sandy. She just hit us with them. What can you say?"

"Nothing. Things change in thirty years. It's called a sleepover, isn't it?"

In the morning, Ann took cups of tea in to the girls' room, but they weren't there. She found them downstairs, in the conservatory, on one of the couches. The two boys were on the other couch.

We all had an early breakfast. Before the boys joined us at the table I asked Alice, "Are the boys for security?"

Sandy laughed. "I don't think they would be very good at that."

Alice laughed too. "They're a bit spindly, aren't they?"

"It's just that if you're with a bloke, the guys in the clubs don't come on to you so strongly. They can be a nuisance," Sandy said.

I assumed the boys were about the same age as the girls, but they looked and acted as though they were younger. They weren't conversationalists. The girls sparkled. They talked about their adventures last night and their plans for studies and vacations.

I drove them all back to the Jenner's house and organised a locksmith. Later, Faith Jenner, whom I would not describe as a fastidious housewife, said to Ann that the four had been 'camping' there for a few days. "You should have seen the mess! I had to have a serious word with Alice," Faith told her.

"A serious word about the fat in the grill, but what else is there to have a serious word about?"

"Bill, you're so permissive!" Ann said.

Barry Machin rang me last night, interrupting the TV news, but at least I had my G&T.

"A couple of things, Bill. Randall has paid up with interest at 15pc to cover the 'misunderstanding'. My lawyers said go no further. Anyway, thanks for your efforts."

"Sounds right to me. What was the other thing?"

Barry hesitated. "It's about Jane. Would it be OK with you if we got married in France when we're there this year. I mean, just come back married?"

"It would be great news, marvellous. Do it, man!"

"We can have a gathering when we're home."

"I can't think of a better way," I said, thinking of the trying formalities which I would avoid.

"Well, don't say anything to Jane because…it's not in her plan at the moment… I'll let you into a family secret of ours. I've been asking her to marry me for the last couple of years."

"And she refuses? She loves you, Barry, or she wouldn't have your babies."

"I know. She doesn't refuse to marry me. She says she's thinking about it."

I was nonplussed, but Jane was very much her own person. "Barry, I'll admit I don't fully understand Jane," I said. It was a giant understatement. "But look at it this way. Things are going in the right direction. You have your beautiful home, your babies, your devotion to each other."

"Yep, I do," Barry said in an uncertain voice. "Thanks again, Bill. I wanted you to know what's happening – or not."

When I had put the phone away, Ann asked me what Barry wanted. She heard me identify Barry when I took the call.

"He was just telling me about sorting that land business out, dear. He's come out very well."

27

I Review a Year or So

I have been keeping this notebook for over a year now. I have re-read the contents to follow Ms Biggs' instruction to review my progress. I'll set out my views candidly:

Reallocation of household chores with Ann: This subject has been too difficult to broach. Unheralded steps like doing the washing, which is really only pressing the buttons on the washer and drier, are not appreciated. The female of the species has marked out her territory. Apartheid reigns between dark and light clothes in the wash and I am regarded as colour-blind. While I clean up the kitchen after our meals, I am not encouraged to put the dishes in the cupboards when they come out of the dishwasher. The reason for this has been plainly and politely put to me: I put them in the wrong places. *Resolution: work on this, but I have little confidence.*

Voluntary work: The food bank ended badly, and I have been pushed into a nasty place on the Drugfree board by Becky. She is displeased at the uncertain outcome of the Nestor sex allegations, although it seems the two girls are satisfied. She really wants to get rid of Nestor and that's a battle for her to fight. I foresee my tenure on the board will be short lived, but there are hundreds of voluntary jobs I can do. I will learn something, as I go from one to another. *Resolution: resign and seek another post.*

Financial affairs: My savings and investments, such as they are, are stumbling along, and I have been too busy to attend to them. Not really too busy but impelled to find tasks which enable me to avoid other tasks that don't interest me. I do what I'm advised, although I know I am being gouged. *Resolution: make a thorough study of this in the next year.*

Consider a radical lifestyle change*: This has not been a good year for such a thought, but in the ensuing year Ann and I might embark on some new adventures. Ann is showing a tendency to relax her rather puritanical view that cruise holidays are something for the idle rich and not for us as resolute workers for a better local community. *Resolution: keep under consideration. Send for cruise catalogues and continue to provide discreet propaganda in discussions with Ann.*

Consider accepting lucrative consultancy roles*: I have not exactly been deluged with opportunities, but I haven't sought them. I had only to raise my eyebrows to Ms Biggs to obtain some. It troubled me when I retired that I was no longer 'needed'. It's nice to be needed. But I soon began to appreciate that there are thousands of us former executives who need to be needed, in fact so many that my need was diluted. As for the money side, which is the other reason for flogging on with work: the truth is I'm happy enough with my income. I should be so lucky! *Resolution: forget it!*

The Chandler affair*: Chandler has been banished and my marriage saved. I have regrets about some of my methods to accomplish this and the collateral damage caused to Ann and Thelma Chandler, and to be fair, to Carol too. I sound like a general assessing a campaign! But what's done is done and had to be done. *Resolution: try to be a little less emotional about my marriage.*

Drinking*: I need further time and some real evidence to consider whether I drink too much. For example, if my annual medical overhaul reports a clear blood test, it means my liver is good. Why be drastic and reduce my intake? *Resolution: defer for later consideration.*

Peeing in the night time*: This is very confusing. It can't be that I drink too much water or coffee because when I have drunk a lot, the number of times of peeing is not proportionate. For no reason that I can find, there will be occasional nights when I only go to the bathroom twice. I think this is one of those problems which some friends talk up as a *big problem* (loss of sleep, disturbance of the wife etc.) and when I remember who they are, I realise they are amongst the worriers. I will not join them. *Resolution: keep under observation for further action if necessary.*

Sex: I have my doubts whether the Carol experience has dealt effectively with the admittedly small concerns which I have about my sexual abilities. It may not have been worth all the trouble it caused me. My feelings were spurred on by the lustiness of certain situations – after having a *final* lunch and a shared bottle of sauvignon blanc for example, or sliding into bed after being told to forget the condom! These sort of occasions don't arise in a marriage of 30 years. Ann is a willing and accomplished lover and a woman who enjoys sex. She can't be faulted. I can. But I will not plead guilty to erectile dysfunction, the medical problem. I will admit to very occasional inabilities which Ann always treats light-heartedly. *Resolution: unearth sex manual in the garage and study for information.*

My dealings with my son: I have qualms about Nick because I love him and I don't want to hurt him, but I remain resolute about not being his money-box except to the extent that I already am. Love in this context means a deep and somewhat mysterious psychic involvement. His failures hurt me. I have made George my executor instead of Nick. The one decisive improvement in my affairs this year!

I think of my responsibility as a parent for the way Nick behaves. He's intemperate. As a selfish young animal that had to be trained, he never learned the overarching lesson that his own security and comfort can only be achieved if he compromises with the security and comfort of others. Why has he never really learned that lesson? In the very uncertain ground that all children have to cover progressing back and forth between home, school lessons and the playground outside, when they can't choose the quality of any of them, something has gone wrong. Or is it something in his head, a clinical defect? Or is it just a malign satisfaction in abusing, upsetting and rejecting others, short of such a defect? He gets his satisfaction this way?

I acquit myself on the home front as basically a kindly and indulgent parent – and Ann too. Schools? They were adequate scholastically. Playground? Here is the Wild West where no kid ever knows quite how he will survive. He can be lauded by peers, and Nick was by some; he can be bullied and Nick was – no serious repercussions as far as I know. Or he can be ignored. Nick was never ignored. Most kids go through this mangle without undue harm. More than a few times I have had to write to his headmaster and visit his schools to plead that he should not be expelled for some outrage. The truth is that while I claim to be a good parent, I really haven't a clue about the value of my parenting. Am I letting myself off too easily? *Resolution: keep under consideration with a view to resolving confusion.*

Lisa Hurst's death I have grave doubts about the effectiveness of my involvement. No, I *know* it was wholly ineffective. I could have acted in a more macho way, as probably her father would have done. I could have dragged her out of the tent and forced her to come home with me. I treated her like a rational adult – which she was not. What harm would it have done if I had kicked her arse? Suppose she screamed her head off and I was forced to desist. A little pain and agony and a few hurt feelings, but possibly a life saved.

I talked to Ann and she said: "You're a permissive guy, *always* too permissive, Bill, but you were in no way responsible for what happened to Lisa." Comforting? Not much. I'll confess to something that I can't mention to anybody. I felt that although Danny was a nauseating wreck, Lisa had found comfort with him in her torment, not with me or her own mother. *Resolution: review my permissive attitudes and assess later.*

In what way have I reshaped my day over the year? Not at all. I continue to meander through much the same routine. I enjoy it. The basic shape of the day is there, but events seem to manage me, rather than the other way round. *Resolution: consider further with a view to improvement.*

Am I a serious person? In my first entry in this notebook, I said Ann did not regard me as a serious person. She apparently does not regard this as a damning criticism. I am in her eyes, in so many ways, a lightweight. Perhaps her life is easier married to a person who is not serious. However, this was one observation of Ann's that I have borne in mind in my review.

Well, am I serious? The answer I conclude is, probably not. But am I very different from *any* ordinary guy? None of us around here are very serious as a general rule of attitude and behaviour. We are very ordinary people concerned with our children, family, job, and whether to paint the house or buy a new car. The implications of the never-ending wars, mass migration and the debates about Brexit and fake news are peripheral. For a while, politicians and journalists persuade me that worldly affairs beyond my ken are proceeding in a rational way and then it becomes glaringly obvious that they are not.

When I home in closely on humankind with a magnifying glass, I see its affairs are arranged in selfish groups which resolve themselves in conflict and compromise. The effects are devastatingly illogical and often cruel. If I back off and look from a distance, I see the rational principles which we pursue in the west as a community (like emancipation of women and equal rights). I persuade myself that these are progressing year by year. I am blurred in this bifocal view of reality and rationality, thus not serious. Humans seem to me to be the same everywhere on the planet in their selfish, and entirely natural, instinctive drive for security.

A word about how serious the residents in and around Amherst Street are: It's true that some are relatively well off, but we are indisputably nondescript and our pursuits are common-and-garden. Forget the literary novels we may read and the galleries we may visit. A few may be big cheeses in pharmaceuticals or banking – until they retire. When we greet each other in the street, we sigh at the latest terrorist threats, or political posturing, then shrug, smile and walk on. Serious people?

Of course you could say that my remarks are made from a perspective of unashamed privilege, that my words come out of a comfortable, white middle class bubble. I accept that I am privileged. I don't feel ashamed about it. I have been conditioned to be what I am. I agree that I live in a middle class bubble, but doesn't every community live in its own bubble.? I can be disturbed or alarmed by people who are unlike me and I expect it's the same with every community. My bubble is not particularly white or English. There are a few Asian, Indian and Middle Eastern families in the street, as well as French, American and Russian. And the majority of Brits. We greet each other cordially. I meet them at street parties and fairs and at the market in Bishop's Park. Some join us at our house. The subject of conversation is usually health and holidays (after the weather). It's a bubble of class, in the basic meaning of that word, referring to common characteristics. Skin colour, religion, philosophical and political beliefs are *not* common characteristics of this class, only the broad level of income and education.

I wouldn't call Sophie's husband (the lawyer) or Mr Daniels *serious*. I would rather say surly and preoccupied – and I would not criticise them for earning a couple of million pounds a year or desiring a car that shines like a jewel.

Surely, not being serious is helpful. In the absurd turmoil of the world, it is difficult to be serious. It was in 1960 that Phillip Roth argued that American reality was so crazy that it almost outstripped a writers' imagination. In 2018, he acknowledged that he was miles short of the mark. I doubt that Britain can be much different.

I wonder where these thoughts place Ann. I think she's more serious about everything than I am, but when she sees nonsense (and I have to point it out to her sometimes) she, equally, appreciates how difficult it is to be serious. George is certainly not serious.

G*overnments and their departments*: I tend to think of governments and their departments collectively as gothic constructions which cannot see themselves and in that sense, not serious. The overloaded House of Lords is barmy but what a cosy club for the needy.

Conclusion: Honestly, I recognise that my findings on self-improvement are not entirely satisfactory, although it is instructive (to me) to measure how little progress I have made in spite of my earnest desire at the time of writing. Have I just been beating the air like a chick trying to fly?

28

Change in Amherst Street
Versus the Status Quo

It's possible to see how Amherst Street has changed over the years by observing the change in house-owners. I suppose Ann and I have met many residents around here at the annual cricket match, housewarmings, or street parties, but they remain relatively distant. London is like that. I have been focussed on our street. I'm not conscious of what happens over the back fence, except for the occasional noise of their dogs, the occasional children's ball over the fence, and the occasional cutting of trees. The back gardens are deep. I guess that conditions over the fence are not dis-similar to Amherst Street.

The 'settlers' in Amherst Street if I can call them that, have been here for 50 years and they are dying out. Craven Cottage bears a shield dated 1895 so life started long before the settlers. The Cottage, intact and circled by the sheds which make up a stadium, with a façade protected by a conservation order, has a statue of Johnny Haines, 'The Maestro' outside, Captain of England 1934. Craven Cottage also used to have a statue of Michael Jackson because the then owner of the club was a fan. For some reason, interesting to speculate about, the statue was moved from a position of prominence inside the front fence, to a lonely position at the rear of the stand, facing the Thames. I liked the statue; it was painted in bright colours. Perhaps the fans thought it was inconsistent with the serious business of football. It's gone entirely now, replaced by a statue of a bare-chested young man in shorts – facing the Thames.

Johnny Haines' earnings as the first footballer in England to earn over 20 pounds a week, contrast with an Amherst Street home where a Chelsea footballer lived who was said to earn a hundred thousand pounds a week. His fans used to walk along the street to photograph the house, such was his fame.

I have said Andrew Muir is a settler. The Fosters are settlers. They are in their nineties. They probably have money but they have eluded the continual grind of maintenance. The roof of their house is covered with moss, the garden full of weeds. The woodwork around the windows is cracked and faded. Their only child, incompetent. *Some* houses in Amherst Street are like this, in a row of cleanly painted town houses with immaculate window boxes, clipped hedges and flowers, behind back-painted iron railings.

Lucinda Helman, once an operatic singer, nearly 90 and nearly blind, who lived opposite us, was another settler. Her house, of which she could only manage to occupy the kitchen and a makeshift bedroom in a downstairs reception room, was in a similarly decrepit condition. Lucinda had co-opted me to adjust the worn out gas boiler in her cellar which I had to attend to frequently. She died suddenly. A developer acquired the house and it metamorphosed into a palace suitable for a footballer or a banker.

The next generation are represented by people like Ann and me, the Clitheroes, and Mr Daniels. Business people near to or in retirement. Our homes and gardens are well kept. Peer pressure (imagined) may have something to do with it, but pride in the place has a part too.

The subsequent generation are the youngish ones, probably 35-ish, with slender blond wives who drive their monster cars with elan, two or three young children and two dogs. They want to be near good schools. They have good incomes but the Bank of Mum and Dad plays a part. There is a sprinkling of French, Russians and Americans (as well as the British) often lawyers and bankers. Some of them are gypsies at the behest of big corporations who will move them on in a year or so. The British in this younger generation, believe they are doing very well, and mark their territory by stripping out the kitchen when they move in, even if it was installed last year, and laying astro-turf in the garden for the children.

We all seem to rationalise where *we* live as the best place for the moment, town or country. Most of my work colleagues claimed that it was better to commute from outside London. They had spacious houses in leafy lanes. Now that they are retired they seem to be stuck a long way from the adventures of London. Meanwhile, Ann and I hunkered down in Fulham which can be noisy and dirty despite the efforts of the local authority. We watched the marathon opposition to Heathrow airport expansion, always hopeful over the 20 years we have lived here that it would succeed. But no.

When London and other major cities were found to infringe pollution laws, it seemed that as with Heathrow, the economy trumps public health. That's a strange priority in a democratic society. You could make a comic opera along the lines of *'Oh, What a Lovely War'* about the argument and prevarication over Heathrow in the last forty or more years.

One can't help but be struck by the element of absurdity. We burrow like rabbits for more space where we live, we drive cars that are too big for the streets, and we tolerate high levels of noise and toxic air pollution. But Ann and I still count our blessings about where we live. We think we live in the *best* place for our practical purposes. At times, I ask whether what we have is a genuine compromise between what is good and bad, or whether we are all a bit nutty around here and ought to move out.

I have to admit that if I was a politician with a shared responsibility for the state of the nation, I would, like the rest, press for measures which support my career and the accretion of my pension. I don't blame politicians. It's the nature of human beings and the necessarily short termism of democratic society – lots of often conflicting selfish interests which lead to skewed decisions rather than beneficial compromises. Don't ask a small businessman in London about increasing the congestion charge!

I saw Carol this morning. I had slipped into a café in Parson's Green for coffee, cake and to read the paper. When I had paid the check and was getting ready to leave, I noticed her on one side of the room, head to head with a man over a small table. She saw me too. She looked well-groomed and composed and I thought absorbed in her companion. Her glance had just broken away from the man, and there I was about 15 feet away. Our eyes locked for the merest fraction of a second. Her composure was unchanged by this. She moved her attention casually back to her companion as though I didn't exist. When I was outside the café, I untied Rex's tether and led him home with a jaunty feeling. I was out of her life.

Is Mr Bhatta back? A marvellous card came through the post box in the front door the other day. I took it to the potting shed and leaned it against my pencil box where I could see it as I work or think. It would be classified as junk mail. Many residents in the street have a notice over the postal slot in their front door saying, 'No junk mail'. The size of the lettering of each individual notice is probably proportionate to the temper of the owner.

I like to glance at the whole deluge of junk mail, and regrettably those who have elected otherwise will not have seen Mr Bhatta's card. Could it be the same Mr Bhatta? He announces that he is a clairvoyant, spiritual healer and expert in black magic. He can deal with every problem relating to love, sex, relationships, finances, litigation, addiction, and protection against enemies. He can cast powerful spells and results are guaranteed. Prices are reasonable.

There is hope yet.

I think of Lampedusa's saying, that to stay the same, things have to change. The process of change may be self-evident to me but it's salutary to consider what a wobbly, quirky space I occupy. Not merely changes in deserts and oceans, cataclysmic wars, revolutions, cosmic upheavals and the decay of the human body, but the momentary changes of mind and action of the people I interact with. What will happen next? I nerve myself for surprises. Faced with this quagmire of events, what I do is to strive to maintain a comfortable status quo. I am lucky enough to have attained one, just, but can I sustain it? – and that ironically must mean accommodating change.

I want this comfortable status quo above all, the plain damn ordinariness of it all, the usual, the typical, the everyday, the nondescript. I have had to repel the Bernard Chandler invasion, I have had to accept that Ann wants to continue her professional career, I have had to retire thankfully from the corporate rat-race despite the manner of my going; and to acknowledge that Jane and Barry can live together informally and have children and a happy life. I have to understand that George is immoral (forgetting my own sins and crimes for a moment) but extremely likeable, I have to accept that my son is not me and will never be like me, and to realise that persistence with Carol would wreck my marriage.

The comfortable status quo for me is lithe and moving like a snake, while I embrace all these different and changing events and more, and continue to live in this agreeable home with a special person.